Annie's Christmas Plan

A MORNING LAKE NOVEL

LORRAINE PATON

ISBN: 0991994051
ISBN-13: 978-0-9919940-5-2

Print Edition.
Printed by CreateSpace

Visit Lorraine at **www.lorrainepaton.com**

DEDICATION

To my wonderful family and friends,
Because of you, my dreams take flight.
Thank you.

ACKNOWLEDGMENTS

To everyone who read my first book, *Devin's Second Chance*, I thank you! You are amazing and wonderful for taking a chance on an unknown writer! And to those who contacted me to say how much they enjoyed it, you'll always have a special place in my heart!

To my family, who continues to support this wild endeavor, I want you to know I love you so much!

To my friends, whether we've shared real or only virtual coffees, you are forever special to this process. I appreciate the support you've offered me.

To my fearless beta readers and editor, I want to express my heartfelt gratitude. Without you, *Annie's Christmas Plan* would be a poor shadow of what it has become.

To everyone who picks up this story, I hope you enjoy Annie and Quinn's story!

CHAPTER 1

Heritage Day Long Weekend

"Annalisa?"

Annie bit her lip. Her ex was the only one who ever called her that. Nope, she was just plain old Annie now.

Besides, she hadn't been down here *that* long. All she needed was a minute or two. Why couldn't he give her a few moments to regain her composure? She stiffened her shoulders but didn't look up. Not yet. She'd almost positioned the Santa and reindeer atop the paper house, the last details of her Christmas village. How odd that she would finish her idealized winter world today.

She dipped her index finger into a glob of white glue, then she dabbed the adhesive along the edge of the sleigh runners. Annie held her breath until she had the object resting on the snowy roof. A thin gold thread tied the reindeer to the sleigh and to one another.

With Santa's sled in place, there were still eight sets of little hooves to affix.

"Annalisa, did you hear me?"

Crap, he was coming downstairs.She gritted her teeth and rubbed her forehead with the back of her hand. The figures lay cockeyed and drunk across the glittering roof, and they'd have to stay that way. The summons, and the summoner, would not be ignored.

"I'm coming," she muttered, as the hesitant footsteps on the stairs continued their descent. She waited with her hands folded in her lap. Jack's polished oxblood shoe inched into view, as if he wasn't sure if he should enter. Ha, that was unlikely. "I said I was coming."

He stopped a foot inside the rec room. "It's changed down here."

Annie shrugged. It really hadn't. "How do you remember it?" Gah! She shouldn't have asked that.

Jack stroked the wood panel wall. "We never did get time to reno this, did we?"

"No, I guess we never did." Annie stood from her craft table, which once upon a time had been the jigsaw puzzle table where she and Kelly had pieced together European landscapes while Jack cheered for his favorite hockey team on TV. Things had changed—no more hockey, no more puzzles—but the room was still the same. "What do you see when you come here?" Again with the questions? She couldn't stop her curiosity.

He pursed his lips, which wasn't exactly a declaration of how much he missed their former life—but he did, she truly believed he did. He was simply better at containing his emotions.

"Never mind—"

"I guess I see a house where I used to live," Jack said.

"Remember when Kelly used to make forts out of the sofa cushions? Or when we tried to get your uncle's pool table downstairs and put the hole in the wall? It is still there, you know," she said, "the hole."

"We're almost done." Jack indicated to the activities upstairs with a nod.

She adjusted her glasses. He must have noticed she'd retired the old plastic frames for a smaller, sleeker set. He used to comment on her previous pair often enough.

Annie waited for a remark but nothing came. He glanced toward the stairs, a sure sign he was feeling impatient. The inevitable was upon her. She brushed the bits of paper from her pants as she crossed the room. Little clippings fluttered to the carpet like confetti over newlyweds. "All right. Let's go."

"Listen, I realize this is hard."

Annie straightened her back. She itched to cross her arms, but Jack watched her too closely. She couldn't shake the impression he was trying to read her like one of his bigwig clients—if only she found that flattering.

"Try to look at this as an opportunity," Jack continued.

She wanted to scream at his condescending tone. Through everything that had happened between them over the years, she couldn't remember ever wanting to scream at him like this.

But today wasn't about them.

"Kelly's a good girl." Thank heaven, her voice didn't waver. "We've raised her well." She touched his forearm, but her hand lay there dead and out of place. "Take care of her."

"She's my daughter, too, you know."

"I know." Annie patted his arm. When had touching him become so awkward? "I just thought I'd have another year before she left."

"This has been a tough time for all of us."

"Sure—but who keeps getting left behind?" She pressed her fingernails into her palm. Why had she said that? It was stupid.

Jack frowned.

Circling him, Annie climbed the stairs, the ascent to her nearly vacant house. When he sighed behind her, she wanted to grab him and shake him, but she managed to keep walking.

"Stop for a minute," Jack said, but he didn't touch her, didn't try to make her stay. "If you need anything, anything at all ..."

What a meaningless thing to say, especially today. No one ever listened to what she wanted or needed. If they had, he would still be her husband, and the light of her life wouldn't be packing to live with him, in Edmonton … more than three hours away from Calgary. Kelly wasn't really moving to the other end of the province of Alberta—it just felt that way.

When she crossed through the kitchen, she could almost pretend nothing had changed, but then Kelly darted into view with a box in her arms.

Annie's chest tightened. How was she going to survive this?

"Guess what, Mom? My room is almost clean," she said, before disappearing out the front door.

Annie loosened her clenched hands and trudged toward Kelly's room, while Jack followed Kelly outside.

The door to the formerly overflowing, poster-clad, music-blaring room gaped open. She stepped inside. Her knees were suddenly weak, so she leaned against the wall. When Kelly returned a moment later, Annie forced a smile.

One hundred and ten pounds of excited teenager bounced around the room. A big grin lit Kelly's face. "Looks different in here, doesn't it?"

"It sure does."

"You'll never guess what I found, or should I say *who* I found." She plucked a dusty purple rabbit from the floor of her naked closet. "Feather."

"I never did understand why you gave him that name." Annie walked over to touch the stuffed animal. She could remember Kelly sitting at her feet, talking to the stuffed animal like a dear friend, while Annie braided her long dark hair. "You used to take him everywhere."

Kelly grinned and tossed Feather to Annie. "He's staying here, where he belongs." Then Kelly's cell phone vibrated. She scanned the screen and smiled. With one hand, she keyed something into the phone, while she seized a half-filled plastic bag with the other.

"Looks like you're almost finished." Even to Annie's own ears, her enthusiasm was false, a lie.

"This is the last of my stuff." Kelly shoved her phone into her back pocket. "You should see Dad's truck. It's overflowing. God, I hope we don't lose anything." After ramming one last pair of shoes into the bag, she tied it closed. "I can't believe I'm starting a new school."

"You'll meet lots of people. Have you decided what clubs you want to join?"

"I don't even know what's available, but I bet there is better stuff than Humphrey High."

Annie trailed behind her still chattering daughter as she exited the gutted room.

"Heya, Mom, don't be sad. I'll be home at Thanksgiving. I've already talked to Dad about it."

"Right." Oh, heavens, Kelly was filling her last bag. What would happen if she clung to it? Begged her to stay? "We can go away for a girls' weekend. I can book it now."

"Well, I'll have to hang with Becky and Eve, too." She raised her phone and jiggled it as if the other girls lived in the phone itself. "They can't believe I'm leaving."

"Right," Annie said, "Becky and Eve."

She had followed Kelly to the front porch, but didn't go to the truck. Jack was already in the driver's seat, ready to go and leave her alone all over again.

Her heart pounded inside her chest. It ached. Goodness, how it ached.

"I'll talk to you tonight, 'kay, Mom? Oh, wait—it'll be late by the time we drive there and unpack, so I'll phone tomorrow instead."

Annie forced herself to blink. To breathe. If everyone else could leave, why was she still here? "Kelly, I need to talk to you for a minute, before you head out."

"Sure, but I'm not changing my mind."

"Do you have everything?" She tried to think about her little Christmas village downstairs. Perfect. Peaceful. Quiet. It was a place where good things would happen, where people cared for other people, a place imbued with family traditions. Oh, how she wanted to be there. "I ... I ... Kelly, I'm selling the house."

"Mom, you've been threatening that for ages, but you know this is the place for you. Besides, where would you go?" Her daughter shook her head. "I need to be with Dad right now, but I'll be back."

"Right ... to see everyone."

"Exactly."

Her ex honked the horn, like the most heartbreaking moment of her life didn't deserve a little respect.

"I'll call you soon." Kelly hugged her.

Her suddenly stiff and heavy arms clung to her daughter, and then Kelly pulled away. "Day or night, you call me. Even just to say hi."

"I know, Mom." Kelly's phone vibrated again. She read the text message, laughed, then glanced at Annie. "I love you."

"I love you, too," she said. Tears were streaming down her face now, but Kelly didn't notice since she was already rushing down the stairs, typing something on her phone.

Annie stepped inside after the truck disappeared around the corner, out of the cul-de-sac. Out of her world. Cradling Feather as she would a crying infant, Annie slid to the floor.

It had happened.

The home she and Jack had created was now a house—a house where a family used to live. Now she and a dusty rabbit were the only residents.

She stroked the rabbit's matted fur and stared at the painting in the hallway of a beautiful stone house nestled in a snowy winter landscape. Its windows shone with yellowy warmth. Nothing bad happened in those houses. No, in those kinds of places, families curled up in front of fireplaces to play board games, laugh, and drink cocoa.

She needed that kind of house, a place in the country where people had good family values and simpler lives. She studied the picture. Each detail of the cottage beckoned her. Each brush stroke promised a gracious welcome.

What if she traded everything in for a slice of an ideal world? What if her Christmas village existed outside of the depths of her imagination? What if holiday magazines spoke the truth? Maybe eternal cheer, shimmering hope, and glittering joy existed year-round. She wanted that. If everything were perfect, Kelly would want to come home. She'd want the tradition. She'd want Annie's love.

Jack would come, too. He'd realize how perfect they were together. Divorced couples reconciled all the time. She would forgive his leaving, and they would be a happy family again.

That's what she wanted—to have her family back again.

Maybe someone would even come and photograph the perfect holiday festivities at her home. Their holiday would be featured on the cover of a magazine.

Everyone would see everything was okay.

Annie hugged the bunny close when she stood. As she passed by Kelly's hollowed-out room on the way to the office, she shut the door.

Yes, she needed a new house and she knew where to find one. Her fresh start existed in cyberspace somewhere, just waiting to be found.

After a few hours, she was thrilled with her results.

"Look at this one, Feather," she said, each time she found a charming little cheap house in a small town. She didn't want to move too far away, just far enough to find *a charming little cheap house in a small town.* She printed the information for each possible home, collecting a handful of postings.

Maybe this wasn't the most horrible day of the year.

She'd spread them out on the floor to evaluate them all side by side when the phone rang. She raced to the telephone. "Kelly? So soon?"

"It's Merry, dear. I guess she's left by now, right?"

Annie took a deep breath. "Yes, a few hours ago. She's supposed to call."

"How are you doing?"

"I'm selling the house and moving to the country."

Merry cleared her throat. "Is it wise to make a big decision right now?"

"I have to," she said.

"Sweet pea, they don't have many corporate accountants in small towns."

"I ..." Huh. A job? True, a paycheck might be important. "I'll figure it out."

"Well, good. No sense you holing up in the place you're in now. You've spent enough time in your basement full of crafts. Time to get out and live a little."

"I need to get a life. That's what Jack said when he left. Right after he said Mrs. Claus wasn't sexy." Oh, she should have remembered that earlier. She glanced down and cringed at the sheen of silver glitter covering her clothing and skin.

Merry chuckled. "Well, Santa likes the Mrs., but do you like Santa?"

Annie rubbed her hands on Feather, but the sparkles seemed to have taken root in her skin. "I've found a couple of places."

"What's that now?"

"Houses to buy. I've found a few on the Internet."

"You're moving? Milt and I were saying you needed a change. It's unhealthy for you staying in that basement of yours. Good for you."

A pang of worry raced through her heart. "How are you?"

"I repeated myself, didn't I?" Disgust coated Merry's words. "Don't you fuss. The doctors have me a bit doped up, that's all. Everything's good. You sound better than I'd expected. I'm proud of you. It's hard, but apron strings are meant to be cut."

Annie glanced toward Kelly's room across the hall and gripped the phone tight. "I'll be okay."

"We'll get you through this, kiddo."

Annie stared at the papers strewn across the floor and prayed she was making the right decision.

CHAPTER 2

Labour Day Long Weekend

After Annie handed the keys of her city house to a property manager, she jumped into her new-to-her pickup and headed north from Calgary on Highway 2. Her destination was a little town over an hour closer to Kelly and Jack. An orange tarp, which covered a few precious belongings in the truck bed, flapped in the wind as she traveled through the countryside. The air hinted at autumn's imminent arrival. A moving van would deliver her furniture and other possessions later in the day. She couldn't wait that long.

She'd seen her new home—not a house, her beautiful little two-story was already a home to her—once before, three weeks earlier. During that short viewing, Annie had measured all the rooms and taken copious digital views of the yard. Then she'd carefully laid out the scaled drawing of her new house, tacking little cutouts of the furniture in place with tape. She was ready for this. Everything would be wonderful. This move was exactly what she needed.

Over an hour later, she left the main highway, and another half-hour after that, she guided her truck off the secondary highway and into the little town of Morning Lake—what a perfect name for her paradise. This place didn't even have traffic lights—just a few four-way stops.

When she parked her pickup in an angled stall on Main Street, people on the sidewalk watched her with undisguised curiosity. On her previous visit, the streets were packed with summer tourists, but it was September now so these people were probably the locals. Her neighbors. If she ever moved again, maybe they'd all be friends. Then they might help her and she'd feed them beer and homemade chili as a thank you.

In the meantime, she waved at a couple of the unabashed observers and suppressed the urge to dance as she hurried to the realtor's office. The bells on the door jingled as she pushed it open.

The front desk was empty. "Mrs. Jury?"

"Back here, dear. Oh, Mrs. Bingley, hello." Mrs. Jury glanced at her watch. "My, but you've made good time."

Annie grinned. "I'm here to collect the keys. Are they ready?"

"Of course. Let's settle these last few documents, then you've got yourself a new home."

Ten minutes later, she was back in her truck, heading homeward over unfamiliar roads. The landscape had changed in those few weeks. The green aspen groves were tinged with yellow, red machinery dotted the open fields, and the sky was a brilliant blue. Although she wasn't anxious about her decision, she figured this riot of beauty and color was yet another good sign.

The last time she'd been to the house, she'd noted the way by local landmarks. Annie now read those transcribed directions. "Pass two intersections going east on the highway. Turn left at the red Quonset. Then follow the gravel road until you go over the railway tracks. From there, the first house on the right side of the road is mine." Easy peasy.

When she turned off the highway onto the gravel road, the steering wheel tugged under her loose grip. She hadn't driven on these types of road much in her life, but it didn't take a genius to figure out the wheels were catching on the loose gravel at the sides of the worn grooves. She tightened her hold and watched the road ahead for the railway tracks. Houses were quaintly placed in clusters of trees across the gentle rise and fall of the golden fields. Perfect and peaceful. She rolled down the window to breathe in the goodness of the country air.

Then she saw it.

Dirt and rocks billowed behind a mechanical beast on the road ahead.

Move over already. You don't need the whole road. She directed her vehicle closer to the shoulder.

The steering wheel tugged again.

What was going on? The truck wasn't obeying. Brakes! Gah! She wasn't stopping. No, her foot was pressed on the accelerator. Shoot, she wasn't on the shoulder anymore ... The ditch was right there ... No ...

She was in the ditch.

Still clutching the steering wheel, Annie blinked. She had stopped. A filthy fog of dirt and rock floated around her—up her nose, in her eyes, down her throat. She choked and coughed, vaguely aware of the sound of the other vehicle stopping on the road above.

"Jesus Christ." The man slammed his door. "What the hell were you thinking?"

"*Me?*" She wiped the dust from her nose and mouth. "What were *you* doing?"

Crap, the door wouldn't open—it kept hitting the slope in the ditch. She was trapped in her truck at the bottom of the ditch with some lunatic who didn't drive properly. Tears rushed to flush out the grit in her eyes. Great—dust smears were probably running down her face, and he'd think she was crying. She blinked again rapidly, trying to hurry the process.

A moment later, the dust had settled and the world was quiet.

She assessed the man on the road in a quick beat—his baseball cap had probably been in service for the last fifteen years, his faded jeans fit snugly over lean hips, and the creases around his eyes suggested he'd spent his life squinting into the sun. He was one of the sexiest men she'd ever seen outside of movies.

And now he was focused on her.

When the corner of his mouth kicked up in a lopsided grin, heat rolled over her skin as if he'd caressed her. Annie swallowed and looked away, mortified by her immediate heated response to him.

Maybe she was going through an early menopause.

She pushed on the door again.

"Don't move so fast now." The man scrambled down the steep slope of the ditch toward her. "Check to make sure you're okay before you go flailing around."

"I'm not flailing." Annie retorted, but she stopped trying to reef the door open. A snicker drew her attention back to the stranger. "Are you laughing at me?"

"Are you okay? You look fine, but let me know if you have any bumps on your head or aches in your bones."

She checked her limbs, even though she knew she was okay. The real issue was that he'd driven her off the road.

"The only pain I have right now is you. Oh, my ... I'm sorry ... I ..." She covered her mouth with her hand. She never said things like that. Ever. What was wrong with her?

But of course she knew what the problem was. He was an attractive man, that's what. Men like him made her lose her mind.

Now he really was laughing at her. Out loud. Right outside her window. "All right, then," the man said. "I haven't been called a pain in the ass in a good long time. I guess I was due."

"I didn't call you that. I ..." Heat rushed to her cheeks. She hadn't called him a pain in the ass, only a pain. She was certain. She banged her shoulder on the door again, hoping for some give. "I'm sorry, really."

"Relax. We'll get you out of there. First, let's see if you can reverse out of the ditch."

The engine was still running and her foot still pressed on the brake, so she changed gears and peered over her shoulder to see if anyone else was coming on the road. The orange tarp blocked her view.

Oh, no! All the precious glass and breakables she hadn't trusted to the moving company would be jostled and askew.

"What's the hold up? No one's coming. Come on, let's go." The man hit the hood of her truck as if he were prodding a donkey or cow or some other kind of dim-witted animal.

She bit her lip and pressed the gas pedal. The truck rocked once and then stopped. Nothing. She closed her eyes for a moment before opening them to beg the universe silently for another idea. She turned off the ignition. The universe wasn't answering. "Now what?" She pushed against the door again.

The man started to reach through her open window.

"What are you doing?"

He pulled his hand back and rested it on the window instead. "I was reaching in to undo your seatbelt."

"Oh. Um, I can do that."

The man shook his head as he braced himself on the frame of the truck and watched her. She knew he watched because she didn't take her attention off him while she fumbled for the seat belt release.

"You're the one who bought the old Geller place, aren't you?"

Annie nodded.

The man's smile threatened to open into laughter again. She didn't like being laughed at, but then again, who did? Besides, what was so funny? She lifted her head and scowled, using the same expression she'd perfected on Kelly when she drank milk straight from the carton. He laughed. Again. Well, wasn't that special?

"Listen, I'm sure you have better places to be. I can manage on my own." The seatbelt clicked and immediately loosened across her chest.

"Sure, but how could I resist this? After all, I was wondering what I was going to talk to the guys about today. I didn't want to hear about Ryan's conquest of the underwear model again."

Annie stared at him, mouth gaping.

He was still laughing when he reached in and nudged the bottom of her chin with the tip of his large thumb. "Don't look so shocked."

She pulled back and rubbed her chin, which tingled from his brief contact. His skin had been so rough. And no one touched her. Not anymore. Then again, that's what she wanted to change, wasn't it?

"All right, then," the man said. "Let's get you out."

"Let's."

"Go to the other door. Maybe it'll open."

A truck had two doors. She rolled her eyes. God, she was an idiot. This wasn't menopause. She'd obviously sniffed too much glue over the last year.

She collected her sketches of the house and the sheet of directions from the passenger seat, and placed them in a pile on the dashboard. She slid across the bench seat to the passenger side. That door didn't open either. "Nope."

She glanced back to find the man eying her, and crossed her arms in front of her chest. "What's your name?"

"I didn't think the door would open, but it was worth a try. These ditches should be rebuilt—they're too steep. I'll talk to Mitch at the County Office again." While he spoke, he continued to look her up and down. "Oh, and the name is Quinn. Well, my parents named me John, but everyone around here calls me by my last name. It's probably 'cause of my high school football years."

"Umm ... Why are you eying me up?" She swallowed. Under similar circumstances, other women would probably think he was making a pass at them. Annie knew better.

Quinn grinned. "Well, we have two options. You either jump through the window and then I pull your truck out of the ditch, or you stay put and I drag the truck out with you in it."

"So you were deciding if I'm too big to fit through the window? How charming."

"That's not it at all. You've got some nice curves, nothing out of place as far as I can tell." He winked at her. "I was just thinking you'd probably prefer to stay in the cab because of your fancy clothes."

He was right. She had dressed with care, wanting to strut into her new life with a bit of attitude. At this rate, though, she would never get there. Wait, did he say he'd tow the truck out of the ditch? Not with her inside. No way. "I'm coming out."

"I'll make sure you don't fall."

She bit her lip as she pivoted toward the open window, toward him. She avoided his gaze—he was too close, too much, at this proximity—but she knew he watched as she knelt on the driver's seat. When she tried to crawl forward, her foot became tangled on something. God, now what? Annie glanced down.

Cleavage!

Her hand flew to her chest to clutch her shirt closed—albeit belatedly—as she kicked her foot to free it. When the passenger side seatbelt flung against the far door with a clunk, Annie spared a quick glance at Quinn. His gaze was fixed on hers, as if he struggled not to look lower. His brown eyes were darker than a moment ago and he grinned—yes, indeed, he'd seen straight down her shirt. Some small part of her was immensely relieved she'd grabbed her lacy bra instead of the frayed cotton one she usually wore.

The other part wished she'd worn a turtleneck.

Truck windows weren't meant to be used as doors, at least not by her and not while she still clutched her shirt closed. She'd managed to get her upper body through the opening, but when she tried to pull her leg around, her knee kept hitting the steering wheel.

How did they do this on *The Dukes of Hazzard*? Maybe it would be better if she backed toward the window, bum first.

When she started to crawl back inside to reorient herself, Quinn cleared his throat and she froze.

Then he reached for her.

"Stop that." She jerked away, banging her back on the truck in her effort to pull away.

"Jesus, woman, relax. I'm trying to help." He stepped forward to place his hands on her waist. "Put your hands on my shoulders."

His voice was so close to her ear now that his breath tickled her neck. With one hand on his shoulder and the other still clenching her shirt, she wiggled and kicked her legs, trying to inch her way toward the window again. Then she stopped. What was she doing? Swimming to him?

Closing her eyes, she let go of the front of her shirt and placed that hand on him, too.

Within seconds she was free of the truck. His hands were on her waist still as he lowered her to the tall grasses. "You can open your eyes now."

She blinked as she yanked her hands off him and adjusted her shirt.

He turned away from her and strode toward his truck.

"Wait. Where are you going? Are you leaving me here?" How far was the nearest house? A mile? Two? With her luck, she'd arrive at her place and have to keep hiking somewhere else. "Listen, I'm sorry—"

"Do you want to have your truck pulled out or what, lady?"

"My name isn't lady, it's Annie."

But as far as she could tell, he was ignoring her now. He reached into the flat bed of his truck and brought out a chain. Good, he wasn't abandoning her.

Giving up on Quinn, she gave into the temptation to check her boxes. She loosened one of the corners of the tarp, fearful of what she'd find. She peered under it. Everything was better than she had imagined. The box with her glass angels was still snug in the corner. Beside it, the carton with the Santa figurines appeared okay, but the Christmas balls ... Her heart sank. That box had rolled toward the bag with the wreaths. She reached in to tilt it back, but it was too far away.

Meanwhile, Quinn had pulled his truck around and started to hook the chain to his hitch. "I don't understand what you're so worried about. I haven't seen anyone creep into a ditch like that before. Probably didn't even spill your coffee."

"I don't drink coffee." She climbed onto the bumper and fixed the box of balls. Wait a minute, why did he get to blame her for this?

"What were you doing anyway? You were right in the middle of the road with that big thing of yours. I had no choice but to move to the ditch."

He raised an eyebrow. "How long have you been driving this truck?"

She drew the tarp over her boxes and tightened it again. "Two weeks."

"I don't think you have any idea how much room you need on the road, or rather how little room ..." When Quinn returned, he carried one end of the chain with him as he walked. The thick metal links snaked across the ground behind him.

Was he trying to make her feel stupid? If he was, he was successful. But she didn't have to let anyone poke fun at her any more. At least that was one good thing about Jack leaving. No, that was wrong. She wanted Jack back. They were family.

Annie raised her chin. "Obviously, neither do you."

"I'm not the one in the ditch." He reached under her truck.

Annie crossed her arms and watched him with what she hoped was indignant silence. She did not think about his nice butt. Nope—not once.

Within five minutes of him fiddling with this and that, her truck and precious possessions were back on the road. She and her truck were almost free from him.

"Thank you for hauling me out of the ditch." Her relief eroded her indignation. She reached out to shake his hand, but he lifted his baseball cap instead.

"No problem. Be careful now."

She walked toward her truck.

"Listen, Annie."

She stopped.

"If you need some help with the Geller place, I do some home repair work now and again."

"Do you have a card?"

When he said sure, she was surprised. He didn't seem the type to have a business card. Then he extracted a battered, dirty cream-colored card from his wallet.

"Thanks." She took the card and stuffed it into her pants pocket without reading it. Part of the pride of ownership was doing renovations—a whole industry of hardware stores was built around do-it-yourself projects. She didn't want to call in someone else to do this for her. She had a metaphorical chisel in her hand ready to carve herself a new life. A better life.

This man underestimated her, which she supposed was no great surprise after this whole ditch fiasco.

CHAPTER 3

Driving onto her property for the first time as an independent homeowner sent a typhoon of satisfaction through her heart. The house was old enough to be steeped in historical charm, worthy of a magazine cover. A ladder leaning against the front porch had vines growing around its base. Sure, the vines were weeds, but those could be picturesque, too. The barn at the far end of the yard leaned to the left, but that was okay, too. It had character.

Annie hopped from her truck. The troubles with Quinn and the ditch were almost forgotten as the hollyhock flowers bowed toward her from their cluster at the side of the house. She curtsied back. A girl with a new dollhouse wouldn't be happier.

Fishing the house keys from her pocket, she glided over the broken sidewalk blocks to the steps leading to the porch and front door. What should she do first? She could paint the outside before winter hit, weed the garden or plant perennials. The yard was bursting with possibilities, and she could do whatever she wanted.

"Hi, honey, I'm home." She slid her hand across the weathered handrail. "Ouch." Annie jerked back and squinted at her finger. A sliver. She'd live.

The treads groaned as she climbed the steps to the front door. Then there was a creak, then a crunch. "What the—?"

The heel of her shoe had sunk into a rotten wood plank.

She tugged her foot from the shoe. Then she reefed her shoe free. The heel was scarred, but better that than her ankle. She scanned the expanse of wood leading to the front door as if she could judge its structural integrity. When she finished her renovations, she'd be more knowledgeable. But right now? She didn't have a clue. With careful gentle steps, she crept to the front door.

The key slipped into the lock with ease, and her heart lightened again. Home—her ticket to the life she deserved. When she reconciled with Jack and they were living as a family again, they could keep this as a vacation property. They could return for holidays and summer vacations, and rekindle all the memories they'd make here this year.

Her mind whirled with a blur of decorating ideas as she stepped into the front vestibule. Its white painted trim, leaded glass door, and built-in shelves for wet shoes were just so welcoming. The space begged for something special.

Everything was how she remembered it. Sort of. Now that the Gellers' furniture was removed, a few problems she hadn't noticed before were visible. The hardwood floor had a big black stain right in the middle of the living room, and the plaster walls were pockmarked with gaping wounds. Dusty outlines showed there had been pictures hanging over the injured walls. She touched one of the holes. The plaster turned to dust under her fingers, a little avalanche of powder that cascaded to the floor.

A picture would be okay there, in the short term anyway. She turned around in the beautiful room. The fireplace's smooth white mantel drew your eye, the plaster at the ceiling rounded where it met the wall framing the room, and the windows faced the garden. She'd plant roses out there. Big yellow roses. Yes. This would do wonderfully.

She went through the house room by room and although little problems cropped up here and there, nothing could bring her spirit down. She had her beautiful, quaint character house in the country, and with a little elbow grease, it would be perfect.

She had brought in the bucket of cleaning supplies from her truck when her cell phone rang. The display announced it as Merry.

"Are you all moved in?"

"Hi, Aunty. I'm getting there. It is wonderful." Annie took her armload of supplies to the kitchen.

"I'm glad it is."

"Listen, I would love it if you and Uncle Milt came for Thanksgiving," Annie said as she removed the soaps, powders and brushes from the bucket, setting them in a line on the counter.

"Will you be all settled in by then?"

"Of course." They talked for a few minutes more, before Annie ended the call. She already knew how she would decorate the porch for Thanksgiving. She set the bucket in the sink. The tap sputtered and groaned before spewing out brownish, orange liquid. She suppressed the urge to gag at the smell. Leaving the bucket in the sink to fill with what Annie could only guess might be water, she considered her new home. This might be too much. She was all for DIY, but even in her naïve I-can-do-this attitude, she knew a few too many things were adding themselves to her to-do list. She had to get this Thanksgiving perfect.

Yes, the first step was Thanksgiving, then the clincher would be Christmas. By New Year's Eve, she would have her family back.

She pulled out Quinn's card and placed it on the scarred countertop.

A ripple of unfamiliar sexual awareness swept over her as she remembered the feeling of his breath on her neck when he pulled her from the truck—

No, she wasn't attracted to him. It was just a little normal, everyday reaction to having a handsome man touch her. It would have happened to anyone.

Mr. John Quinn would help her with her house, and that was what she needed. He would be a good person to know. "It is wonderful here, really wonderful. Everything is going to be all set for Thanksgiving."

Even if she had to hire someone to make it happen.

CHAPTER 4

Annie sat on the edge of the front step and looked at her list again. If only she had thought to pack a lawn chair in her truck. The moving company was delayed, and with it being the long weekend she didn't hold much hope that they'd arrive before Tuesday.

Last night, she'd had to sleep in the truck. It was almost as uncomfortable a sleep as the night Jack told her he would be moving out the next morning, then rolled over and promptly started snoring. She probably should have driven to a hotel—on both occasions—but she hadn't.

Please let the kink in her neck work itself out soon. She needed to get working!

At least that John Quinn man hadn't hung up on her when she'd called him. Even better, he said he could meet her today to discuss what work she might like to have done. Why did the thought of seeing him again send a shiver over her skin? He was a stranger. And she wasn't supposed to be attracted to him—she was married, for heaven's sake.

No, that was wrong. She shook her head. When would she remember she was single? You'd think the hole in her chest where her heart used to live would be reminder enough.

The quiet of the morning was interrupted by the roar of a familiar truck. John nodded as he parked behind her vehicle. The driveway could have still held another ten or more vehicles, and from what she'd seen driving through the countryside, that was pretty typical. What a waste of space. Maybe she could reclaim some of that space and put in more flowers—

What was she doing? She needed to get the house under control before she tackled the outside.

Annie stood and crossed to meet John halfway. She held out her hand. "Thank you for coming on such short notice, Mr. Quinn," she said.

His mouth turned up in that lopsided grin. Gosh, he was cute when he did that. His hand wrapped around hers and they shook. His grip was strong, but gentle. She liked the feel of his hand around hers. "You can call me Quinn."

"Oh, right," Annie nodded. She pulled back her hand. "You ... um ... can call me Annie." Why was she so flustered? She'd shaken hands with hundreds of people over her lifetime. She nodded, but then winced as the motion sent a flash of pain up the side of her neck.

"What the matter?" His forehead was creased with worry when she managed to blink away the tears.

"Just a little kink. It'll go away." She rubbed the tight muscle.

"Let me see," he said as he stepped forward.

"Really, it'll be okay."

He ignored her, and attempted to walk around her. She turned to follow him, but he stayed her with a soft touch on her elbow. When he lifted her hair off her neck, she froze. She should stop this—stop him—but she couldn't. She held her breath and waited to see what he would do next.

His fingers brushed along the tensed muscle, sweeping over the most sensitive area of her neck. Of anything on her body, a kiss on her neck had always been her undoing. But this man—this stranger—wasn't going to kiss her.

He pressed small circles along the muscle, following the tight cord up and down—and she let him.

Her breath came out in jerky spasms.

"That's it," he said softly. "Relax."

He seemed to say that to her a lot, and they'd only known each other one day.

She stared straight ahead, fixating on his truck, while he stroked her neck. She didn't dare close her eyes. Heaven only knew what fantastical images might fill her head if she did. Her body was zipping to life with alarming speed. Parts of her body that hadn't tingled in years were suddenly fiery hot.

This was bad. So very, very bad. She should stop him.

But she didn't.

When he lifted his hand from her skin, she swayed back toward it again.

"Whoa," he said, grabbing her by the waist. "Steady now."

Easy for him to say. Annie stepped away from him on legs as strong a pipe cleaners from the dollar store. She slowly tilted her head from side to side. The muscle was still tight but the pain was minuscule compared to a moment earlier. It could just be that her body was now preoccupied with re-routing her adrenalin and endorphins. She cleared her throat, and turned to him. "Thank you. That might just do the trick."

"Okay, then." He smiled. If she wasn't mistaken, he looked a little flushed. At least she wasn't the only one. "So you have some work to do?"

When they got to the bottom of her list, he wasn't smiling anymore. They were sitting next to one another on the step, and he'd been stroking his chin for the last half of the page. "Unless you want to hire more people, you're going to have to choose what your priorities are."

"You don't think we can do it all before Thanksgiving?" Annie bit her lip. She did want all of those things completed. What could she live without?

"We?" One of his eyebrows curved up high on his forehead.

"Well, sure, I'll help you."

He took the list from her hand then, and drew a finger over the page. "I'm still not sure we can do all of it, but it'll go faster with two." Annie had the sense he still thought her list was crazy, but he didn't feel he knew her well enough to say so. "Listen, why don't we start with some of the big things? I can start on the porch, the floor, that kind of thing. And you can look after the painting."

"What about the water?"

"We'll have to head into town on Tuesday and see if we can find a water distiller or something. And we'll get someone around to test the water."

Annie nodded. "Okay. Shall we go look through the house?"

He stood and extended his hand to help her up. Annie stared at him for a moment before placing her hand in his. Jack hadn't helped her stand for years. Quinn's strong fingers wrapped around hers, a little hug for her hand. Her pulse fluttered at the touch. She pulled away from him as soon as she was standing and tucked her hand into her pocket.

A few steps inside the house, he turned to her. "Where is your furniture?"

"The moving company is MIA." She crossed her arms. "When I talked to their main office this morning, the woman said their truck broke down en route and that all their other trucks were booked until Tuesday."

He narrowed his eyes. "Which hotel did you stay in last night?"

She laughed. "Hotel Truck."

"So that's why you had the kink in your neck?"

Annie rubbed her better, but still tender neck. "I guess so."

"You're staying in a hotel tonight, though, right?"

She smiled and walked into the kitchen, ignoring his question, and proceeded to describe what she thought needed to be completed in the room.

Five hours later, she was surprised at how much they'd accomplished. The nail holes in the walls had been filled with mud Quinn happened to have in his truck, the broken and rotten boards on the porch had been removed, and a makeshift bridge had been built over the hole as a temporary way out the front door. When they said goodbye at the end of the day, Annie was incredibly happy with her decision to hire Quinn. He listened to her ideas, and when he offered advice he wasn't the least bit condescending. In fact, he made it seem like they were just having a conversation and talking through the options. Jack could probably learn something from him to use in his business meetings.

Her stomach rumbled, so she grabbed a granola bar and went to sit on the front step again. She'd need to get more groceries soon. The few apples and granola bars she had packed for her drive wouldn't sustain her for long.

Annie reviewed her list as she munched. Quinn was probably right. Her wish list was ambitious. She'd crossed off two items when a truck pulled into her drive. He was back. A tarp covered something in the back of his truck. When he jumped out, he waved at her.

"I didn't expect to see you back here tonight. Is something wrong?"

He shook his head and started to release the ties holding the tarp down.

"Quinn?"

"I couldn't let you sleep in your truck again, could I?" He winked at her as he threw the tarp off his load to reveal an old-style cot with a striped mattress. "That *is* what you were planning, right?"

Heat rushed to her cheeks. "Um … maybe. But you don't—"

"Yes, I do." He opened the tailgate and jumped into the bed of his truck. "Are you going to help?"

"Oh, of course." Annie dashed to the truck and helped him lift the bed out.

They carried it into the living room.

"This should be okay," she said.

He shrugged. "It is up to you. Now, if you want to set up the cot, I have to run out and grab a few more things."

"What—?" But he was already through the door.

The cot's metal hinges creaked as she unfolded it. She stared at it. He had brought her a bed so she wouldn't have to sleep in her truck. Tears welled in her eyes. He was the nicest man she'd met in a long, long time.

She wiped away the tears when she heard him return. The lack of sleep and her excitement were making her emotional—she had to get control.

He carried three plastic shopping bags and a pillow. "Here," he said as he tossed one bag to her.

Oh, he'd even remembered to bring linens. Her tears resurfaced. She turned away from him and fumbled to remove the sheets from the bag.

Behind her, she heard him continue into the kitchen and open the refrigerator. A moment later, he was back at her side. She took a deep breath and prayed she had her emotions steady again.

"What was that?"

"Nothing much. A bit of bread and milk and such," he said. "Here, let me help you make the bed."

Annie hugged the sheet to her chest. "Why?"

"Why what?" But, of course, it was clear that he knew what she was asking.

He didn't evade her study. For such a simple moment between two near strangers, an unexpected intimacy seemed to blossom.

"Why are you helping me like this? You don't even know me."

"Sometimes people need a little help, even if they won't ask for it." His words were soft, and suddenly the air between them seemed alive with possibility. He stepped closer to her—was he going to kiss her?—and then he reached for the corner of the sheet she'd balled in her hand. "I'm just trying to help. Besides, it is hardly like I needed the cot tonight."

She blinked through blurry eyes. "Thank you."

"You're welcome. Now let's get this cot prepped and then I'll leave you in peace."

CHAPTER 5

Days slipped away quickly. The end of September meant only a few short weeks remained before her house would be bulging with family. Annie stared at the calendar every morning, counting the days and thinking about all the work still to be completed. Motivation, tinged with panic, propelled her through the day.

Well, that and Quinn's steady presence.

He was a godsend. He worked right alongside her through the long exhausting hours, but managed to convince her to stop for a grocery run now and again. One night he even packed up the paint cans and took them with him when he left so she wouldn't paint through the night.

He was so sweet.

A great neighbor.

Nothing more.

Honestly.

And to be fair to him, Annie insisted that he take the weekends off. He agreed to take Sundays. So when his truck pulled into her yard that September Sunday afternoon, Annie's heart fluttered in her chest. If he wasn't there to work, that meant he was there to see her …

Of course she wasn't interested in him. No, that was silly. And he was probably just being a friend, checking to make sure that she, too, was taking a bit of a break.

He couldn't have known she'd been awake all night, thinking about him.

The truth was that she hadn't realized how labor-intensive all this house renovation work would be. Her body ached every night. And she couldn't help but remember the way he'd soothed away that kink in her neck.

Her skin tingled at the thought of it.

Only because he'd done such a great job.

But for some reason, the dark quiet of night, which in the countryside was really dark and really quiet, liked to take that innocent memory and play with it. In her half-awake-half-asleep state of mind, it almost seemed as though his hands were touching her again … but they strayed to the most delicious places.

Those wayward imaginings were difficult to shove on her mind's shelf, the one with the lock and key, each morning before he arrived. And it hadn't helped that whenever he was there, they worked side-by-side.

Perhaps most surprisingly, her fantasies weren't always sexual.

No. Now her fantasies were starting to morph into speculating on what a future might look like with him.

It was all perfectly crazy.

Annie tossed her clothespins into her laundry basket on her way to the truck. Thankfully, she was only hanging sheets.

"Hey, stranger," she said, "I didn't expect to see you here today."

Quinn jumped out of his truck with a contagious smile and a spring in his step. "You'll never guess what I found today."

"A whittling kit?" For some reason, her latest fantasies had them sitting on the porch, she looking through holiday magazines while he whittled. He *was* quite talented with his hands …

He cocked his head. "Um, no. Whittling? Do people even do that anymore?" He walked to the back of his truck and started loosening straps on something that was sticking out over his tailgate. Then she saw table legs sticking up in the air. "No, I found something a helluva lot more useful than that."

"A table?"

"I was driving through town when I came across a fundraiser at the elementary school. They were getting rid of some of their old furniture. I'm pretty sure I sat at this table in art class in Grade Two. Anyway, I saw it and I thought it'd be perfect for your craft studio."

"You bought me a table? For my crafts?" Her old craft table had been a folding one with a wonky leg, and it hadn't made the move to Morning Lake.

"Don't get all teary-eyed." Quinn's words teased, but his tone was soothing and he looked pleased with her reaction.

Annie rushed over and hugged him. "Thank you! I don't know how to thank you enough for this. I—"

When Quinn's laughter rumbled beneath her cheek, she realized what she'd done. His strong arms wrapped around her, warming her. She hadn't even realized the fall breeze was quite cool until she was sheltered by his body.

Every tingle-inducing, sizzle-evoking fantasy surged through her mind. She closed her eyes, and the unbidden thoughts seized the opportunity to flash their explicit offspring across her vision.

Whatever she'd been saying, the words were forgotten.

And Quinn was returning her hug.

Those powerful hands of his pulled her snuggly against him, his fingers splayed across her back. If she held her breath, bathed in his tantalizing scent, she could almost pretend this moment could live a little longer.

Or, what if this was the moment their relationship shifted? What if—

Wait, she wasn't in a relationship with Quinn. She was supposed to be thinking about her family, and that included Jack.

Annie swallowed and broke the embrace.

"I appreciate this," she said, turning her attention to the table. But she couldn't resist sparing a quick glance at him. She could almost pretend that he looked like he wanted to kiss her the way she would have liked to be kissed. He didn't look at the table, no, his entire focus was on her. As if the rest of the world didn't exist around them. And now that she'd looked at him, she was pulled into his magic.

"I couldn't pass it up." His voice was deeper than usual, and his gaze drifted over her upturned face.

She licked her lips as he leaned closer.

Then a siren screamed through the air around them. She hadn't heard that sound since she'd moved.

Quinn spun toward the road as a fire truck passed by her house.

"Shit."

"Oh, no."

"Okay, let's that's get this off the truck, then I've got to go. I'm a volunteer fireman, and they've probably been trying to get hold of me. I forgot my cell at home this morning. Shit." He shook his head.

When they pulled the table off the truck, she urged him to go.

He nodded. "But don't take it into the house by yourself. It is too heavy. I'll be back to help you."

He studied her for a long moment, then he raced to his truck to track down a fire.

Panic surged through her heart as she watched him leave. She prayed he would be safe.

CHAPTER 6

The big city television news shows had only a passing reference to a wildfire in the county, so Annie had dug out a radio and dialed it to the local station. It wasn't much better, but at least they kept confirming that everyone was safe. Apparently the grass fire had been started by a bit of straw getting caught in one of the machines used to take the crops from the fields.

She'd fallen asleep listening to the radio, and her dreams were a mishmash of dark images and strange, frightful emotions. So very different from her other dreams.

Morning arrived and she still hadn't heard from Quinn.

She stared out the window at the table he'd brought her, a reminder the previous day really had happened.

It was impossible to concentrate on anything when she didn't know what was happening with Quinn. She paced, she tidied, she paced, she scrubbed, then she paced some more.

By mid-morning, the crunch of tires on her gravel driveway had her running outside.

Quinn's hair was damp, like he'd just hopped out of the shower, but otherwise he looked the same as always.

He waved at her and walked to the table.

"Are you okay?"

"Good enough."

"The circles under your eyes suggest differently."

He shrugged. "I'm glad you didn't try to move the table."

Okay, so he didn't want to talk about it. "I tried, but it was too heavy."

"All right, then, let's get it inside." He seemed different this morning, which was good. She wasn't sure how she was going to talk to him about their almost-kiss the day before. Nothing had happened. And it couldn't. Not when she was implementing her big plan in a few weeks. Her family had to be her priority, and she wasn't sure how to explain that to Quinn.

And she wasn't even sure if she had to. Maybe she'd been imagining that he'd been about to kiss her. Her imagination did seem to be quite active lately.

They each grabbed an end of the table, and after a few tight corners through the house, they managed to get it into her craft room. It was perfect for the space.

Quinn nodded when they set it down. "I thought it'd fit."

"Thank you again," she said. The table was stretched between them, and for the moment that seemed a safe distance.

"Okay, we've got some work to do, don't we? Today I wanted to get the baseboard up again."

"Right," Annie agreed. Had she imagined the near-kiss? "Um, Quinn?"

Quinn stopped at the threshold and looked back.

"I'm glad you are okay."

He shrugged. "It took longer than I'd have liked, but we got it under control."

She cleared her throat, as heat stole over her cheeks. "I was worried about you."

His forehead creased as he studied her face, like he was trying to figure out what she meant by her confession. "I'm sorry I worried you," he said. His voice was soft.

"Do fires happen a lot around here?"

He shook his head. "No, but we had one last year and now this one."

"Was it a grass fire last year, too?"

"No, my buddy Devin's place caught on fire. Special circumstances on that one. Actually, I became a volunteer fireman after that. And when I helped him rebuild his place, I discovered that I liked doing stuff like this." Quinn knocked on the doorjamb that he'd replaced the week before.

"Okay, good," Annie said, "so not too often then." That eased some of her worry. With any luck, that would be the end of fires for the season.

"Let's get to work."

And with that, the conversation was closed, and it seemed they were both eager to get their friendship back onto familiar ground. Their easy camaraderie returned by midday, and it was only in the depths of the night that her imagination explored what might have been.

CHAPTER 7

Thanksgiving

The cold north wind howled each night, keeping Annie and Quinn company as they worked long hours to get the house ready for Thanksgiving. The days were still warm, but coolness had seeped into the air and bit at her ankles at the start of each day.

When Quinn opened the front door and called to Annie, the drone of nearby combines and balers filtered in. She hadn't known what those machines were a few weeks ago, and felt absurdly proud of herself for knowing that now—although she couldn't shake her worry of another grass fire each time she saw one go by. "Come out and have a look."

After having worked together for so many weeks, his voice was as familiar to her as her family members'. With those few words, she could tell he was excited. She rushed to the front door and pushed it open. "Is it done?"

"You bet."

She plucked up one of the outdoor arrangements she'd made for the front step and scurried outside with it. She positioned it on the side of the step and turned to the porch itself. "You did a great job."

He shrugged. "I don't know about that, but at least you won't lose children and small animals in it anymore." He was being modest again. He did that a lot. But the angle of his chin and his strong posture told her he was proud of his work.

"I'm more worried about Uncle Milt. He isn't a small man, if you know what I mean." Then she gave into the temptation and jumped on the porch. Three times.

He watched her for a minute before shaking his head and bending to retrieve his tools. His eyes twinkled when he looked at her. Gosh, every time he looked at her like that her insides went gooey like melted marshmallows. But they shouldn't. He was a friend, and she was doing this work to get her family back together—including Jack.

"Is it okay?"

"Perfect!" Annie gulped. She needed to steer her thoughts back to her family. Badly. "Everyone will be impressed. Especially Jack. He isn't very handy, but he recognizes skill when he sees it."

Quinn cocked his head, and the twinkle in his eyes faded. "You've mentioned that a few times." He cleared his throat. "If you think the two of you'll need more work done later, I'm around."

"Great!" She nodded. Even Quinn knew Jack was coming back into her life—her ex didn't stand a chance against all the charm she was determined to infuse into the weekend. So, when this was what she wanted and planned, why did it feel awkward talking to Quinn about it? He had endorsed her plan from the beginning—not that he needed to, since they were hardly more than acquaintances, but it was good to have his vote of confidence. So again, why was it increasingly uncomfortable to talk to him about Jack and her grand scheme?

Probably because she'd dreamed about her sexy handyman every night since he'd pulled her from the ditch. And they weren't the innocent, acquaintance-like dreams they should have been.

Heat crept over her body. Oh, no, she couldn't think those kinds of thoughts now, not when he was standing there all sexy in his worn jeans and button-up plaid shirt. "Wait a minute and I'll get my check book." Annie ran into the house and slid across the newly polished floor in her sock feet.

When she returned to the porch, she brought the other arrangement for the other side of the step, too. Quinn had already brought up one of the deck chairs she'd had him make from a pattern she'd found on the Internet. "Wow. Just like a magazine spread." She sat on her new chair on her new porch, a queen sitting on her dais. She opened her checkbook and wrote out the payment for him. "Here you go," she said when she handed it to him.

He took it after he set down the second chair. "This is more than we agreed to," he said after a quick peek at it.

She shrugged. "I suppose, but I've had you do a lot of other extra work around here."

"We're … neighbors. You need to make the check right." He held it out to Annie to take back.

"I wouldn't have made it out for that amount if I hadn't wanted to."

He set the check on the empty chair. "I don't take charity."

"No. It isn't charity. What an odd thing to say." She grabbed the check. "I'm sorry if I offended you. I mean I wouldn't have been able to have Thanksgiving without all of your work and I think you worked longer hours than you'd expected when we started this."

He packed up his remaining tools and descended the steps.

"Wait. You can't leave with nothing. See? I've ripped it up." She raced down the stairs after him. "I'll write another one. With the agreed upon amount."

"You must have had some life in the city, to be tossing money around like that." The implication that their lives were polar opposites begged to be refuted, but Annie kept her mouth shut. How would Jack feel about the fact that her closest friend in Morning Lake was a man? He was prone to jealousy, so perhaps she needed to distance herself from Quinn.

Her hand quivered, but she grasped the checkbook tighter and wrote out a new check. "Here. Peace?"

He placed the tools in his truck and took the new check. "I'll go get your turkey tomorrow."

"Thank you, for everything. I didn't mean to offend you."

"No harm done." He patted his shirt pocket where he had placed his payment. "We're all square now."

"Listen, I was serious before. I want you to come to Thanksgiving." Maybe he and Jack would hit it off. "You said you didn't have plans." Annie followed Quinn to the driver's side of his truck. Gravel and twigs jutted into the bottom of her feet through her socks.

He didn't say he was coming, but he didn't say he wouldn't either. A moment later, he was gone. She hoped he came. This was going to be the best Thanksgiving she'd ever hosted.

She suspected he didn't want to come, though. Her efforts to distance herself had obviously worked. A peculiar hurt shot through her chest, not unlike the ache that rose when she thought about Jack.

Annie shook her head. A twinge of apprehension was natural after weeks of planning such a special event. There was one day to go before her life was set right again. With a few more decorations, everything would be ready outside, and a few more hours inside and her house would be set for her first bunch of company.

How exciting to have everyone together again. That's what she needed to think about.

They could have a bonfire and roast marshmallows one night. The nights were getting colder, but with blankets and a fire it'd be okay still. Then they could marvel at the stars, watch the satellites zip through the night sky, and roast chestnuts. Hmm ... Morning Lake's grocery stores might not carry chestnuts. She'd have to check when she did her last minute shopping.

Annie climbed the stairs and did a spin on her porch before entering the house.

Inside she went to the kitchen and put chestnuts on her grocery list before going into her craft studio. She was almost organized. This was the last room in the house to get ready, and it was the most precious. She had given her studio what was rightfully the master bedroom. The big windows facing onto the yard were perfect … plus, the room was huge.

She and Quinn had built storage shelves along the longest wall, and the big table Quinn had found at the school thrift sale held a place of prominence in the center. It would allow her to work on either multiple projects at once or one large one. He'd said he knew it would be perfect for her when he'd seen it, and he was right.

She had five boxes left to unpack, which was quite a feat. It had been time-consuming, but she'd stowed her supplies in clear plastic bins with crisp little labels and photos of the contents fixed to each container. Christmas ornaments took three-quarters of the shelves. Her Victorian Christmas, her mountain Christmas, her paper Christmas, her purple Christmas and more were all carefully sorted. Yes, the year since Jack had moved out had been busy. Most of the ornaments had never been used, but that'd change this year.

Pushing the last box into place, a sense of peace and accomplishment filled her. The house was ready. Everything was ready. The decorations were in place. The turkey was on its way.

Jack wouldn't imagine such a perfect holiday as this.

CHAPTER 8

Where had the time gone? Everyone would be getting there soon and there wouldn't be enough time to run to the grocery store for chestnuts. Maybe at Christmas.

The house was picture perfect, and now that she'd had her shower and done her hair—well, she'd never be a model, but she'd done okay. She wanted Jack to remember how perfect she was at hosting his functions, how presentable. She'd heard time and again at those little evening soirées that she was a great executive's wife. It was time to remind him of that. Smoothing her skirt again, Annie tried to steady her nerves. She couldn't wait until they arrived. She leapt down the stairs to the kitchen to the steady beep of the oven timer, which announced the last pie was done.

She plucked her apron off the chair and tied it around her waist. The apron, with its brown-and-gold-colored leaf pattern, matched the tablecloth and napkins. Would anyone notice?

Lined on the counter, the pies smelled wonderful. Why didn't she make them more often? The expression on everyone's faces when they came in the door and spied the treats would be well worth the effort. The pumpkin was for Milt, apple for her sister Jenna and a chocolate one for Kelly and Jack. Merry would try one of everything. Hopefully Quinn liked one of them.

Quinn. He should be there with the turkey soon. She turned off the oven, then checked the fridge. Yes, there was plenty of room for the turkey. She'd stuff it in the morning, and—

Oh! A car was coming down the drive. Her heart skipped. Straightening her shoulders and taking a calming breath, she tugged the kitchen curtain aside for a better view.

An old seventies style sedan crept into view. Merry and Milt. She waved to them.

Forcing herself to walk, not run, to the door, she opened the door as they popped the trunk open. "You found the place."

"Your directions were clear," Merry said as she waited for Annie to come to the car and help with the luggage.

During their quick hug, something in the back seat caught Annie's eye. Milt set one of their bags on the drive. "Oh, now, Merry, you haven't introduced our girl to Tiger and Dumbbell yet."

"Tiger and Dumbbell?" She broke the hug with her aunt. "Are those animal carriers?"

"We couldn't leave them at home," Merry said, worrying her hands. "I hope you don't mind."

"Tiger is a sweetheart. He's about your age in cat years, with a heart of a lion." Milt closed the trunk and came around.

"Well, go on, tell her about Dumbbell."

"That isn't its name, is it?" She stepped back to let Milt open the rear door. He lugged out the first carrier. An orange cat yowled pitifully from its prison. "I'd heard cats prefer to stay home when their owners go away."

"I knew she wouldn't want them here," Milt muttered.

"Oh, no. Not these two." Merry ignored him, poking her finger inside the carrier to rub Tiger's chin. "We'll just get them inside before ..." Merry glanced at the barn fearfully.

"They aren't going to get out unless we let them out." Milt's words were muttered with a tone that suggested they'd had this discussion several times already. He hauled out the second carrier, which held a spaniel. The small dog whined while scratching at the side of the carrier. Its body wiggled so much the carrier looked like a shaken pop bottle about to explode. "Here's Dumbbell."

Her aunt lifted the carrier with the cat and cradled it in her arms. "Be a dear and bring in the luggage."

"Of course." Annie nodded, watching her frail aunt step over the uneven ground leading to the porch. Thankfully, she'd had Quinn replace the broken sidewalk blocks.

Milt stepped up beside Annie. "The nurses told her animals would be good for her health, so we went to get one. You know Merry. She couldn't decide what she wanted so she got these two."

"How long have you had them?"

"About two weeks."

"She didn't say anything," Annie said as she retrieved two small suitcases. She left Dumbbell for Milt. Gosh, these cases were heavy. Her muscles, still tight from the renovations, protested the load.

"She wanted to surprise you."

"That she did." How could she turn away the animals now? Well, she couldn't, could she?

When they got to the front door, Milt stopped. The dog whined in its carrier. "Suppose he needs a potty break before we go inside."

Annie agreed. She didn't need any extra surprises, particularly on her refinished floors. She returned to the house and left Milt to tend to the dog.

"Merry?" Annie called as she entered the house. In the living room, she found her aunt perched on the side of the sofa with a straight back, arms still wrapped around the carrier.

"We need to get Tiger settled and then let's us humans have a cup of tea."

She tried not to think about the fact Merry hadn't said anything about her place yet. She would. It was only a matter of time. "Milt is with the dog."

"Doing his business? Good."

"Okay, let's go to your room." Annie hauled the luggage up the stairs. The look on Merry's face when she entered the beautiful guest room would be worth all the extra time it'd taken to finish it. Well, normally it would be Kelly's room, but for the weekend, it would be Merry and Milt's.

Merry followed her silently. When they got to the room, Annie placed the luggage on the trunk at the end of the bed. "Thank you, sweet pea. Now close the door and we'll be all set to let Tiger out."

Annie pushed the door shut.

The guest housecoats she'd found at the discount store swung on the back of the door. The guest towels were folded neatly on the dresser top with a small basket of toiletries, in case they'd forgotten anything. She'd bought some fresh cut flowers for the bedside tables and they were still perky and pretty.

"Thank you, dear."

Annie waited by the door and watched Merry wander around the room.

"Now we have to make a few adjustments ..."

Merry plucked the housecoats from the door and rolled them into a ball, which she then pushed into one of the dresser drawers. "Tiger climbs things … and if we …" Merry picked up the end of the pressed drapes and twirled them into a knot. Then she handed the towels and toiletries to Annie. "We'll get what we need from the linen closet, dear. No sense bothering with this for us. Oh, and ..." Then she seized the flowers. "These need to go away. Dumbbell chews on fresh plants and flowers, and then he gets such an upset stomach."

"No one wants the dog to be ill." Annie agreed. "I'll take these out." With full arms, she stepped from the room and shut the door behind her.

The guest room was awful now. She'd wanted everything to be perfect, but what could she do? She bit her quivering lip and straightened her shoulders.

After finding homes for all the bed and bath products, she stopped to straighten a picture on the wall. At least that didn't need to be hidden and tucked away.

Milt shouted her name from downstairs.

"What is the matter?"

"Come here a moment, will you?"

Something about his voice made her feet adhere to the floor.

"Annie?"

"Coming."

She found Milt holding a miniature pumpkin, which was covered in holes and slobber. "I'm sorry. Dumbbell took off with it before I had a chance to stop him." Milt held the battered little pumpkin out to her. The culprit was beside him, his tongue was hanging out, and he was looking as happy as a dog could.

Trying to touch as little of the pumpkin as possible, she took it from Milt. "Oh, it's okay. These things happen. I'll take care of this ..."

He stared at her, as if wanting something more.

"Umm ... Aunty Merry is upstairs. Go to the first door on the right." She pasted a smile on her face for Milt, but inside she couldn't believe how nonchalant he was about his dog destroying her hard work.

Milt, with the dog at his heel, passed Annie to go up the stairs. Her heart started to pound. The pumpkin could only have come from one place—the front step and her newly crafted entrance arrangements. The arrangements had been in place for less than twenty-four hours.

She returned to the porch and reluctantly assessed the damage. What a disaster. On the left, the little pyramid of pumpkins she had wired and attached to the topiary form was toppled. It didn't take Sherlock Holmes to determine this was the one with the missing pumpkin. Perhaps the arrangement was salvageable, but the other one ...

The other one sat in a puddle. Only one thing could cause a puddle on a day like today, and it had everything to do with the dog.

She set the mangled pumpkin on the step and tried to stay calm. It would be okay. Little glitches came up all the time. It'd be fine. She straightened the toppled topiary, realigned a pumpkin or two, and shoved the injured pumpkin to the back. *Voilà*. It was serviceable again. No one would know there'd been a problem with that one, but the puddle was still there, seeping into the planks of her new porch.

After washing everything with a hose, Annie itched to scrub her hands, but someone new had arrived.

It was Quinn. Shoot—she had to disinfect before she could even peep at the turkey. She waved to him and raised her index finger. She mouthed, "I'll be right back."

When he nodded, she ran into the house to pour antibacterial soap over her hands and forearms. The house was quiet. Milt and Merry were probably having a nap. They'd have to meet him later, like tomorrow at Thanksgiving.

Hearing the front door open, she said, "Do you have my turkey? Bring it into the kitchen."

"Are you sure?"

He arrived in the kitchen with empty hands.

"Where is it?"

"In the truck," he said.

"Well, it can't stay there."

"Annie, did you know you ordered a living turkey?"

She shook her head. "What do you mean, *living*?"

"It made turkey noises at me the whole drive back. It wasn't happy about the wind, by the way."

"It wasn't … happy? What do you mean? It's *alive*?"

"I guess I should have called, but I figured it seemed like something you'd want, what with you planning a traditional Thanksgiving and all."

"Authentic is different from a bloodletting. I can't ... I can't kill ... Oh, my God ..." Her head spun. "I have a dog and a cat and now a turkey. I have no dinner. There is no Thanksgiving without a turkey."

"Why don't you sit down a minute?" Quinn guided her to a chair. "It isn't the end of the world."

"Oh, no, don't laugh at me, not today. Today wasn't supposed to be a funny sort of day—it was supposed to be a perfect and wonderful day." Then the dog bounded down the stairs barking, his feet slipped on the hardwood floors and he slid into the wall with a thud.

"When did you get a dog?"

"He must hear the turkey." A crushing, tight pain seized her lungs. She was breathing too fast. "I could handle the pumpkin, the unexpected tag-alongs, and even the puddle on my new porch, but no dinner? You can't coast through Thanksgiving without dinner. Thanksgiving is all about the dinner."

"Annie." He placed his hands on either side of her face. "Annie, don't be so melodramatic."

"I can't get to the grocery store before it closes, and nothing is open tomorrow. If we were in the city ..." She stopped then. Quinn's face was so close. He was touching her. Her heart pounded with new panic—no, panic wasn't the right word—excitement? Would he kiss her? His gaze strayed down her face before becoming snagged on her lips. She opened her mouth. "Oh ..."

His quick intake of breath caused an erratic jump in her stomach that felt suspiciously like butterflies. She leaned closer. He blinked.

"Um." His eyes widened, then he removed his hands from her face. In the next moment, he had stepped away, well beyond reach. "There, you're returning to earth now." He cleared his throat. "I have stuff in my freezer. You're welcome to it."

"*Stuff?*" Annie rubbed the ache in her chest that she wasn't sure was from the turkey problem or yet another near-kiss with Quinn. The dog stood on the threshold and barked.

"I've got roasts of pretty near every description. I know it isn't a turkey, but—"

"A roast? No, a roast is good." She nodded quickly. "Dumbbell, enough!"

The dog's barks quieted to a whimper.

She rubbed her forehead. "Quinn, would you adopt my turkey?"

"I can take the turkey." He grinned and shook his head.

"Thank you."

"I'll be by later with a roast."

When he left her in the kitchen, she jerked a cookbook off the shelf. So help her, the beef dinner would be perfect.

"Who was that, dear?" Merry asked, as she entered the kitchen.

"Quinn. I think I mentioned him." She dragged her finger down the table of contents of her favorite recipe book.

"Quinn. Hmm ..." Merry's tone caught her attention.

"He's helped me around the house a bit. He's a neighbor."

"He seems to be an exceedingly helpful neighbor. He seems to know you quite well, too."

Good grief, what had Merry seen? Had she seen Quinn almost kiss her?

Merry's eyebrows lifted high on her forehead.

"It isn't like that."

"I won't say a word." Merry nodded conspiratorially and put her finger over her mouth. "We all have our little secrets."

CHAPTER 9

With Merry's speculations foremost in her mind, Annie didn't know how she would react when Quinn dropped off the roast later. The last thing she needed was Kelly to think she'd taken up with someone new. It didn't seem like something Kelly would accept. He was so different from her dad. Then again, that was probably a good thing. Good grief, what was she thinking? She wasn't getting together with Quinn! She was going to reconcile with Jack.

At dusk, she'd just poured herself a quick little glass of sherry, when a car turned into the drive.

After swallowing the drink in one gulp, she waved at Jenna from the window. Jenna wasn't alone—Kelly was here! Her heart thrummed with excitement as she rushed to greet them. "You found the place."

"You're in the boonies," Jenna proclaimed. as soon as she exited her car. Her long blonde ponytail swung gracefully down her back. It'd probably taken the better part of an hour for her to get her wavy hair that straight.

"You didn't get lost, did you?" Annie went to the passenger side of the car and waited for Kelly to climb out.

"Heya, Mom."

Annie pulled Kelly into a big hug, whether she wanted one or not. "I haven't seen you in forever."

Kelly wiggled from the hug. She didn't say anything.

"Is your dad coming later?"

Kelly glanced at Jenna. Annie followed her gaze.

Jenna hauled a bag from the trunk and set it on the driveway before she met her gaze. "He isn't coming, sweetie."

"I see," Annie said to cover the sound of her heart crunching. It looked as if she wouldn't need to have that awkward conversation with Quinn about borrowing his cot again after all. "Okay, let's get your stuff inside. Merry and Milt are already here."

Annie pulled out another two bags—and there were still more. The weight of one almost made her lose her balance, though that wouldn't explain why she was a little dizzy, too. Annie set it down and leaned against the car for a second to regain her balance. She probably should have rested a bit more before everyone arrived.

Jenna and Kelly were so much alike, unable to pack for a weekend without needing ten shirts and four pairs of shoes. It was surprising they had managed to fit their luggage into the car without strapping more to the roof. Maybe it was better that Jack hadn't come with them—he needed almost as much luggage as they did. Annie was still hauling bags to the house when another set of headlights turned into the drive.

Jenna, who had pulled the last bags from the trunk, pivoted to see the new arrival. "Expecting someone else?"

"No ... Yes ... The roast."

"Meat products drive trucks out here? Cool. Wait—did you say roast?" Jenna frowned at her. "That better be for tonight, because I want my turkey on Thanksgiving."

Annie smiled. "Well, you are welcome to prepare the turkey if you want. It's at my neighbor's house, still clucking or gobbling or whatever turkeys do."

"Oh." Jenna's face screwed up in disgust.

"I'm going inside." Kelly took her bags from her mom.

"Where are we sleeping?" Jenna asked. "I want to take the bags through."

Quinn's truck crept down the short drive. He must see them all standing outside and not wish to intrude. Annie waved at him. "Jenna, I'll be there in a minute, but in the meantime, because of Merry and Milt, I think you'll be in the basement on the sofa bed and Kelly will be on the couch in the living room."

Jenna and Kelly had opened the front door before Quinn brought his truck to a stop. Milt and Merry's dog greeted the girls with a bark. "What's that smell?" Jenna asked as they disappeared into the house.

The dog had probably peed again. Annie scowled.

Given Quinn's cautious approach, she'd expected him to toss the roast to her and bolt back down the drive. Instead, he stepped out of his truck. When she got close, he passed her a plastic bag. He nodded toward the other cars. "It looks like you've got a houseful."

"Yep. Everyone's together for the holiday." She peered into the package. She'd never seen a roast so large in her life. It was wrapped in brown paper and stamped in black ink: *Uninspected.* She'd have to hide that label from Jenna and Kelly. The last thing they needed was a hunger strike based on unfounded fears of BSE. At least, she hoped it was unfounded. Of course it was. Quinn was still alive. He seemed fine.

It was probably better not to think on it.

"All right then, I'll be—"

"You're welcome to come in for a drink and meet everyone," she interrupted.

He glanced at the house and then back at Annie. "Not tonight."

"I'd like you to come to dinner tomorrow, if you want. We'll sit down at two or so."

He shrugged, which seemed to be his favorite answer to that invitation.

"Thank you, again, for everything." She stepped forward. "I'm sorry about earlier."

"We've already settled that." It took a moment for her to realize he was talking about the check.

"No, I mean about me, my panic attack or whatever you want to call it."

He leaned against his truck. "Nothing to apologize for."

"I'm embarrassed."

"It's the first time you're having people in. I suppose it happens."

Annie leaned forward to kiss him on the cheek. He pulled back, moving out of reach.

"Oh, I ..." Her cheeks were burning. What was she doing? A kiss on the cheek, that's all she had been thinking, as a thank you. She'd do the same with her uncle—but Quinn wasn't Milt.

Then he touched her cheek. His eyes were so intense ... so beautiful ... They whispered of some great question. A question she should know how to answer.

"I was going to—"

He bent forward, and her words were forgotten. He lowered his lips to hers. Annie leaned into him, fingers tangled in the handles of the plastic bag. She kissed him back.

He smelled of sawdust and some kind of enticing musky aftershave. His lips were strong, but they moved with exquisite gentleness. He teased her, and she opened herself to him. His tongue darted in and out of her mouth, and she sank closer to him with a soft muffled groan.

She heard something in the distance, but the path his hand followed from her cheek to her neck was more important. Oh, mmm … He'd found that sweet wonderful place on her neck—

"Mom, are you still out there?"

Annie jumped. Kelly had caught her smooching with Quinn in the driveway. In a blink, he was in his truck and she was racing to the house. Her heart slammed against her chest. She tried to dry her lips discreetly. "What is it?"

"Come quick, Mom, something's happened."

CHAPTER 10

She had kissed Quinn, or he'd kissed her, or whatever. There was a kiss.

What a mess. She couldn't get involved with one of the only people she knew in the community. She was trying to create a perfect life for herself. The woman who was getting her family back.

Annie fumbled up the stairs to the front door with the roast swinging at her side. Even if Kelly hadn't seen her canoodling with Quinn, the whole family would be able to tell from her lips or cheeks or something as soon as she entered the house.

"What is it?" Her voice squeaked.

"In the kitchen." Kelly held open the door and she scurried inside.

Everyone stood in a cluster around the counter. Had they been spying on her out the kitchen window? Her heart pounded.

Jenna turned to Annie. "Now, we don't think this is as bad as it looks, but ..." Then Jenna waved to the pies.

Little cat-sized paw prints meandered through the pies. All of them. A couple of hours ago, she would have had another panic attack, but now this didn't seem like the worst thing in the world. She took a deep breath and tried to view the pies objectively.

"I'm sorry," Merry said. "Tiger doesn't go on the counters at home. I don't know what got into him."

"No worries," Annie declared. "We'll eat around the paw prints, and if that grosses anyone out—well, there is always ice cream."

"It must be cold outside, dear." Merry smiled. "Your cheeks are bright red."

She wanted to crawl under the table as everyone turned to study her face.

"You were out there for a long time." Jenna shivered. "It was too cold for me."

If she didn't say anything, it wouldn't be a lie. "I'm going to put the roast in the fridge." She turned away from the inquisitive eyes.

"Your neighbor friend didn't want to come in?" Milt asked.

"Not tonight."

"I bet he's off to push over sleeping cows or sew another patch on his jeans or whatever it is farmers do at night." Jenna laughed.

Annie's jaw dropped.

"Jenna, that's rude," Merry scolded. "Farmers work hard to provide us food. You are a teacher, for heaven's sake. What do you teach the children in your class?"

"I was joking," Jenna muttered, as she strutted to the living room.

With the pie crisis solved, everyone followed Jenna to the living room. Annie had the kitchen to herself again. She touched her lips and studied her reflection in the window over the sink. Her cheeks were still burning hot and her knees were wobbly, but at least from what she could tell her lips weren't swollen.

She shook her head and turned to the pies. They were a mess. At this point, her only option was to put them away so the cat didn't get to them again. She lifted the first pie, and her hand shook. Clutching the pie with both hands, she put it into the cupboard. Her hands continued to shake as she put the others away. The chocolate pie even jiggled when she placed it in the fridge.

She needed something for her nerves. Another sherry sounded perfect. After retrieving the glass she'd used earlier from the sink, she poured another little swallow of sherry. Everything would be okay. No, everything would be perfect.

She swallowed the sherry in one gulp. Everything was in order for the next day. The linens were folded on the end of the table, the place settings were stacked beside the linens, the silverware was polished and now the pies were stowed away.

Annie took off her apron. It was time to make some memories. She grabbed a deck of cards from one of the kitchen drawers. As she walked into the living room, she held up the cards. "Let's play a game."

The drone of the television continued and no one responded. Milt was sleeping with his feet propped on her vintage coffee table. Merry and Kelly were curled under a blanket, enthralled in their program, and Jenna wasn't there.

"A game?" Annie asked again, louder.

"Milt and I are heading off to bed as soon as this is finished," Merry said. "You don't need to fuss over us. We can amuse ourselves."

Kelly still didn't respond.

Behind her, Jenna stomped up the stairs from the basement. Annie turned to intercept her before she lost Jenna to the TV, too, but Jenna was already lost under an overflowing armful of blankets and pillows.

"What are you doing?" Annie took the two pillows from the top of Jenna's pile. "We can turn up the heat if you are too cold."

"No, this is for tonight." Jenna tossed the crisp pressed sheets into a rumpled pile on the floor.

"I don't understand. There is a bed—or was a bed—made up downstairs."

"It smells down there. I tried it. I stretched out on the bed and everything. I turned off that thing humming in the corner." *What thing in the corner?* "It didn't help. Did I mention it smells?" Jenna squished her nose. "No worries. I'll sleep on the floor up here."

"You'll be all stiff and sore." Annie sighed. "I'll sleep downstairs. You can have my bed."

"I don't want to kick you out of your bed." Jenna watched her gather the linens and blankets again.

"I'm sure."

Kelly held up her hand from the couch and grabbed Jenna's shirt. "Jenna, come check this out. You'll never guess what the psycho did since you left."

Jenna turned to the television while Annie hoisted the blankets and hauled them downstairs.

Throwing her armful onto the bed, she inhaled deeply. There was a slight smell, but nothing obnoxious. It'd be fine to sleep there.

She bit her lip as she shook out the sheets again. Her lips still tingled. That was some kiss.

She sat on the chair beside the naked mattress. What was she going to do about Quinn? She just needed to think for a minute in the quiet. She sank deeper into the chair. It was awfully comfy.

The quiet seeped over her as the chair cradled her in its soft, worn cushions. She put her head back, fingers still curled around the edge of the sheet.

Whispers were coming from the direction of the step.

"She's sleeping. Let's leave her."

CHAPTER 11

When Quinn hadn't arrived by two-thirty, Annie knew he was skipping Thanksgiving dinner. Had the kiss been that bad? Her hand trembled as she removed the place setting as discreetly as possible. The animals had been secured, with Tiger in the spare bedroom and Dumbbell in the car. Thanksgiving would be a success from this point forward.

The roast carved beautifully. Everything was almost as good as it could get. She splashed some wine in the gravy, then poured a glass for herself. This would be great—she deserved a quiet toast.

Stirring the gravy with one hand while sipping her wine, Annie silently toasted her first Thanksgiving in her new home. Did it matter that no one commented on the little paper pilgrims' hats she'd made to use as place card holders or the centerpiece of orange-colored roses? Come to think of it, no one had commented on anything, but they would have seen it. It was part of the—what's the word?—*atmosphere.* That's it. She topped up her wine glass, then raised it. To atmosphere.

"I'm starving." Kelly poked her head in the kitchen and rubbed her stomach.

"Soon." Annie smiled and turned back to the roast. "Listen, if you want it faster, you can ..." Kelly had already left, probably to sit in front of the TV again. They'd even dragged out a laptop. Couldn't they unplug for one day? "Never mind."

After five trips back and forth to the kitchen, everything was out, including the cranberry sauce she'd made yesterday to go with the missing turkey. "Let's eat."

"In a minute, Mom."

Annie groaned. More TV programs? She sat at the table in front of her place card and waited. She poured a glass of wine for herself and toasted the empty seats.

After refilling her glass again, she spied the rest of the family shuffling into the dining room.

"Looks good," Milt said, as he sat.

Annie finished her wine and glanced at the bottle. Oops, she'd have to open another for dinner.

Milt opened the second bottle without comment and filled the glasses. Milt's hand was unsteady, but in the end, only two small splashes had christened her grandmother's lace tablecloth. Good thing she'd purchased white wine, though with roast it should have been red. Annie shook her head, wishing she'd thought to buy more wine.

Minutes later, with heaping plates of food in front of them, everyone was chewing. No small talk. Just eating. Within another ten minutes, everyone pushed away from the table.

"That was great," Kelly said.

"Yes, ma'am," Milt agreed.

"Milt, dear, we should check on the animals. They're all cooped up."

Jenna and Kelly collected the plates, while Merry gathered the salt and pepper shakers.

Annie sat and stared at the empty table.

Where was the laughter? Where were the memories? Did they even notice what they ate?

Swallowing the rest of her wine, she picked up the little pilgrim's hat and put it on her head. Then Jenna returned to the dining room. "Annie, are you okay?"

"Fine, fine." She waved her hand at Jenna. "Come here." She plucked another hat from the table and put it on Jenna's head.

"How much wine have you had to drink today?" Jenna whispered.

Puzzled by the question, Annie didn't say anything. Instead she straightened Jenna's hat again.

"Oh boy, that much, hey?"

Annie shook her head. Her hat fell off. She bent to retrieve it from the floor and banged her head on the side of the table. "Ouch."

"Okay, we'll take care of everything. I think you should rest a bit." Jenna made her stand and steered her toward the basement.

"My hat—"

"Here, have mine. I'll get another." Jenna propelled her forward.

"Mom, are you okay?"

"She didn't sleep very well last night. You wouldn't have either on that chair. So she's going to rest for a bit," Jenna said, as she helped Annie down the stairs.

"I'm fine, you know," Annie whispered as her sister pushed her onto the bed.

"I know, but you've been working hard these last couple of days. So put up your feet for a minute or two while we clean up."

She closed her eyes. "Okay, just for a minute."

When Annie woke, she was disoriented and had a terrible headache.

Then she was wide awake. Oh no, she'd passed out at her own Thanksgiving dinner.

Racing upstairs didn't help the ache in her head. The house was bizarrely quiet. Where were they all? What time was it?

"Kelly? Jenna? Anyone?" She flew into the living room.

"Heya, Mom. You look like you're feeling better."

"I guess." She rubbed her head. "You aren't leaving already?"

Kelly zipped her luggage closed. "Jenna said we need to get going before it gets too late."

Cards and snacks were spread over the dining room table. "You played games."

Kelly nodded. "TV was a bore this afternoon."

She wanted to cry. "Where is everyone else?"

"Packing up, I guess."

She sat on the sofa and patted the couch beside her.

Kelly trudged forward. As soon as she sat, she crossed her arms. "What?"

"I haven't had much chance to talk to you."

"We talk on the phone all the time." Kelly shrugged. "There isn't much to say."

"How is everything?"

"Fine. Like always."

"I know I surprised you by moving. We haven't talked about it much."

"Really, Mom, everything is fine." Kelly straightened. "Listen, Uncle Milt wanted me to take Dumbbell out for a minute before they load him up."

"Okay, but now you know where I'm at—"

"I know where you live, I know you're a phone call away, I know. You say the same thing all the time."

"As long as you know." She reached out to touch Kelly.

"Dumbbell," Kelly called out for the dog, which materialized within seconds of hearing his unfortunate name. "I'll be back in a few minutes."

Annie watched her leave with the dog, and a longing built up in her chest. Wasn't there a time when they hugged?

CHAPTER 12

The phone was ringing. Annie blinked at her clock. Who would call at eleven-thirty at night? No one—unless something happened on the drive home.

She threw off her covers. The sheets were tangled in her legs, and she jumped on one leg to the landing. "I'm coming," she muttered to the phone. Kicking off the sheet finally, she scrambled down the stairs to the phone.

"What's happened?"

"Annalisa?"

"Jack?" She gripped the phone tight. "Is something wrong? Where is Kelly?"

"Kelly's gone to bed. Jenna dropped her off a while ago."

"Oh, thank goodness." Her heart settled back into her chest, but her blood still raced. "Why are you calling?"

Jack was silent for a minute and then he cleared his throat. "Is there something you need to talk to me about?"

"Is this about Kelly? Did something happen?"

"No. This isn't about Kelly. It is about you—" Jack cleared his throat again. "—you … and your habit."

Annie sat on the chair and tried to figure out what Jack was saying. "My habit? You mean my hobbies? I know I've been doing a lot of crafts in the last year or so—"

"Are you drunk right now?" he snapped.

"Drunk? Me?" She shook her head. "I don't understand."

"Kelly said you were drinking when they arrived. You had alcohol on your breath when you hugged her yesterday. Then today you passed out after lunch and didn't wake until they left."

Her jaw dropped. "She told you *what*?"

"I see you can't deny it." Jack's sigh was clear through the receiver.

"Why would she say that?"

"I'd love to say she was worried about you, but she thought it was all great fun. Is this the kind of role model you've become?"

"How dare you say that to me." Her hand trembled, but she was wide-awake now. "After you leave and get your little midlife crisis tattoo and your sleek little condo. Heaven knows what kind of—" She stopped. This wasn't going to help anything.

"Sure, blame it all on me." Jack huffed into the phone. "It was unhealthy when you hid in the basement and sniffed glue all day for your little crafts. Now you've moved out where no one knows you. You can drink and pass out all day, every day."

"I'm not an alcoholic."

"You are OCD. I've known that for years."

"OC—? Obsessive compulsive? I don't think you know what that means."

"I was scared this would happen when Kelly decided to move in with me. At least you could try to be discreet in front of our daughter."

"I can cope just fine. You have no idea about my days or nights ... and you never have."

"Nights? What, do you have some lover out there? That isn't what you need."

"*What I need?* When did *you* care what I need? I think this conversation is over, Jack. You can't tell me what I can or can't do anymore. I can dye my hair purple and wear miniskirts, and you don't have the right to say anything to me about it. You lost that right when you left me."

"You need help, Annalisa. I can help you."

"Jack, the only person you like to help is you."

The blood roaring in her ears filled the silence that followed her declaration.

Then Jack sighed. "I'll pay for your medical help. It won't be covered by my health care, but for the sake of my daughter …"

"This is done. We are done, and so is this conversation. It is all done." Annie wanted to hang up, but some part of her wanted Jack to admit he was the reason their marriage fell apart. It was his fault. There was a time when she'd figured it'd been her fault, but things had changed. A sudden clarity rose in her heart.

"Fine, but I'm going to take you up on that invitation for Christmas. We'll talk more then."

The line went dead.

She started to dial Jack back. What had she been thinking? What had she said? Then she stopped, one digit away from finishing his number. Wait a minute. What had he said to her?

She forced herself to set the phone on its cradle. She stared at it. Waiting for it to ring. Waiting for Jack to call back.

Silence. No apology. She let out a ragged breath.

That son of a … son of a …

She covered her mouth. What was wrong with her?

Then it hit her—Christmas invitation? So much for the two of them sitting around, laughing about the good times and deciding their divorce had been a mistake.

He thought she needed an intervention.

CHAPTER 13

Christmas

By the time the snow fell and coated the earth with a healthy veneer of glistening perfection, Annie was sure she wasn't an alcoholic. Things had gotten out of hand at Thanksgiving, but Christmas would be different. Christmas would be stunning. Busy in her craft studio from morning to night, she worked on all the shimmering, glittering, wonder-inspiring creations she would need to decorate the house from hardwood floor to ceiling light fixture.

With new decorations alongside all the decorations she'd made the year after Jack divorced her, she could decorate each room with a different theme. The spare bedroom would be done in blue and purple, the living room in Victorian, the kitchen in decorations made from popcorn and cookies, her bedroom in paper ornaments, the basement in candy canes, the dining room in gold and silver, and the rest of the house from hallway to bathroom would have everything else.

Jack might think he was staging an intervention, but when he stepped into the house, he'd know no drunk lived there.

After a couple of days of cleaning and scrubbing the house thoroughly, she pulled out the first of the decorations. Wreaths were hung on every door and bells on every doorknob. Velvet stockings hung on the living room fireplace and felt stockings hung on the dining room cabinet. Large glass bowls were filled with shiny things of all sizes and descriptions.

The paper white daffodils she had forced were starting to nod awake, and she wrapped the stems in a deep burgundy ribbon. Glass ornaments were hung from every window, candles arranged on every surface. Christmas CDs, DVDs, magazines and books were arranged in vignettes throughout the living room. A wire puzzle in the shape of a Christmas tree, which Annie had never been able to figure out, sat on the coffee table, as an invitation to anyone who might like to take up the challenge.

A couple of weeks before Christmas, when she was sure the selection wouldn't be too picked over and not too early to bring in, she bought a truck full of trees and boughs.

Another three days were needed just to decorate those. When she had finished, her craft studio was nearly empty, and the house was overflowing—a cornucopia of good cheer.

The day the last present was painstakingly wrapped and placed under the tree in the living room, she wandered through the house with an empty heart—all of this effort and no one was here to enjoy it. Christmas was still days away, and a decorated house should be shared. Good friends, good food, goodwill toward men and all that.

She put on one of Bing's Christmas albums and sat back. All she needed was a nice glass of Merlot and a friend with whom to talk. No! No Merlot.

However, a friend ...

Annie set the local phonebook—it was a marvel that the town still published one—on the coffee table and flipped through the pages. Who could she invite? Since moving to Morning Lake she'd met a few people. Perhaps ...

The only person who kept coming to mind was Quinn, and he was the last person she ought to call. Sure, they'd shared an hour or two of coffee conversation and he'd helped finish a few small projects around the house over the last few months, but she couldn't help but feel he had disappeared like a dollop of whipped cream on hot chocolate after their kiss at Thanksgiving. The twinkle in his eye, which had been so prevalent in the days leading up to Thanksgiving, had vanished, and oh, how she missed it. She'd messed things up between them by kissing him.

The idea of calling him took root, and was rather insistent about not being ignored.

What would he think if she called him? She had to try.

She grabbed the phone and dialed his number before she lost her nerve. No answer. She left a message on his voicemail. Immediately after she hung up, she hated herself.

A minute later, the phone rang.

"You called?" Quinn's voice was muffled by noise in the background. Wherever he was, people were having fun.

"I was wondering if you wanted to come over for some Christmas cheer." How desperate did she sound?

After what seemed a gaping chasm of awkward anticipation, he cleared his throat. "Sure, when?"

"Whenever you like." Desperate again. Shoot.

"We're at Cathy and Chris's place, up the road from you. I don't think you've met them yet."

"No."

"Well, at Christmas we sometimes go around to a few houses and—" His voice disappeared.

"Hello?" Another voice—a woman's—came on the line.

She never should have called.

"You're Annie, right?" the woman asked, but she didn't wait for an answer. "We'll be over in a bit." Then the line went dead.

We? In a bit? Did that mean right now?

She jolted off the couch and dashed into the kitchen. People were coming. Her neighbors, her new community members … strangers would be at her house tonight. What did she have to serve? Nuts? Cheese and crackers? Veggies and dip? Little Christmas oranges? Chocolates? Thankfully, she had already bought some groceries for Christmas.

Rushing through the kitchen from pantry to cupboard to fridge, she tossed food on plates and serving trays. Please let there be enough for a group. Of course, she had no idea how big of a group to plan for, but they would have some morsel at least.

When the first set of headlights appeared in the drive, her whirlwind ceased. She set the bowls and platters out on the table before rushing to the door to greet the first arrivals.

When Quinn strode into the light, her heart skipped. Their kiss was foremost in her mind. Behind him, others exited his truck and then more trucks and cars came into the drive. Annie couldn't believe it. Her yard was filling with a little convoy of Christmas celebrators.

CHAPTER 14

"Santa's place at the North Pole is a dive compared to this," one woman with a red parka exclaimed as she stumbled behind Quinn.

Another man grinned. "All right, where did you hide the elves?"

"Hi, Annie," Quinn greeted her, before pointing to his companions. "This is Rita Winston, and Cathy and Chris Carr. There are a couple of others coming, too." Judging by the number of cars, his assessment of the quantity of revelers was a bit of an understatement. "Hope you don't mind."

"Is this the porch you built?" The blonde woman named Rita put her hand on his arm.

Quinn nodded, then moved out of the way of a petite woman being led up the stairs by a big man in a cowboy hat. Rita followed Quinn like her hand was soldered to his parka.

"Heya, guys," Quinn said to the couple. "I thought you were ducking out and heading home."

"Well," the woman said, winking at Annie, "I couldn't leave the new girl here on her own with all you locals, could I?" She reached her hand out, while her escort muttered beside her.

"Couldn't we do this inside? Off the ice and snow?" The cowboy frowned.

The woman laughed—her voice had a light lilting quality—but she didn't retract her hand. "I'm Claire, and this ogre of a cowboy is my husband Devin." The woman grinned at her, with a conspiratorial angle to her head. The ogre in question tipped the edge of his cowboy hat to Annie. "He didn't used to be quite so protective, but then—" She motioned to her belly. There was a slight mound. A baby mound. Then the woman laughed again. An indulgent smile suffused the cowboy's face. His love for his wife was almost tangible.

"It is a pleasure to meet you," Annie said and she shook the woman's hand.

She opened the door for her guests as the "Twelve Days of Christmas" started on the stereo. She followed everyone inside, except

Quinn and Rita, who seemed to be hovering on the porch. She wanted to stay and speak with Quinn, but she was raised to be a hostess first, so she went with the others and took their coats, while he stayed out and spoke with the blonde.

Before the carol came to the *five golden rings*, her bed was mounded high with parkas and jackets of every description. Some people even tossed their coats on the floor, scared of staining her eyelet white duvet, despite her assurance it would be fine.

No one was dressed up in anything special—there wasn't a velvet gown in sight, not like the magazines—but some of the women wore Christmas sweaters. She was glad she hadn't changed.

They all moved into the kitchen—a herd of cattle to the trough.

"Help yourself," she called to them, although they didn't seem to need the invitation. Any food in sight seemed to be fair game.

When she made the last trip to the bedroom with jackets, she paused on the stairs to marvel at her houseful of people. She'd never had so many people in her house all at once, even for one of Jack's snooty office parties.

The Christmas CD had been removed from the CD player and the local country music radio station played over the speakers now.

"Hi, Annie." Cathy waved at her as she entered the kitchen. "We were going to call you and introduce ourselves, but we didn't know your number. We used to stop here all the time when the Gellers had the place. Honestly, I'd never imagine this was the same house if I hadn't seen it with my own eyes."

"Thanks." Annie beamed. "It was a bit of work—"

"That's what Quinn told us on the way over. I can't believe he kept it a secret that he knew you." Cathy shook her head.

"You live up the road?" Annie tried to change the subject, although she also wanted to know why he would keep it a secret.

"Yep. Up toward the highway." Cathy took a swig from a beer bottle. Annie didn't have beer in the house, so they must have brought their own. "Anyway, Quinn, he sure did turn red when we took the phone from him when you called."

"Oh ... I ..."

"He's quite a catch if you can land him." Cathy nodded conspiratorially. "Of course, he's had his share of problems, but haven't we all. You're divorced with a teenage daughter, right?"

Annie rubbed her hands on her jeans. "You've heard?"

"Everyone knows things in small towns. Don't be worried." Cathy patted her hand. "Divorced, right? For long?"

"A year, I guess."

"Hmm ... that's pretty recent." Cathy stopped when another woman stepped up.

"Is Cathy giving you her fifty-cent shrink session?" The woman laughed.

"I'm Annie." She extended her hand and smiled.

"I know. I'm Sandra," the other woman said, shaking her hand.

"Oh, don't listen to her," Cathy said. "She thinks I watch too many daytime television talk shows."

"I suppose she filled you in on all the goods on our Mr. Quinn. Terrible shame about his wife and kids." Sandra shook her head, then popped a nut into her mouth.

"I hadn't got that far yet," Cathy said.

"Oh." Sandra shrugged. "Well, never mind then. Actually I was going to ask if you'd ever participated in a Christmas tree auction."

Annie had no idea Quinn had a wife, let alone kids. They'd spent so much time together, but it had never come up. What had happened? Were they still in the picture? No, they couldn't be—Cathy had suggested Quinn was eligible. Annie burned to ask for details, but the subject had been changed and it'd be too obvious to bring the conversation back to him now. "An auction?"

"Every Christmas in Rosemount there is a big auction for charity. It is tomorrow, so it is a bit short notice for you, but next year—"

This was an ideal opportunity to get to know people in the community—she couldn't let it go by without jumping at it. "I could enter a tree this year. I don't need this many trees for myself."

"*This* many?" Sandra and Cathy said in unison.

Then Cathy cleared her throat. "How many do you have?"

Annie grinned. "I can show you if you want."

After twenty minutes, Annie had taken half the women on a tour of her house. Claire, the pregnant woman, hadn't come through the house with the rest, but she did ask if she could commission a special stocking for her baby. Two other women offered to buy sets of her ornaments, and another asked how much she would charge for a wreath.

"I've never given any thought to selling things. Would you really want to buy something I made?"

"Yes, but we don't want to pressure you. Think about it," Sandra said. "We'll get you registered in the auction tomorrow. You know, you could set up a table at the craft fair, too, if you wanted."

"Tomorrow? All tomorrow?" Ideas spun through her head. What could she put in a craft sale tomorrow? At least four boxes of ornaments were still tucked away in her studio, unused.

"Annie might not want to sell her things," Cathy said. "Don't push."

"No, I do. Thank you."

Returning to the living room, she let her gaze flit from one decoration to the next. There was meaning in this. All of her efforts weren't for naught. She couldn't wait to tell Jack she was making money from her silly, glue-sniffing activities.

When had she grown so irritated with Jack?

Then her gaze fell to Quinn. He was leaning against the dining room wall, surrounded by men ... and Rita. As if sensing her watching him, he turned and smiled at her. She pulled her gaze away and forced herself to walk into the kitchen.

A minute later, he was at her side. "You've met everyone?"

"I think so. It is quite the crowd."

"They're good people—not glamorous and polished, but good people."

"What a strange thing to say. Do I seem glamorous or polished?"

"Your house could be in one of those magazines you read." His tone suggested his observation might not be a compliment. It was probably safer to change the subject.

"You've been busy?" she asked. Her gaze slid over his face, taking him all in. He was as handsome as ever. Those lips, which were right in front of her, had invaded her dreams far too many nights.

Quinn seemed to know she was thinking about the day they'd kissed. He took a swig of his pop, then wiped his mouth with his thumb. "A couple in town have me framing and dry walling their basement."

Annie nodded. Her hair tickled the side of her neck and she rubbed it. He watched her fingers and she found herself leaning in closer to him.

"All right," someone shouted from the living room, "on to the Schneiders'." Within minutes, everyone had tugged on their jackets and were heading out the door.

People shouted over their shoulders as they exited the house. "Thanks." "Great place." "See you next year."

Quinn hadn't moved. "Are you coming?"

"Sure!" Then she remembered about the sale. "Oh, no, I can't. I have to get organized for tomorrow. I'm putting a tree in the auction."

"Sandra got to you, hey? That didn't take long."

"No, I want to donate one. It'll be fun," she said with conviction, even though she wanted to go with Quinn on a whirlwind tour of the neighborhood more than attend the auction.

"Hurry up, buddy, you're our DD." Chris tossed a coat at Quinn.

She half-expected Quinn to kiss her goodbye, but of course he didn't.

"Thanks, Annie," he said. Then he donned his jacket and exited the kitchen. "Come on, then, you lush bags. There's more drinking to be done," he said. Then he grinned at her for a moment before disappearing into the night with the others.

She waved at the closed door. Everyone was out having fun, and here she was stuck inside with her Christmas trees. "Wait!"

She grabbed her coat from the hook in the vestibule and scrambled to find her winter boots, which took her precious seconds to remember were at the back door.

"Wait. I'll come," she said breathlessly as she flew from the house in time to see his taillights disappearing around the hedge.

Everyone was gone.

CHAPTER 15

Annie shook her head and tried counting her inventory again. Inventory? Perhaps she was getting a little carried away. What was she selling? Goods? Wares? Trinkets?

More importantly, though, why couldn't she count? She was an accountant, for heaven's sake. Just because it was three a.m. didn't mean basic math skills should abandon her.

She stifled a yawn. She had to make sure she woke up in time, but what time would that be? Sandra hadn't told her what time any of this started—the auction, the sale or the set-up. She rubbed her neck.

It would be fine. Quinn seemed to know about it. If all else failed, she'd phone him in the morning. Of course, he was probably still out with the partyers ... and Rita. She rested her head in her hands. *Quit thinking about Rita and Quinn.*

When had she started devoting more thought to Quinn than Jack?

She forced her thoughts back to the auction. What if she wasn't allowed to sign up so late? No, it was fine. Everything was fine. It was the same thing she'd told herself over and over again since Quinn and the others had moved on. She hadn't done anything more than move the abandoned drinks that weren't on coasters before slipping into her studio to figure out what to take.

Ringing ... Was that the telephone?

Her legs felt trapped in papier-mâché as she tried to find the phone in the living room. Where had she left it? Oh, right ... beside the couch, where she'd left it after she had called Quinn earlier, hours ago.

"Hello?" She was winded and scared as she held the phone. Who would call at such a time?

"Did I wake you?"

"Quinn? Umm ... no, I was awake." Her heart danced at the sound of his voice. "Are you coming over?" She clapped her hand over her mouth. What was she saying?

He laughed. "You're getting ready for the sale tomorrow, aren't you?

I'm not getting caught up in all that."

Thank goodness he'd laughed it off, even if it wasn't what she'd meant. Her hand inched off her mouth and closed into a fist. "How did you know?"

"I noticed your light on when I drove by after dropping off Cathy and Chris."

"Right," she said. "I'm on your way home." Was that Rita woman still with him? "You're just getting home?"

"Sandra wanted me to tell you to show up at nine in the morning at the school gym in Rosemont."

"Right. The school gym in Rosemont tomorrow at nine a.m. Got it."

"You have no idea how to find the school, do you?"

"I'm not even sure where Rosemont is, but I've got a GPS."

"I'll be at your house at eight."

"I don't want to be a bother. You don't need to—"

"Annie, go to sleep. I'll pick you up in the morning."

She grinned as she disconnected. She was spending the day with Quinn tomorrow. Suddenly she wasn't sleepy at all.

CHAPTER 16

Big speakers blasted out Christmas carols from the stage where the school band was practicing. Every squeal of the second clarinets and off-key trombone notes ricocheted through the concrete-block gymnasium. Sandra sat at the front door accepting registrations for the auction and the tables. Each Christmas tree team received Santa hats to wear. Annie pulled hers on proudly.

At the back of the gym, which had children's drawings plastered to the walls, a little forest of Christmas trees had sprouted on the hardwood floor. In the middle, between the band and the trees, sales tables were set in rows. Table 33, her home for the day, was tucked onto the end of one of the lines. Sandra must have arranged it first thing this morning.

She laid a patchwork tablecloth of velveteen squares across her display table. There was a lot to do before the doors opened at ten. Quinn brought in the boxes and she gently uncrated each piece. She'd brought some small pine boughs to arrange in a big masonry jar to resemble a makeshift Christmas tree. Each tree ornament hung on a bough. The wreaths were displayed on a coat tree she'd tucked into Quinn's truck as a last-minute idea. The paper Christmas village sat amid glitter and mirrors, and the real treasures, her Santa sculptures, were placed throughout the table arrangement and on the floor in front of it.

With the table arranged, she went with Quinn to unload the tree for the auction. He'd been sweet, taking care to avoid potholes on the paved roads. She hoped the tree, cocooned in plastic wrap, had survived the trip. She'd used every roll of plastic in her kitchen to try to secure the tree. She would need to get more before she had to deal with Christmas leftovers.

Last night she'd added to the candy cane tree, which had been inspired by Clement Clarke Moore's line about a child's sugar plum dream. Now she cut away the plastic to reveal the tree—phew, it had survived intact. When the lights were hooked to the extension cord, it glittered and shone just right.

Annie sighed. So far so good.

Quinn left her to fuss with the tree, saying he'd be back later. He'd been quiet, but she concluded he wasn't particularly interested in Christmas, which made his offer to drive her and her trinkets all the more thoughtful. Jack wouldn't be seen in a place like this unless he calculated the odds of running into the CEO of some company. She paused. Lately she was having an increasingly difficult time remembering Jack's assets, and wasn't that bizarre?

A man by the band announced over a loud speaker that the doors were about to open to the public. She glanced around. The public all seemed to be inside already. People milled about between the rows of crafts, sampling fudge and hot chocolate, and someone was even taking photos with a big expensive-looking camera. Would she be in the local newspaper?

She smiled to anyone who happened to glance her way, but tried to give people space to browse without being intrusive. She should have brought something to do or make. Next time she'd be better prepared.

Next time? Did she want to be one of those women who peddled their crafts? People would probably point at her stuff saying, "I could do that at home," or "I'm not paying that kind of money for that." She shoved those thoughts aside. Sure, she hadn't any sales yet, but then again it was only quarter after ten.

A few minutes later, Sandra greeted her with a big smile. She held a clipboard and seemed to be making the rounds through the sales tables. "Quinn told us you were up half the night, but I'd never know it to look at you. You wear that hat perfectly. You're a real Mrs. Claus."

Annie cringed. How could she have forgotten? Mrs. Claus—that's what Jack had called her when he wasn't being flattering. Suddenly the cheap felt itched, and she twitched. Annie forced a smile to her face. "I'm glad you told me about this."

"God, I feel like shit today. The Christmas open-house circuit isn't for the light weights, that's for sure." Sandra rubbed her forehead. "Oh, speaking of which, in the teacher's lounge we've got coffee brewing, and in the cupboard there is almost anything you could want to mix into it. There is Irish Cream and, I don't know, all kinds of liquors."

"Oh, I don't drink coffee, but thanks."

"I don't drink it for the coffee, either." Sandra winked at her. "Well, my dear, I'm off to make the rounds. Let me know if you need anything." Sandra walked down the aisle of tables, and people waved to her, trying to get her attention.

Annie sat on the chair behind her table. What would Jack and Kelly think of her now? She stood again. What was the proper etiquette at a small town craft sale?

"There she is, Claire," Cathy said, as she guided the small, pregnant woman from the previous night to her table. "Isn't her table great? It is too bad you didn't take the house tour with the rest of us last night! You can't imagine it."

Annie wiped her forehead. It was getting hot with so many people milling about the gymnasium. "Hi, Cathy. How are you doing today?"

"As well as I deserve." Cathy groaned and rubbed her ample stomach. "It'll be four o'clock before I'll be able to walk by the food tables, but that's what happens this time of year. Annie, this is Claire. I think you met her last night."

She shook the woman's hand.

"But I don't think it came up last night that Claire is a photographer and has started writing articles for magazines, too. Since she was pretty wrung out last night by the time we'd arrived at your place, she didn't see everything, so I was telling her about it today."

Annie's heart flipped and she wiped her forehead again. Was this leading to where she thought it was? "A photographer? Wow, that must keep you busy."

"I freelance." Claire handed Annie a business card. "I'm always hunting for story ideas and great photo opportunities."

"I'll let you two chat. I've spotted Sandra and I needed to talk to her about getting power to Table Twelve." Cathy surveyed her table first, though. "Be a dear, Annie, and hide those three stockings for me. I'll be by later to pay for them."

Annie removed the stockings from her display. As she folded them to tuck them in one of the boxes under the table, she tried not to watch Claire poke through the remaining items.

"Do you participate in craft fairs regularly?" Claire asked.

"This is my first one." She shrugged. "I guess I'm a virgin." Heat rushed to her cheeks as soon as the words were out.

"I'd never have guessed." Claire laughed. "I have to say, it is pretty funny to hear someone who could be a stand-in for Mrs. Claus say 'virgin.' "

The heat in Annie's cheeks could melt the North Pole. She rearranged some of the other items on her coat rack to cover the hole created by the stockings.

"I think Cathy mentioned that you did a tree, too?"

Annie discreetly rubbed her hands on her pants. Sweaty. "Over there, the candy one."

The woman glanced at the tree, then back to her. "Cathy said you have a bunch more trees in your house?"

She tucked her hair behind her ear and nodded.

"Annie, would you mind if I came by sometime? Cathy raved about everything I didn't have the chance to see. And I loved your living room. And your porch. And ..." She laughed. "Well, you get the idea. I would love to take some photos of your place."

"You'd want to do that?" Annie was as giddy as a kid on Christmas morning. "Sure, when?"

"Just a warning—I can't seem to shake Devin these days, so he'll be coming, too. How about tomorrow?"

CHAPTER 17

Their booth in the diner had a view of the snow-covered parking lot, where Annie's few remaining Christmas ornaments were strapped down beneath a tarp in the bed of Quinn's truck. Annie let out a big sigh and kicked her feet up on the bench seat beside him. Her feet tingled from standing on the gym's hardwood floor for so many hours, but it had been a wonderful day and she wouldn't change a thing about it.

She grinned. "You were right, I am starving."

"See? You should listen to me more often." He winked at her, and a little flutter tickled inside her chest. "This place has the best burgers. You won't be disappointed."

The small diner was decorated in what most designers would call vintage, and she suspected much of the decor might be original. Someone had even dragged out holiday decorations that looked of the same era. The place was buzzing with people talking all around them. The exceptions were two teenagers, who were sharing the booth adjacent to theirs. Their awkward lack of conversation was palpable. Annie's thoughts turned immediately to her own teenager. Only a few days now and Kelly would be home. Annie smiled at the kids when the girl glanced her way.

Was it the kids' first date? The girl's incessant giggling and looking around, coupled with the boy's beet-red cheeks suggested it might be. Ah, that was so—

Wait—was she on a date with Quinn?

Her gaze shot back to Quinn. He was looking over the menu. He wasn't blushing. She wasn't giggling. But ...

Holy cow, they were on a date.

When was the last time she'd been on a date? Twenty years ago? She wiped her palms on her pants, and wished she'd thought to fix her makeup before leaving the school. She was probably covered in glitter, too.

Jack would have told her to wipe her face and hands by now to dislodge the shiny specks, but she knew Quinn wouldn't, and that realization eased her worry. In fact, it was a relief. Was it weird that she was more comfortable on a possible first date with Quinn than she had ever been with Jack?

Of course, Jack hadn't been perfect, but somehow Annie had believed Jack was perfect for her. Had she been lying to herself all this time?

Now wasn't the time to ponder questions like that, but the thought allowed her to relax into this time with Quinn. She was a divorced woman. Eventually Jack would realize he'd made a mistake in leaving her, and then he could be the one to ask forgiveness for once in his life. But maybe she'd have already moved on with her own.

After they ordered, Annie told Quinn about Claire asking to take photos of her home.

"That's great, if that's what you want," he said. When she didn't respond, he said, "You're thinking about what you are going to change before she comes over tomorrow, aren't you?"

She laughed. "Am I that obvious?"

"Probably not to everyone, but I know you—"

He was interrupted by their bleached-blonde, wrinkled waitress, who set their orders on the table with a thud. The plates were heaped with food.

"That's why I didn't let you order the milkshake like you asked," the waitress said in a raspy smoker's voice. She cackled as she walked away.

"Wow, how am I ever going to eat all this?"

He grinned. "Dig in."

After the first bite, she nodded. "Oh, my, this is great. I haven't tasted a burger this good since I was a little girl."

He winked at her again, probably because his mouth was full, but she sensed he was pleased with her enjoyment of his restaurant choice.

And Annie *was* enjoying. Even more than the behemoth of a burger, she was happy the awkwardness that had surfaced at Thanksgiving had subsided. His eyes were twinkling again, too. Just like they had before.

Maybe he didn't think this was a date.

"She's a light-weight, isn't she?" the waitress said to Quinn when she returned later to remove Annie's plate, still half covered with fries and burger. "The bill's at the front when you're ready."

Annie took one last swig of her iced tea, then they stood. She peeked over her shoulder at the kids on the first date. They looked a little more comfortable now.

"What's up?" Quinn asked.

"Those kids are on their first date, I think."

"That's what I thought, too." Quinn nodded. At the counter, he motioned the waitress closer. "You see those kids in the corner?"

"Yeah, so?"

"I'll buy their burgers as well as ours."

The waitress's over-plucked eyebrow shot up as if she didn't approve, but she didn't say anything as she tallied the bills together. The fact that Quinn had paid for her meal also made Annie wonder anew if they were on a date like the kids.

When they climbed into the truck a minute later, she turned to him. "That was very sweet to pay for their meal."

He shrugged as he started the truck. "It was a first date. It should be memorable."

Was he talking about theirs or the kids'?

"Quinn, I've been meaning to ask you something," she said as he guided their vehicle onto the narrow secondary highway that connected Rosemont to Morning Lake.

"Oh?"

She swallowed. "Why didn't you come to Thanksgiving?"

He whistled, and his eyebrows rose. "You have to ask?"

She waited because she didn't consider that an answer.

After a long silence, he glanced at her. "Are you getting back together with your ex?"

"What?" She stiffened.

He rolled his shoulder and tapped the steering wheel. "Well, you'd said that was your plan, and I figured it might be awkward if I showed up."

"Oh."

"So are you?"

"No." The word was out of her mouth before she realized what she'd said. It probably would have been better to think about that first, but in the heartbeat after she'd said it, she knew it was true. She'd been clinging to a memory that may have never happened. A life without Jack suited her perfectly.

"Okay then." he said and he reached over to turn on the radio.

"Okay then." Annie mimicked.

But what did Quinn mean by that?

CHAPTER 18

A writer for a magazine had taken pictures of her house for an article, she had over five hundred dollars in her pocket from the craft sale, and she may or may not have been on a date with Quinn. He hadn't kissed her after they'd unloaded his truck, so she'd been awake all night going over the various interactions they'd had since they met, searching for clues as to what had happened last night. By daylight, she still wasn't certain.

Lack of sleep may have made her a little giddy today. Claire had laughed at her exuberance more than once. And now she felt compelled to share her news, at least the part about the sale and the magazine, with someone. She wouldn't talk about Quinn—she needed to have a better handle on what was or wasn't a date first. Her hands shook as she dialed Merry's number.

"Guess what?" she asked, as soon as someone answered.

"Annie, is that you?" Milt sounded tired.

"Yep. You'll never guess what happened. Is Aunty Merry there?"

"Annie, dear, I meant to call you." Something was wrong.

"Is she not doing well?"

"No, that's not it." He was lying. She could tell by the tone of his voice. "The weather is supposed to be turning tonight and, well, we don't want to risk the roads."

"I heard a forecast for a little snow, but—"

"We're not getting any younger, and icy roads, well, they sure do a number on my Merry's nerves."

She nibbled on her lip for a moment. "What if we bring the food to you? I can make it all here, then we'll pack it up and there won't be anything left to do but eat."

"No, no. Annie, I think we'll sort ourselves out for Christmas. Merry's friend Mabel is going to have us over for dinner. She came by when we were trying to decide what to do."

"Oh ... of course ... but are you sure we shouldn't come? For a visit?"

"Merry's doing fine, dear. I'd have you talk to her, but she's out with

Dumbbell for a walk." That was an outright lie. She knew Merry had hired a local teenager to walk the dog since the day they'd adopted it, but what could she do?

"Uncle Milt—"

Milt was silent for a minute. Then his voice was soft, "Merry doesn't want you to worry. She says she's a bit worn out since the doctor changed her pills on her. She needs to have a bit of time to adjust to all the side effects. Our Merry, she's a strong old goat. She'll be fine, but if you come in all trumpets blazing, she'll think I told you she's dying or something. That's not the case, but it might do her more harm than good while she's adjusting, you know. These meds are doing strange things to her spirit, but this depression stuff is temporary. The doctor said she'll be back to herself right away."

Annie's heart broke. Every bit of her body screamed she needed to be there for Merry. "What if I came without the trumpets?"

"Let's leave it up to Merry to decide. I'll talk to her, but for now this is what she wants."

Futility gulped over her heart and sank it to the pit of her stomach. "I understand."

"Now, you were saying you had some news. Is it about that Quinn fellow?"

"No." Her voice squeaked over her lightning-fast denial. "What a funny thing to say. You know what, never mind, it can wait. I'll tell you when I see you." She gripped the phone. "Now you take good care of my aunty, Milt."

"Of course," Milt replied. "Oh, wait, she's come into the room waving at me. She has something to say to you."

"Annie, dear?" Merry's voice was barely audible.

"Hi, Aunty. I'm sorry you can't come because of the roads. I understand."

"Roads?" There was a lengthy pause. "Oh, right, there'll be snow tonight. Hold on a minute now." Then another pause. "Milt, sweetie, get my slippers from the other room."

Annie waited silently.

"Okay, he's out of the room. Now, sweet pea, I have something to ask you. I know it is a bit morbid this time of year, but—"

"You can ask me anything." She pressed the phone closer to her ear.

"You promise me. If something happens to me, you'll take care of my Milt. We rent this apartment, so we don't have any equity and, you know, the medical bills have been so high."

"What is it that you're bothering our Annie with?" Milt sounded angry.

"Annie?" Merry prodded.

"Of course I'll help Milt." She took a shallow breath. "Do I need to come? Do you need me?"

"Oh, hosh posh." Merry cleared her throat. "I just needed to know, that's all."

"Know what?" Milt's voice was clear. He was obviously standing next to Merry now. "What did you need to know?"

"Our Annie will take care of you when I'm gone."

"That's years away. And who's to say I won't go first?" Milt said.

"Thank you, I knew I could count on you, dear." Merry said and then the line went dead.

Annie sank into her sofa, still clutching the phone, while she gulped for air. "What should I do? What should I do?"

A minute later, Milt called back. "Now I know she's probably upset you with all this nonsense talk."

She sniffed and clutched the phone. "A ... a little ..."

"It is the drugs, nothing more. The doctor said so, I promise you. That's why we need to stay home for a bit, but there isn't anything for you to worry yourself about."

"Oh, Milt, I can be there in a couple of hours."

"No. Now you stay. That's what I told you to do. Stay home and have a good holiday with your daughter. We're fine."

"Fine?"

"If there was something wrong I'd drag you here in a jiffy, but there isn't. I wouldn't lie."

She wiped the dampness from her cheek.

"Right?" Milt prodded.

"Right."

She sat on the sofa for a long while after Milt hung up the phone. Kelly ... Kelly was coming. She needed to have a good Christmas with Kelly. On Boxing Day, though, she would go to Merry's.

Where were the others? Jenna should be here by now. Kelly and Jack would be here after that. She wiped her eyes again. She needed to do something to keep busy.

In her craft room, after pulling out the wire, the dark green velvet and the glue gun, she started making a wreath similar to one she'd seen on a television show. The velvet was soft and thick. It reminded her of the dress she'd worn to her first Christmas party when she was ten. Merry had put matching ribbons in her hair that day. She swallowed. How was she going to keep the holiday spirit when Merry was so upset?

She shook her head. No. She needed to think about other things. Boxing Day would be here soon enough, and they'd all go to Merry and Milt's.

After gluing the last velvet leaf in place, she rolled her head from shoulder to shoulder and glanced outside. The darkness was obscured by her own reflection. She stepped closer and realized puffs of snow fluttered to the ground through the blackness outside the window.

She hadn't realized how late it was. Where was everyone? Worry curled around her heart.

She went to the kitchen to get a drink of water and was startled to find bags at the front door. "Hello?"

"She's alive." Jenna sat up from the couch, putting a book down on the side table.

"Jenna? What time did you get here? You should have come and told me you were here."

"I did, but you were so absorbed in your velvet thing you didn't hear me. By the way, your humming is out of tune."

"I don't believe you. You must have just arrived."

"I bet the snow has covered my tracks." Jenna extended her hand as if to shake on the wager.

Annie ignored her sister's hand and went to the front door. Sure enough, Jenna's car was covered and her footprints were lost under a fresh coat of snow.

"I wonder where Kelly and Jack are," she said as she turned to Jenna. Jack was sometimes an impatient driver, but he was usually careful on icy roads. Still, they should have arrived by now.

"You should call Jack's cell and check on them. The snow made the roads kind of dicey in a few spots." Jenna's words sent Annie's heart to a gallop.

She dialed Jack's cell. "Jack?"

"Hi, Annalisa. Listen, sorry about this weekend, but you know how things come up."

"Sorry about this weekend? What do you mean? Are you not coming?"

"Didn't Kelly call?"

"No."

"Becky and Eve invited her to go skiing. She said she'd call you. I just put her on the bus."

"But it's Christmas."

"The ski hills are open."

She could imagine Jack shrugging. "What about you?"

"Well, I'm not coming without Kelly there. That'd be a bit awkward, don't you think?"

"You're right."

"You aren't going to get drunk, are you?"

"Oh, for Pete's sake, you have no idea. Listen, Jack, next time *you* call, okay? I have all this food and—" she waved her hand around the room, "—

and everything. It would have been good to know before I went and spent—"

"Are you strapped for cash?"

"The point is everything is going to be wasted now. All the food, everything."

"Are you wasted?"

"Do you have any idea how annoying you are? Have a Merry Christmas, Jack."

"Merry Christmas, Annalisa."

She ended the call, then threw the cordless phone onto the counter. It clattered across the chipped laminate and hit the wall. Jenna gaped at her.

"They aren't coming." Tears brimmed Annie's eyes. "Kelly is going off with her friends. It's Christmas and she isn't coming."

"Oh, hon, we'll be okay without them. Kelly will go away this year and she'll be back like an oil stain on a silk shirt next year. You don't spend many Christmases away before you appreciate the ones at home."

"I haven't seen her since Thanksgiving," she said. "And that was a disaster."

"When are Merry and Milt coming?"

Annie bit back a sob. "They aren't coming either. Merry's too sick, but they blamed the roads." She waved to the counter, which was overflowing with fresh buns, snack foods and pop bottles. The food was the least of her worries, but it was one tangible thing she could focus on. "What a waste."

"Is Merry okay?" Jenna asked.

She shrugged. "I thought we'd visit them on Boxing Day. Milt says we aren't allowed to come before then. They've already made other plans."

At least Jenna was settled in for the duration since her school was closed until January.

"Okay. So, it's just you and me, baby," Jenna said, opening the cupboard over the sink where Annie stored the liquor. "Let's have a little Christmas cheer."

"I can't."

Jenna ignored her and pulled out two glasses.

"Seriously, I can't. Jack thinks I'm an alcoholic because of Thanksgiving."

"He wasn't even here." Jenna poured rum into the tumblers. "Besides, I bet he doesn't know you were necking with that neighbor of yours. Speaking of which, he looked like a hottie. Anywho, that'd make anyone's knees wobbly. You needed a drink."

"I never told you I kissed Quinn."

"Well, Aunty Merry said you did. You did, didn't you?"

CHAPTER 19

New Year's Eve

Annie flicked on the television and wondered what Quinn was doing. Was he watching TV, too? "The New Year's Eve shows should start soon."

"You're kidding me," Jenna said.

"Tell me you don't want to go out. It has been such a dreadful week. I can't believe Merry … I think she was getting worse by the time we left, don't you?" She wrenched the blanket to her chin and settled deeper into her cocoon on the couch.

"Merry wouldn't want you moping around."

"Jenna, she's not going to be here long. I'm not in the mood to go out with people."

Jenna crossed her arms. "I can't stay in another night. Merry isn't dead. For Pete's sake, Annie, what the hell? I have to get out of here before I lose my mind." Jenna waved her hands through the air and started to pace. She had already peered out the window five times in less than a minute. "We spent three days with them and now how many more days cooped up here?"

Annie took a deep breath and tried to ignore her irritated sister. "Oh, look, there are fireworks going off somewhere." Annie pointed at the television.

"I'm going out." Jenna stomped upstairs. "You can get ready and come out with me or not. It is up to you." Once in her room, she slammed the closet door so hard it rattled the light fixture in the living room.

"Jenna, quit making so much noise." Annie yanked the blanket over her head.

When Jenna started running the shower, Annie considered putting her fingers in her ears and humming, but Jenna would go out with or without her. Gah! She couldn't let Jenna go out alone, and Jenna knew it. A young woman out on her own in a town where she didn't know anyone? Who knew what kind of people she would meet?

Annie flung off the blanket. One night. What was so freaking special about this one stupid night? Jack never wanted to go out and there was something nice and comfortable about the tradition of sitting at home having champagne at midnight—all safe and warm in your own house.

Obstinate, foolish, stubborn Jenna. She would get an earful ... all the way to wherever they ended up. When the shower stopped upstairs, Annie turned off the television. Where would they even go? Most people would be having house parties or something. Going to the bar at the hotel, hanging out with heaven knows who, sounded horrendous. Besides, it'd be full of all the people who didn't get invited into other people's homes. If Jenna thought about it at all, she'd know that wasn't a good idea.

Then Annie remembered part of a conversation. Someone had said something about New Year's when they had stopped by her house before Christmas. Would it be better to crash a party of near strangers or go to a dive with *complete* strangers?

Annie went to the kitchen and dumped her purse. Sandra's number was on a piece of paper somewhere. Upstairs Jenna was blow-drying her hair. She needed to find Sandra's number before Jenna left to find her own fun.

Aha! She found it on a crumpled piece of paper mixed in with old receipts. She dialed the number quickly before she came to her senses. While the phone rang on the other end, she closed her eyes to calm her nerves.

"Happy New Year!"

"Sandra? This is Annie. How are you?"

"Happy New Year, sweetie." Sandra shouted over the din of music and laughter.

"Happy New Year to you, too." She held the phone out from her ear. "Listen, someone, maybe it was Cathy, mentioned there was a get together tonight."

"Are you coming? Good. The more, the merrier. See you soon."

"Wait! I don't know where to go."

Annie scribbled the directions and hoped Sandra was sober enough to have given them correctly. When Jenna appeared in the kitchen, she hung up the phone. Jenna crossed her arms.

"Fine, we'll go out," Annie conceded. "Some people I know are getting together. We can go there for a while."

Jenna smiled. "I knew you'd come around. You need to get out."

"I'll be down in a few," Annie shouted over her shoulder as she dashed up the stairs.

Would Quinn be there?

CHAPTER 20

Snow whisked across the road and over the car, so Annie put on the windshield wipers. It didn't help. "Why are we doing this again?"

"Because it is New Year's Eve and we need to bring in the New Year properly in order to get the year off on the right foot." Jenna grinned from ear to ear. "I can't believe you're coming out with me." She turned up the radio station. The DJ announced number thirty-two of his countdown of the year's hits.

"What did you expect?" Annie turned down the radio. "Wait. Is that a grain bin or a shed?" The crooked structure at the side of the road could be their landmark, but Annie wasn't sure.

"I don't know." Jenna rubbed the side of her hand against the frosted passenger window. "Sure."

Annie pursed her lips as she stopped the car and examined the tracks on the road. It looked like they weren't the first ones down this road, so it could be the right place. "We're supposed to turn at a bin. What is a bin? Is it a shed?"

"If we get lost, we get lost." She couldn't tell if Jenna had shrugged under her big parka or not, but it seemed like she had. "At least we're out of the house."

Annie bit her lip and turned down the road. A couple of miles later, a house with a yard light shining over a clump of cars and trucks came into view. "The place is supposed to have a Santa on the roof. Do you see anything like that?"

They squinted through the windshield.

"There." Jenna pointed to the side of the house. "Santa's fallen off. He's dangling by the wall."

"Okay, but if Sandra isn't here, we're heading home."

"You mean if Quinn isn't here."

She ignored Jenna's comment as she squeezed her truck into the packed drive.

Her heart beat fast. She'd never been so crass as to crash a party before in her life. What had come over her? She scanned the assembled vehicles and realized she *was* looking for Quinn's. Jenna may have a point about Quinn, but Annie would never admit it out loud.

"Let's get inside, it's freezing out here." Jenna jumped up and down by the side of the truck, waiting for Annie.

Annie walked to the house, trying to peer into the kitchen window for any familiar heads, but the windows were caked over with frost. The dangling Santa swung back and forth in the wind like a giant hypnotist's watch.

"That's creepy," Jenna said.

She should never have let Jenna talk her into this.

It was bad form to go to a stranger's back door, but she was pretty sure no one had walked to the front of the house since the first snowfall in November. The steps were covered in a pristine, mounding snow bank. Knocking at the back door, Annie clenched her hand in a tight fist. She was such an interloper.

A young girl about Kelly's age, sporting a reindeer antler hat, opened the door. She held out her hand to them, but not in a handshake. "I'll take your coats."

Jenna jumped inside, but Annie lingered on the step. "Is Sandra here?"

"Mom," the girl shouted over her shoulder, "come here."

A second later, the woman who must be the hostess came to the door. She surveyed Jenna up and down first, and her eyebrows rose. Then she caught sight of Annie. She smiled and then Annie realized the woman was Cathy—she hadn't recognized her at first because of the elf hat, complete with ears, that she was wearing. "Oh, Mrs. Claus!" Cathy said. "Come on in."

Jenna laughed beside her, as Annie reluctantly stepped into the house. "Is it okay—?"

The woman waved her hand and cut off her question. "Sandra mentioned you were coming, and you are more than welcome."

"Thank you for having us in." She offered her hostess one of the bottles of wine she'd purchased for the Christmas dinner that had never happened. "I know we're crashing—"

"Don't be silly—I was sure I'd invited you. Everyone is welcome. There's lots of room. Melody will take your jackets and put them on the bed." Cathy took the wine without looking at it. "You didn't need to bring anything."

Annie slipped off her coat and handed it to the waiting girl. Jenna had already disappeared inside. She was many things, but timid was not one of them.

When Annie saw Jenna again, she already had a drink in her hand and a cluster of young men at her side. Annie shook her head and followed the sound of Sandra's laughter. It led her to the kitchen.

"Annie, sweetie, you made it." Sandra gave her a big hug. "Here, I'm mixing something special for us girls. Get yourself a glass." Sandra motioned to the cupboard by the sink.

CHAPTER 21

Annie hesitated. You just didn't go digging through someone's cupboards. She should ask for a glass from Cathy. Seeming to recognize Annie's reluctance, Sandra walked past her and opened the cupboard door, finding glasses on the first try. She pulled out a plastic glass with a cartoon decal.

"I'm glad you came out. Too much time alone will have you bouncing off the walls."

"Oh, it isn't so bad, but my sister, she wanted to go out tonight."

"Sister?" Sandra spun around and followed her to the doorway of the kitchen, where Annie pointed to Jenna. The men around Jenna were putting down their drinks and heading to the porch. Jenna was laughing. "She's a cutie."

Jenna glanced at them then, as if she knew they were talking about her. "They're out to fix Santa," Jenna said, then shrugged. She followed the men to the porch. The thump of shoes being tossed around quickly followed, as they each hunted for their own.

"I don't think that's safe." Annie glanced at the bottles of beer the men were chugging back.

Jenna and Sandra waved their hands at the same moment. Sandra laughed. "Exactly. They can handle it." Sandra turned to the kitchen. "Old Santa is swinging in the wind." She shrugged. "Poor old guy's ready to retire for the season and have a drink."

Sandra set the glass on the counter, poured something green and milky into the cartoon glass and handed it to Annie. It tasted like mouthwash, the icky kind she didn't buy.

"Mint? This is nice." She forced herself to smile—resisting the urge to swish and spit.

Sandra beamed.

"You two need to mingle." Cathy hugged them both by the shoulders. "You couldn't haul Quinn out?" she asked Annie as she guided them to the living room.

"He isn't here?" She hoped she didn't sound too disappointed.

"Never comes out on New Year's," Sandra said before breaking free of Cathy's clasp and moving away to talk to someone else. As soon as Sandra moved on, Cathy's daughter called her into another room.

Annie sipped on her minty concoction and tried not to speculate on why Quinn might not go out. After all, *she* preferred to stay in, so why should his absence be suspicious?

"You don't know, do you?" An older woman, who had materialized at her side like a fairy godmother, leaned in to whisper in her ear.

"Pardon me?"

"We haven't met. I'm Helen Trent," the woman said as she extended her hand. "My son Devin and his wife left a little bit ago." She grinned. "Our Claire is carrying my first grandbaby, so she gets tuckered out a little faster than she used to. They decided to go home early tonight."

Annie shook her hand. "Yes, I met them." The petite pregnant woman and the overprotective cowboy by her side were hard to forget. When Claire had taken photos of her place, the couple had been the epitome of happiness. Had she and Jack ever looked at one another like that when she was expecting Kelly? It didn't seem likely.

Annie murmured her congratulations.

"But enough about me," the older woman said. "We were talking about John Quinn."

"We were?" Her cheeks heated, and she just knew she was blushing.

"His wife and children died this time of year. A real shame."

She blinked. Whatever she might have imagined, it wasn't that. "Oh."

"Now's not the time to talk about it, but ..." Helen patted her hand. "I thought you should probably know."

"Why are you telling me this?"

"Well," she said and smiled slyly, "it is about time John had someone in his life again."

Annie shook her head. After many discreet Internet searches about relationships while Jenna slept in each morning, she'd concluded she and Quinn had *not* shared a first date. "We aren't dating. We're neighbors."

"Whatever you say. All I know is our little Rita has been desperate to get him out and about for years now and he didn't bite, but you managed to get him to the tree auction, of all things." Helen chuckled. "A good man, that John."

Cathy returned to them then with fresh drinks in hand, and heard Helen's last words. Annie wished she could sink into the golden brown wall-to-wall carpet.

"Well, that's not actually dating." She stopped when Cathy kept smiling at her with a goofy, seemingly knowing, expression on her face. "No, seriously."

Cathy and Helen nodded to one another.

She shook her head. This was a ridiculous conversation. Cathy was probably drunk and Helen obviously thought herself to be a bit of a matchmaker. Even if it would have been nice to talk to Quinn tonight, one kiss hardly made a relationship and it was old news. Really old news. Almost forgotten. Annie glanced at her watch. "Wow, it is almost midnight."

"We need to get the champagne out!" Cathy gulped her cocktail while she and Helen moved toward the kitchen. "Somebody get those men inside. Crap, where's my lipstick?"

Annie breathed a sigh of relief at the change of topic. Any further probing of her non-relationship with Quinn was forgotten. Wait a minute—lipstick? Her chest tightened. Kissing at midnight. How could she have forgotten? What a stupid tradition. Out of all the traditions in the world, she could live without this one.

She was about to make her escape to the bathroom, a refuge from the impending kissing activity, when Jenna's laughter tittered through the air. She couldn't leave her alone here.

Trailing behind Jenna, the pied piper of the bachelor world, were the men who had just come in from trying to rescue Santa, probably at Jenna's suggestion. Annie rolled her eyes.

Jenna went into the kitchen, and the men turned back to the living room as if there were an invisible shield at the door. Annie followed her.

"How can I help?" Jenna asked.

That was what Annie should have been doing—helping. Not looking for an escape route. "Yes," she said. "What needs to be done?"

"Start handing out champagne." Cathy poured champagne into glasses of every shape and description—plastic tumblers, dollar-store wine glasses, brandy snifters, you name it. "And tell them not to drink it yet."

Handing out the last of the glasses, Annie discovered she had left herself smack dab in the center of the room as the countdown started. "Ten ... nine ... eight ..." With each number her heart squeezed tighter. Jenna shouted from the sidelines.

At "Happy New Year," streamers flew through the air, the last champagne bottle was popped and someone leaned in for a kiss. Within seconds, everyone had brushed lips with everyone else. She resisted the urge to wipe her mouth on the back of her hand. She guzzled the champagne from her thimble-sized glass.

"Happy New Year, sis." Jenna came bounding up and gave her a big hug. "This is perfect."

This was perfect? "You're having a good time?"

"You'll never guess." Jenna glanced toward a young man still blowing on an obnoxious horn.

"Guess *what*?" As Annie studied her sister, dread bubbled up in her belly. "Oh, Jenna, please tell me you aren't going to do what I think you're going to do."

Jenna smiled.

Annie steered her sister to the corner. "You can't. I live here. You can't go home with someone you just met. You don't even know him. I don't know him. What if—?"

"Annie, it's fine. It's good. Relax." Jenna wrinkled her nose. "Jèsus, you'd think you're my mother."

"Please say you won't—" she leaned closer to Jenna and lowered her voice, "—sleep with him."

"I'm a grown woman." Jenna crossed her arms as she turned her back to Annie. "I'm going to get another drink."

Annie's cheeks burned. People didn't go off and have random one-night stands in little communities like this. No, there were small town values, proper upbringings and salt-of-the-earth folk here. Cathy's house wasn't a seedy nightclub.

With her mind whirling through different options for how to get Jenna to leave and return home without a scene, she bit her lip and rubbed her forehead.

"Annie, dear, come here and have a seat." Helen, the older woman from earlier, waved at her from the sofa as Jenna disappeared into the kitchen.

Sinking into the sofa, she tried to smile. "I'm glad I came out tonight."

"I think Ryan is glad you did, too." Helen gestured toward the young man Jenna had been eying. Then Jenna was back beside him again, already laughing at something he said.

Annie frowned.

"Don't you worry about Ryan." Helen tapped Annie's knee. "It's fine."

"I need to take my sister home."

Helen clucked. "Now, I don't know much about your sister, but I do know a thing or two about Ryan. He's one of our neighbors and a good boy—helped me out on our farm a time or two. I don't think the night will end quite the way you think it might."

"I don't understand."

"He's a gentleman. They might go to his place, but he's a gentleman. Everyone here knows it." Helen winked at her. "I may be an old lady, but I know about these things."

"A gentleman? You mean he won't—" was she really going to ask this sweet older woman about Ryan's propensity for a one-night stand? "—want to sleep with her." She whispered the last part of her question.

Helen laughed. "That's exactly what I mean. I know he's been trying to date women over the Internet, but it hasn't worked out for him. Oh, sure, a girl down in the city was in the picture briefly, but she wasn't the right one for him. Some model or something or other." The older woman shook her head as if the ridiculousness of that arrangement was self-evident. "But if he and your sister hit it off …" She shrugged. "Maybe it'd be good for both of them."

Annie studied the couple in question. Ryan's name was familiar for some reason, but she couldn't pinpoint why. Perhaps he'd been one of the people at the open house. He seemed nice enough. His neighbors didn't shun him or anything, so that had to be a good sign. And then there was Jenna. Jenna had failed in every relationship she'd had. No man kept her interest past a few months, but this Ryan guy might be *the one.* She didn't want to stand in the way of Jenna's potential happiness.

Taking a deep breath, she nodded at Helen. "Of course, I'm sure I'm overreacting. Jack says I do that a lot."

"Oh, now, who is Jack?" Helen cocked her head like a cat ready to pounce.

She leaned into the soft sofa. "My ex."

"Well, there you go then," Helen said, her posture easing. "Perhaps this is the start of a new year and the turning of a new leaf for both you and your sister." Helen patted her arm. "Are you okay?"

Then all the memories from her week of misery caught up with her—Jack's ignorance, Kelly's absence, Milt's worry and Merry's health. "You know, I am a little tired." This Helen woman thought it'd be nice for Jenna and Ryan to get to know one another, and something good needed to happen this holiday. "I'm—"

"You're heading out," Helen finished her sentence for her.

Annie nodded and made her excuses.

Helen patted her on the hand. "Let's go find your coat."

After collecting her jacket, Annie waved Jenna over. "Are you sure you want to stay?"

Jenna rolled her eyes. "You're leaving already?"

"Do you have your cell phone?"

Jenna sighed. "No, *Mom*, it needed to be charged so I left it at your house."

"Jenna …" Annie frowned, but stopped without issuing her reprimand. At least this suggested that Jenna hadn't planned on going home with some guy tonight. "Here, take mine." She glanced at Jenna's chosen guy for the night, then back at her sister. "Just in case."

A moment later, without Jenna, Annie guided her pickup from the driveway and headed home. She'd turned off the radio as soon as she started the truck. It seemed too loud now. The sky was bright and the snow twinkled from the ditch when the headlights caught it just right. She stopped the truck on the road and rolled down the window.

The crisp winter air, filled with glittering crystals, swirled through the still cold cab of the truck. She sucked the air deep into her lungs. The night was quiet, beautiful. A real silent night. She blew the air out deep and slow, and puffs of breath hung in the air in front of her. Home was calling her.

And when she got there, she'd be darned if she wasn't going to open a bottle of Merlot and have a glass in front of the fireplace, all on her own. Jack could go to the devil, too.

CHAPTER 22

She looked ahead. In the distance, the silhouette of her house was a welcome haven in the darkness. They'd turned the porch light on when they'd left. Home, sweet home. It didn't resemble the picture that'd inspired her to move here. No great memories—no inherent draw to family and friends. It was a house, *her* house. Aha, that was the problem—*her*.

She started her truck again. She was getting melodramatic or melancholy, or both. That wouldn't help anyone or anything.

As she drove to the house, something caught her eye—a movement in the shadow by the hedge. Slowing her truck, she felt her heart beat faster. Something was moving over there. Then her headlights illuminated the yard.

Oh, heavens … cattle filled the yard. They were all giant, lumbering beasts. Had she gotten lost? Nope, this was her place. So why were there cattle? She didn't own them, nor did she want anything at all to do with them.

Turning the truck into the drive, Annie shuddered at the casual interest the brutes showed her. What were they doing? Getting closer? Didn't they realize she could run them over? She slammed on the brakes.

The house was still a good sprint away. The porch light beckoned her to come, but in that moment the haven was like the aurora borealis—much further away than it seemed. Cows everywhere blinked lazily at her as if they were trying to lull her into a false sense of security. Then they'd stampede over her as soon as she was three steps from the truck.

She needed an escape plan. Could she scare them away?

Leaning on the horn, she waited for the cows to trot off.

The cow closest to her window lifted its nose and mooed at her. Then it stepped closer.

"Back away!" She pressed the horn again, holding it down. The cows shifted on their hoofed feet and twitched their tails, but they didn't seem scared and they certainly weren't running away.

She took her hand off the horn and swallowed. She was trapped in her truck by a herd of cattle. She could never tell anyone about this. She'd be a laughingstock.

Okay—people dealt with cows everyday. They survived. She shifted in her seat to study the beasts standing in her yard. They didn't seem particularly spritely. Maybe they wouldn't even notice her if she got out of the truck and walked to the house.

She swallowed again. Her heart thudded in her chest. Cows. They were only cows.

She fumbled for the handle of her truck door—not breaking her eye contact with the closest cow. The door creaked open—she waited for a moment. She wiped her palms on her pants.

A distinctly bovine odor flooded the air. She held her breath a moment, but that only made her heart beat faster. Okay—not a good idea.

Annie tried to slide out of the truck. The earth was at least two feet farther away than normal. She stretched her foot down and down until it made contact. A cow by the barn mooed. Another bent its head to chew on a tuft of yellow grass poking through the snow.

She didn't move. One foot was still securely in the truck. She could yank the other leg up and in, in a flash if needed.

With the door open, the light in the cab of the truck shone out onto the driveway, highlighting her presence to all the beasts.

She bit the inside of her lip. Okay, all she needed to do was get the other foot free.

She gripped the door of the truck and started to slip the other leg out. The cow closest to her mooed again and stepped yet closer. No way.

She pulled herself into the truck and slammed the door.

She needed a Plan B. If she wasn't leaving the safety of the truck with the cattle in the yard, then the cattle needed to leave. On the other hand, if the cattle wouldn't leave, then she needed to. She gripped the steering wheel.

"You think you've won, but you haven't."

She started the truck and inched it out of the driveway. The cows had to have come from somewhere. She'd follow their hoofprints to their home and tell their owner to come and collect them.

On the road again, the tightness in her chest eased. *Okay, where do you critters come from?* The hoof marks were easy to see in the snow.

Creeping along the side of the road, she followed the trail. The cows had wandered in and out of the ditch, and Annie retraced their steps along the road until they turned into a field where a fence had been knocked down. There wasn't a house close, and the land could belong to anyone.

She stopped her truck and got out. The tracks went right into the field. She had no idea whose land this might be. Her excursion had not led her to a house.

Darn.

She glanced at her watch in the light from her headlights. It was already half past one in the morning.

Hopefully the cattle had moved on by now.

Still, the excursion wasn't a waste. The crisp sparkling sky was stunning, and she would have missed it otherwise. She couldn't remember the last time she'd stayed awake so late. There was a different quality to the sky at this time of night.

Rolling her shoulders, she suppressed a yawn. Even the idea of the Merlot had started to lose its appeal.

She examined the land one last time for any telltale sign of the cattle's owner. When nothing new appeared to her, she climbed into the truck. She needed to turn around and head home.

Guiding the truck to the side of the road, she initiated a three-point turn, or—more than likely—a nine-point turn. Cranking the steering wheel to the left, she was pleased when the truck turned obediently. Excellent. Then the front tire on the passenger side dropped a little. Okay, she was at the other ditch. Now, reverse. The vehicle kept going forward. What the—? She stomped on the brake. The truck lurched. Okay—reverse. She shifted into Reverse again, and stepped on the gas. Nothing. She wasn't moving.

No. Please. She wasn't stuck, was she? Darn it, darn it, darn it ... and darn those cows. Why was this happening? Letting the truck rest for a moment, she braced her shoulders and tried to think this through dispassionately. She was stuck. She didn't have time to let loose her frustration. She had to find a way out of this predicament.

This was fixable. It had to be.

Annie opened the door and jumped out. Her tire was up to its nether regions in a snowdrift. She kicked at the snow. Then she got back into the truck and shifted it into Drive again. It didn't budge. Then she tried Reverse again. Nothing.

A minute later, she peered under the truck again to find that the tires had sunk even deeper into the snow at the side of the ditch.

There had to be something in the truck to put under the tires for traction. She'd get out of this and then she'd go home and the cattle would be gone and she'd go and have a glass of Merlot and snuggle into her bed and everything would be okay.

She straightened and walked to the back of the truck. The bed was empty. She peered into the cab of the truck again, hoping she'd forgotten about something that would be useful in this situation, but the truck's inventory was limited to sparse essentials like seats and a steering wheel. Behind the seat? Nope.

Resting her head against the doorframe, she sighed. If only she hadn't given her cell phone to Jenna. All she wanted was to be home in her bed, but in order to get there she needed to give her wheels some traction.

Annie removed her jacket. It'd been a gift from her ex, one of those presents she knew he'd selected to make her more presentable to his business partners.

Yes, the coat was an acceptable sacrifice. Besides, if this all went smoothly, perhaps she could get the coat dry-cleaned next week and it'd be fine.

Shoving the jacket against the back of the one front tire as much as she could, she prayed this would work. If it didn't—well, she wasn't prepared to strip everything, so this had better work.

Stepping back into the truck, cold air swirled around her shoulders. At least she shouldn't be jacketless for too long. Taking a deep breath, she started the truck again. It purred under her like an obedient creature—this was it. She edged the gear into Reverse.

"Go slow," she muttered, "let it grab the jacket. Then a little more gas ..." Her gaze stayed fixed on the ditch ahead of her. It didn't go away. Nothing changed. She hadn't moved.

She stopped the truck and jumped out to reposition the jacket. It'd disappeared. She knelt to investigate. One little triangle of fabric remained visible. The coat had been pulled under the tire. She yanked it.

Nothing moved.

Darn it.

Another swirl of cold air crept up around her as she panted with frustration. Her breath hung in the air for a second before dissipating. It was getting colder.

Suppressing the urge to bang her head against the truck, she slammed her hand against it instead.

"Ouch." She shook her hand. "Fine. Stay here," she grumbled to the truck. She yanked the keys from the ignition, hopped out and slammed the door shut. *Take that!*

She would walk to the nearest house. Her sweater was wool, so she'd be okay. The night wasn't that cold yet.

Sure it wasn't.

She would have a conniption if Kelly ever left a perfectly good truck in the winter without a jacket, but there was a light flickering in the distance. It didn't look *that* far away. And all she wanted right now was to be asleep in her own bed. She'd slept a night in the truck once already, and that was enough to last a lifetime.

Besides, her cheeks burned with frustration. She was angry enough to stay warm, if nothing else. She marched in the direction of the home, but she had no idea how far she'd come. She hadn't paid much attention when driving. She'd been concentrating on the hoof marks in the snow.

Ugh. Hoof marks. What if when she got home the bloody cows were still there?

She walked. The snow crunched under her feet. After a bit, she turned around to gauge her progress. The truck was much closer than it ought to be considering the number of goose bumps on her forearms. A shiver shot through her. It was colder out here than she'd thought. What about jogging?

She couldn't remember the last time she'd jogged—High school? Elementary school?—but if memory served, it was pretty straightforward. She tried to put a little bounce in her step. Her lungs and heart ached with the shock of it all before she'd gone a hundred feet.

What did they say? You had to push past the burn.

What burn? Her lungs would shut down and her heart burst from her rib cage way before there was a burn. Now she was weirdly chilled and sweaty at the same time. Maybe she was in the midst of a feverish delusion.

A cramp clamped over her calf muscle, and Annie stopped abruptly. Bending to rub the cramp, she glanced over her shoulder. At least the truck was finally fading into the shadows.

When she straightened, her calf still felt tight, but she couldn't help that right now. She tried to jog again, but she hobbled instead. "Fine. Fine," Annie shouted at the twinkling stars, as if they were the gods tormenting her.

Giving up the idea of jogging, she hopped, limped and skipped as best she could along the road.

On her left, a farm emerged from the shadows. A lone farm light, high on a pole, stretched its warm glow over the farmyard. It was peaceful, enticing. She could stop by, knock on the door and get some help. She had good neighbors.

Then again, most people would be wary of anyone banging on their door in the middle of the night. Some old lady probably lived here alone, and Annie would be greeted by a shotgun in the face.

Okay—it wasn't that kind of neighborhood, but you never knew how people would react in the middle of the night.

The sweat on her brow cooled her skin, and the heat from her jogging and frustration had faded. In the last few minutes, the breeze had picked up. She needed get to her farmyard oasis soon or she'd be covered in frostbite. She'd never had frostbite, but it wasn't something she needed to check off her bucket list.

She hobbled to the end of the driveway and contemplated the house. No late night revelers partied here. The yard light stood silent sentinel over the home and there was a faint sound of a dog barking. She stepped into the still yard. First she'd crashed a party and now she was trespassing. Life was simpler in the city.

At least this place didn't have cattle in the yard—what a novelty. She rubbed her arms to push away the goose bumps as she made her way to the barn. Her teeth chattered.

Earlier she'd been unwilling to step out into a herd of cattle when she'd been a few steps away from her own house. Now she was thinking about spending the night in a barn. Desperation was an interesting motivator.

She trudged toward the barn—she just couldn't bring herself to disturb the homeowners. At least she'd be protected from the wind until morning. Then she'd go and introduce herself and it'd all be sorted. The cows would go away, her truck would be freed from the ditch, and everything would be better.

If only she could get into the barn.

The cold metal latch on the barn door wouldn't budge under the pressure of her numb fingers. She put her shoulder under the latch. *Come on. Come on.*

Behind her the distant barking was growing louder, until there was a bang of a door and the yapping switched to a low but loud growl.

"Hey!" a man's voice thundered over the dog's snarl. "Who's there? What are you doing?"

Fear jolted through her heart.

She spun around as a beam of light shone out from the direction of the house. She blinked when the light shot straight into her eyes. Something nudged her thigh. She reached with one hand to shield her eyes and the other to shoo away whatever pushed against her.

"Digger, heel."

The prodding on her thigh stopped. She blinked, still not able to discern who approached her, but relief at not having to spend the night in the barn flooded through her limbs.

"Don't shoot me. I'm sorry to barge onto your property, but my truck is stuck up the road."

The beam of light shifted down. She blinked. Little squares of color floated in front of her eyes.

"Annie?"

That voice was oh, so familiar. "Quinn? Oh, thank God." Tears sprang to her eyes, and she wiped them away. Her fingers were cold and shaking. She was safe.

"What the hell happened to you?" The concern in his voice wrapped around her like she was sinking into a hot tub.

Annie shrugged. "There were cows."

CHAPTER 23

Quinn braced his hands on his hips, but Annie didn't bother acknowledging the question on his face.

"Get your flashlight and coat and stuff, then we can head to my place. Or maybe my truck. Yes, maybe we should get my truck..." She rubbed her forehead, but it was numb or her fingers were numb—something wasn't quite right, whichever. Then she sensed he was waiting for her to look at him again. "Yes?"

"Come inside and you can tell me how you ended up trying to break into my barn when you were at the party just over an hour ago."

"How did you know that?"

"Sandra called at midnight."

"Oh." She instantly regretted the jealous tone in her voice.

He smiled as he reached out and took her elbow in his strong bare hand. His hand heated her skin, like sinking her elbow in hot chocolate. Everything was going to be okay with Quinn there. She just knew it.

"You're freezing." He took off his jacket and threw it around her shoulders. The warmth, his warmth, enveloped her. Then he grabbed her arm again. "Come."

"Okay," she said, not feeling like she had a choice. She pulled the jacket tighter and reveled in his lingering body heat.

The cramp in her calf had shifted around to a shin splint by the time they reached the porch step. She tried to tug her elbow from his grasp so she could hobble up at her own pace. In truth, even crawling had started to sound appealing. Mental note: Take up some kind of fitness something or other.

Instead of letting her go, he switched his position. He now had one hand on her waist, under the hem of the jacket, and another on her opposite hand. She reached down to feel where his heat seared through her top. His hand was warming her in way too many places. "No, really ..."

"All right." He swept her up in a quick motion, flung her around until she teetered on the fulcrum of his hip, as she imagined he would do with a calf. In three short steps, he was atop the stairs and setting her down again.

"What are you doing?" she responded, perhaps a little too late. "You could have thrown out your back and then what?"

The only acknowledgment she got for her efforts was a grin. She scowled, which resulted in a deep chuckle bursting through the grin. She crossed her arms, but followed him into the house nonetheless.

As Digger circled around them, his big tail whacked her in the leg.

"Digger, go lie down." Quinn commanded, and the dog obediently trotted off to the next room. "Come in," he said to her, in a much less commanding tone.

"But ..." She waved to the outside. "I should get to the truck, or home at the very least." The warmth from the house scalded her cold cheeks, but she didn't relinquish the jacket. Not yet. She was just starting to get feeling back in her fingers.

Even as she spoke, she struggled to keep her eyes open. So tired … so warm …

He exited the porch and turned off the light, leaving her to the shadows of his mudroom. She stifled a yawn and followed him through.

"Seriously—" Another yawn interrupted her words. Where was he? The light was on in a room down a narrow hallway. "Quinn?" She blinked. Curiosity about his house wasn't strong enough to stop her from following the light.

Her eyes burned, trying to adjust to the brightness of the room after being in the dark night for so long. "Quinn?"

Rhythmic thumping emanated from the corner of the room. She squinted in that direction, unsure of what to expect. The dog from outside was now lying on a blanket, wagging its tail hard and fast. It banged against the floor. She nodded at the dog and the tail thumped faster.

Then she realized she was in a bedroom, Quinn's very masculine bedroom to be exact. The heat burning her cheeks grew stronger.

Suddenly the warmth of his jacket felt too intimate, too close. She had to get out of his clothing, out of his bedroom. She shrugged his coat off quickly and tossed it toward his bed. It missed and slid to the floor, but she didn't dare go over to pick it up.

She backed out of the room, straight into his arms. She spun around and he stepped back.

"Here's a T-shirt for you, straight from the dryer." He shook out a rumpled gray shirt, before offering it to her.

"No." She didn't take the shirt.

"It is clean." He tossed it at her. "Take it."

She gaped at the king-sized bed. "Why?" It was the only question she allowed herself to ask.

He smiled. "I'm not trying to seduce you, but I'm not going out in the middle of the night to drag your truck out of the ditch either. I can do that tomorrow."

She wasn't sure what to feel about him saying he wasn't going to seduce her. Disappointment reared its head—however inappropriate. "The cows are—"

"Digger will whine at the door if you shut it, so you'll have to keep it ajar at least."

She pressed her fingers against her scorching hot face. "I can't possibly—"

"Don't worry. I'm not sleeping with you." His voice was dismissive and authoritative, as if everything had been decided and all she had to do was obediently go to sleep. "You can tell me about the cows and the truck in the morning."

"Morning." She nodded. "Wait a minute." Her nodding changed to a shaking of her head. "I can't sleep in your bed." She grabbed his arm to steer him into the room, while attempting to take his place in the hallway. "I'll sleep on the sofa."

"No." He took her hand off his arm and nudged her into the bedroom.

When he stepped into the room with her, everything changed—only the hum of a furnace kicking in broke the quiet. Even the dog's tail had quit thumping. They gazed at one another. The room, the walls, everything seemed to be waiting for what would happen next.

He leaned toward her.

Her grip on the T-shirt he'd given her tightened for a moment. He had kissed her before, at Thanksgiving. Ages ago. Heaven help her, but ever since then, she had wanted it to happen again. Could it be so easy? Unable to stop herself, she leaned forward like he was rum and she was eggnog, and they were meant to be together. The T-shirt slipped through her fingers.

She couldn't stop her hand from going to his face, brushing the side of his unshaven cheek, slipping over his strong jaw to his neck, drawing him closer. Why wasn't she in control of her own body?

He yielded to the soft pressure of her hand at the back of his neck. She closed her eyes as his warm lips touched hers.

He tasted of scotch, peaty and rich. His arms encircled her and she inhaled his scent, the deep masculine scent of a man who had been woken from his sleep, a man not expecting company ...

She pulled him closer.

This was it! She'd lain awake for more nights than she'd want to count wondering if she'd ever kiss him again, and now her fingers were tracing the muscles of his shoulders through the threadbare, velvety soft fabric of his shirt. Then she moved her hands to his chest, molding her touch to his body. Her exploration ended at the hem of his shirt. Without allowing herself any moment of thought or self doubt, which would surely come if his lips ever stopped doing those magical things to hers, she slipped her hand under his clothing and touched his skin.

His quick intake of breath and the tightening of his already hard stomach made her bold. She flattened her palm against him, and his muscles rippled. Although he hadn't touched her, he also hadn't stopped her, which, she decided in that tiny part of her brain that was paying the least bit of attention, was a sign he was happy with what she was doing.

She opened her mouth under his, and was rewarded with the warm invasion of his tongue, which was the first time he'd done anything more than follow her lead. Her body responded like she'd found an unexpected present under the Christmas tree—a very sexy present. She wanted to feel more of him. Daringly, she expanded her hand's journey along his chest to his pecs, letting her fingers slide over his nipples. He shivered.

His arms encircled her a heartbeat later, trapping her hands between them as he tugged her against his body. Excitement surged through her and she pressed against him, encouraging him wordlessly. He was fully engaged now—his mouth stroked hers, his tongue tangled with hers—and she curled her fingers into his chest hair, clinging to him.

He wanted her. He really did. She hadn't thought that was ever going to happen again. She'd been convinced for all these years that she was well beyond someone—a handsome, amazing man—truly being attracted to her. The wonder of being wanted by him became too much to contain, and a cry escaped the back of her throat.

He lifted his head immediately and stared down at her. His panting breath caressed her face. "Annie?"

She blinked. Words were impossible. "Hmm?"

Quinn's embrace loosened, but he didn't let go. If he had, she would probably have collapsed to his floor like a balloon with a slow leak. He brushed his thumb over her cheek. "Why are you crying, babe?"

"I'm not—"

"Yes, you are." He pressed his cheek to hers and held her gently, cradling her in his arms.

"Oh, I didn't know." How could she be crying? This was the most fantastic thing to happen in her world in years. It'd been going so well. She turned her face to his shoulder, and tried to wipe her tears on his shirt discreetly. How could she explain how he made her feel? How could he understand that he was shattering her fears and anxieties? "I … I didn't mean to … I was …"

He stilled, like a man trying to gain control over his body. That was not what she wanted. Not at all.

"Umm, Quinn?"

"What?" His stubble rubbed against her skin with his question.

"Are you going to kiss me again?" Her body tingled at the promise embedded in her own question. "I think I'd like it if you did."

"I don't know that I can." She may have been crying before, but his words made her want to scream. "Annie, I don't think you know what you're doing to me right now. I can't keep kissing you and not ..." He let his sentence dangle, unfinished.

She took a deep breath. Her face was still pressed against his shoulder, so that his scent filled her. Heavenly. "I don't see the problem."

He leaned back so he could see her face again. She met his gaze without turning away, which, considering her words and the implication of them, was no simple task. She'd just told a man she'd like to sleep with him. She hadn't done that, ever. Jack had always been the initiator of their lovemaking. The few times she'd tried to make the first move, subtle though it'd been, Jack had crushed her like wrapping paper on Christmas morning.

"Are you sure?"

She nodded.

"Okay." He nodded in reply. "Me, too."

He actually wanted her! Her heartbeats tumbled over one another.

He scattered featherlight kisses over her upturned face. He murmured soft words about her beauty, which she tried to ignore as silly pillow talk, but the growing lightness in her heart suggested it, at least, wasn't quite so cynical. He made her feel cherished and special, so it was no surprise then that he had to kiss away a few more tears, but this time he didn't pause or pull back.

The pace of their touches and kisses, controlled mostly by Quinn now, was unhurried. It seemed the frantic pull between them earlier had been partially fuelled by a fear that one or the other of them would come to their senses if given the opportunity to think, but that wasn't a concern now. The lure of being wanted by him, the man she wanted, washed over her and added a new element to their caresses.

She pulled his T-shirt up his torso, until they had to break for a moment while he finished pulling it from his body. He was beautiful and strong. At her appreciative caress over his chest, his lopsided grin took on a sexual glint and intensity that made her stomach flutter.

Wow, this was really happening.

He led her to the bed, which was still mussed from his earlier sleep. When her legs hit the edge of the mattress, her heart thundered in her ears. He paused and brushed his fingertips along the side of her cheek. He was giving her the opportunity to change her mind again. She pressed her face into his hand as she began unbuttoning her shirt.

His gaze dropped to watch her fingers work the small plastic buttons free, one by one, seemingly transfixed. A moment later he nudged the shirt from her shoulders, sending it to the floor.

"I want to see all of you," he said.

She swallowed, but reached behind her back and unclasped her bra. At his groan, she realized her action made her breasts thrust toward him in a wanton way. She dropped her arms awkwardly to her sides and stared at him. The front of her bra was still in place, though the ends dangled at the back.

"What's that matter?"

"Umm … should we turn out the lights?"

He cocked his head to the side. "I like seeing you, but—"

She sighed and glanced down at her breasts. "I don't want to disappoint you. My—" she waved at her chest, "—aren't quite what they used to be. They're not quite so—" she pointed upward, "—perky."

He pressed his lips to hers, silencing her. "We can turn out the lights if it'd make you feel more comfortable."

"Oh, thank—"

He held up a finger to her mouth to stop her words. "But before we do that, I want you to know that I would like to see you. You have no idea how turned on I am right now, just having watched you take off your shirt." He traced his thumb under her breast, slipping beneath the bra to touch her skin, but not exposing any additional skin to his gaze. "You are right in front of me and this little bit of fabric is damn near killing me."

Her surprise must have shown on her face, because he grinned again. He turned his hand, so his thumb now rubbed over her nipple. Heat swept over her, landing straight between her legs. Suddenly she felt compelled to do this for him. She wished him to see her, because he really seemed to want it, and she, in turn, wanted to give him anything she could. She bit her lip and shrugged off the undergarment.

His gaze never left hers, though she suspected it was a huge effort on his part. She could melt in his arms for the care he was taking with her—oh, wait, she *was* melting in his arms. He cupped her breasts in his hands, pinching her nipples between thumbs and forefingers. She closed her eyes and leaned into his touch. He nuzzled her neck, and moved his hands to the waistband of her wool slacks. A panting breath later, and her pants and underwear joined her other clothing on the floor. Then he pressed her back onto the soft mattress until she was stretched across his bed.

She opened her eyes when his kisses and touching stopped. He was standing at the edge of the bed, looking down at her, while he pushed his own jeans to the floor. Before panic could blossom in her chest, he was beside her on the bed, without touching her. He propped his head on his hand.

They looked at one another for a moment.

"Hi," he said, which was a ridiculous thing to say when you were naked with someone in his bed.

"Hi, back at you." She grinned, and turned on her side to face him.

"Welcome to my bed, Annie." He touched her shoulder.

She wiggled across the flannel sheets toward him, until her body met his. She set her hand on his hip. "Happy New Year, Quinn."

"Midnight is long gone, but I think I should kiss you."

She nodded, looking at his lips as they drew closer. "You have the best ideas."

The leisurely pace he had set previously was tossed aside as soon as their lips met. His hands stroked her, her legs wrapped around him, and their urgency erupted. His touch sent her every nerve into a quivering, ready mess.

He pushed her back on the mattress, covering her with his body. His kisses never stopped as he positioned himself against her. She drew her legs around his hips, opening herself to him.

He swiveled his hips and guided his length to the entrance of her core.

"Please …" she murmured against his mouth.

He pushed into her, and her body shook with the pleasure of it. He lifted his head then, and gazed down upon her. She wanted to murmur something beautiful, perhaps profound—the moment seemed to warrant it—but then their bodies moved, hers instinctually matching his. She was lost under the quickening in her blood and the joy of feeling his body joined with hers. The rhythmic pressure of him stroking against her stoked the rising heat and need inside her.

When it came, the climax shook her, inside and out. She clung to his still rocking body on a sweet sob.

CHAPTER 24

Warm soft flannel encircled her … A hard body pressed against her back … A delicate trail of soft kisses caressed her neck ... This was the best fantasy she'd had in years. Annie leaned into the body. Wonderful, peaceful, perfect ...

Wait—this wasn't a dream.

She froze. The kisses stopped, but a strange rhythmic thumping noise started. Then it all came back—she was with Quinn in his flannel-covered bed and the thumping was coming from the dog that slept in the corner.

It wasn't that long ago that she'd been plotting how to win back her ex over turkey dinner and cranberry sauce, and now she'd slept with her neighbor. She let out a slow deep breath.

He hadn't moved. Her body was still cradled against his. There was a decision to be made—apparently by her.

"Good morning." She tried to make her voice sound light and cheerful.

He let go and rolled away from her. She twisted to watch him as he got out of bed. Naked. No modesty in that man. Naked. She should look away. Naked. *Think about something else.* "Quinn?" She kept her focus glued to his head as he walked to the doorway where they had shed their clothing last night.

"Let's eat." He left her clothes where they were, only plucking his own from the mess. He bundled his clothes into a ball and turned to meet her gaze for the first time. He still didn't try to cover himself. "Kitchen is down the hall that way." He pointed to his right, then he disappeared. The dog followed him.

She dropped back onto the pillow.

What was she going to do? There was no denying she'd wanted this, but had it happened too soon?

She closed her eyes and tried to sort through her myriad of mixed emotions.

Happy? Yes. Confused? Without a doubt. Scared he'd think this was a mistake? Absolutely.

She needed to quit analyzing it.

Annie scrambled for something else to think about.

This had to be one of the most comfortable beds she'd ever slept in. Jack had had a back injury in his youth, so she'd gotten used to sleeping in the hard beds he needed for support, but this bed was like sleeping in heaven—or maybe Quinn made it seem that way. Her heartbeat sprinted. What had she done? She washed her face with her hands.

People have sex. It happens.

She sat up in bed. He was moving pots and pans in the kitchen. Was he still naked? She shook her head to dislodge the image. At least with him in the kitchen, she could dash to her clothes without the risk of him returning. Why had he left the door open? He didn't seem to mind traipsing about with a bare body, but she wasn't of that ilk.

She threw off the covers and ran to scoop up her clothes. With her clothing in hand, she shut the door, then she let out a deep sigh and leaned against the door. The things they had done last night—she should have had more modesty *then*. It was a little late now.

Annie walked to the bed and untangled her clothes. Then she smoothed them out to ease some of the wrinkles. Oh, who was she kidding? She was wasting time before she had to face him again, wishing she could hide here all day.

The room had a woodsy aesthetic with its big log frame bed and the strange driftwood lamp, but there was something warm and comfortable about it, too. She glanced at the bed, which was a tangle of cream-colored flannel sheets, brown fleece blanket and striped comforter. No individual she knew could make such a mess on their own—it was all due to sex.

She jerked the sheet up and straightened the fleece. Should she strip the bed? She bit her lip. No. There was a strange set of relationship acrobatics she needed to do if she wanted to keep any semblance of a friendship with Quinn after this. Stripping his bed and running from the house to burn the sheets probably wasn't it—not when some other part of her would like to crawl back under the covers and ask him to bring her breakfast in bed. She whisked the comforter over the bed, covering it before there was something else to regret.

No, she didn't regret this.

Once dressed, she crossed to a rustic, unique mirror hung over the dresser. She couldn't imagine him gathering twigs and binding them to the mirror's frame, but that wasn't her biggest concern at the moment. Her hair was a sparrow's nest—more evidence of the night. No comb or brush was sitting on the dresser, and she would not snoop through his drawers. Then a picture on the corner of the dresser caught her eye. It would normally have been the first thing she would notice in a room, but today was not a normal sort of day.

The photo showed him with his family, the family who'd died. They were beautiful—the little girls, with plump cheeks, wide eyes and little mops of cherubic blonde curls, and his stunning wife. He looked different. He was younger to be sure, but there was something else. Perhaps the easy mien of a contented man?

How had he survived his grief? Her heart broke. Just looking at the photo in the sanctuary of his bedroom felt like an invasion of privacy now. She straightened and pretended to ignore the photo as she combed through the knots in her hair with her fingers one last time.

Her results weren't great, but it was a little better. She licked her finger and tried to wipe away some of the mascara smudges from under her eyes. There was a ring of red around her mouth where his stubble had rubbed her skin. More evidence. There was nothing to be done about that without her make up. The smell of bacon distracted her from further evaluation. Her stomach growled.

Then a phone rang in another room. Oh, no, someone had caught them.

What was a stupid thought.

But someone *was* phoning Quinn, and here she was still in his bedroom. It felt a lot like getting caught doing something naughty. With her chest tightening again, she opened the door. There was nothing else to do but to find him.

CHAPTER 25

Quinn was a breakfast god. Annie knew it as soon as she entered the kitchen. He'd donned a pair of jeans, but he was still bare-chested ... frying bacon. Not even the thought of bacon grease splattering from the pan could distract her from the vision of his lean, muscular back, marred by distinctly familiar scratches ...

He muttered into the phone and she didn't think he had noticed her yet. She wanted to duck back out the room, but she was frozen in place. When had she scratched him? She glanced at her nails.

Heat, hotter even than the bacon grease, rushed to her cheeks. What was going on with her? Sleeping with her neighbor? Scratches? A one-night stand?

Was that what this was?

Digger greeted her first. His tail wagged, thumping into his dish, splashing water over the floor.

When Quinn set the phone in its cradle, she cleared her throat. "Good morning."

"I don't have tea, but there is hot chocolate if you want some."

He'd remembered she didn't like coffee. She nodded, but he hadn't turned around yet. "Yes. Thanks."

"Have a seat. It's almost ready."

She sat on one of the vinyl kitchen chairs, vintage. She hadn't noticed that last night. "Listen, Quinn ..."

"About last night?" he prompted when her words refused to come, then pulled out a couple of plates and a cup from one of the cabinets by the sink. He glanced at her.

"No ... That isn't ... Well ... I guess we should ..."

"Get your truck?" He filled the cup with water and put it in the microwave.

"Yes, I think I left it a couple of miles east of here."

"West, actually, and it's about a mile, maybe a little farther."

How could she have been in that much pain from going a mere mile?

"How do you know?"

He dished the food onto the plates at the stove, then set one in front of her and one for himself across the table. When the microwave beeped a second later, he grabbed a can of hot chocolate mix from the cupboard and retrieved her cup from the microwave. After asking if she needed anything else, he sat. From a jar of cutlery in the center of the table, he fished out utensils for the two of them.

"My truck? How do you know where it is?"

"You can see it from here." He nodded to the window over the table. "Both Devin Trent and old Henry Winston found it. The phone's been going since I got up." How had she missed the other calls? "Old Henry said his cows got out last night and he found your truck when he was out rounding them up."

The cows. She shivered, remembering how they studied her last night. "Has he retrieved the cows?"

"Sure. He was more worried about you."

"Me?" She stopped measuring the chocolate into her water. "I don't even know 'Old Henry'."

Quinn shrugged.

"What did you tell him?" The whole neighborhood would know she'd spent the night at Quinn's. She'd lost count—was that the third or fifth spoonful of chocolate?

"Henry is Rita's dad. Nice man. He farms the place up close to where you stalled out your truck that first day."

She took a sip. The super sweet chocolate sat like a lump of cookie dough in her stomach. Rita's name brought with it a wave of insecurities, though she wasn't sure why. Everyone had said Rita and Quinn had never dated. "Oh."

Quinn ate. She tried to eat, too, but the food wasn't enticing just now. Perhaps they needed to talk about last night.

About last night ... What an awful phrase.

Should it have happened? Probably not. Did it happen? Yep. There wasn't much either one of them could do to change that.

He had barely looked at her since she'd walked into the kitchen. He was waiting for her to take the lead. Either that or he was regretting things. Was she?

No, she'd already decided she didn't regret last night, but she didn't have the guts to explore why. Even worse, it was obvious by the prolonged silence that he did.

After making the bacon and toast into a little sandwich, she cleared her throat. "I suppose we should talk." Then she took a big bite.

He looked at her. This time they both knew it didn't have anything to do with her truck. Well, truth be told, she wasn't meaning to ask about her truck the first go round either, but she'd chickened out. He waited for her, and she waited for some new conversational thread to strike her. It was difficult to think about talking about last night with him when he was focused on her. Particularly since he sat there shirtless. Right there beside her. His scent lingered on her skin, even obliterating the breakfast smells.

"Why weren't you out last night?"

He leaned back. "I don't do New Year's."

"Oh," she said. She wished she could think of a way to talk to him about his family, but he didn't seem open to that. She wanted to comfort him, but wasn't sure how to do it, particularly when she'd learned of his tragedy through rumors not from Quinn himself. So she let the topic drop.

"I didn't expect last night to turn out the way it did."

His eyebrows rose as if to say, *And I did?*

"No," she said quickly. "What I mean is, I didn't stumble into your yard hoping to sleep with you."

He laughed.

Heat rushed through her again. Only this time, there was something in the way he eyed her, in the timber of his laugh that sent heat circling, spiraling down, stirring some internal sex beast she had forgotten about until last night.

"I didn't think you had," he said after a moment.

There was tenderness there, and something sexy. Definitely sexy. Suddenly she wished they were having whipped cream and pancake syrup instead of bacon and eggs. Something she could lick seductively from her lip, something she could lick from his skin—

She had to quit doing that.

"What are you thinking, Annie?"

Some things you didn't say aloud, particularly when you didn't know what was going on in a relationship. They shouldn't have slept together. Not like this. They should have courted. Worked up to sex. Understood their feelings for one another first.

Courted? What century did she live in?

His fingers nudged her chin up and turned her face so she met his gaze.

"Yes?"

"Annie ..."

She half expected some words of reassurance, or maybe affection. She waited.

"You have some ketchup here. Let me ..."

He touched her cheek. At the soft rub—ketchup or no ketchup—that same carnal beast inside her stretched and sniffed the air. Yep, it was definitely charged with something—something decidedly tantalizing.

She leaned toward him. "You want to know my thoughts?"

He smiled. His eyes told her he knew exactly what she'd been thinking.

Annie whispered in his ear.

CHAPTER 26

Three hours later, under Quinn's tutelage, the truck behaved like a chastised child and jumped out of the ditch. Annie kissed Quinn goodbye on the side of the road and left for home. She couldn't remember if Jenna had a key to the door or not, and if Jenna couldn't get into the house, Annie would have hell to pay.

With the radio blaring and an exuberant surge of excitement in her heart, she turned into the yard. A car idled in the drive—it must be Ryan. Wow, he drove a pretty nice car. She'd misjudged him.

Then again, she couldn't very well come down too hard on Jenna, given what had happened with Quinn. She was never going to hear the end of it as it was.

She parked beside the car and started to wave to Ryan and Jenna—except it wasn't Ryan and Jenna in her driveway.

Nausea swept over her, swift and compelling. Jack sat in her yard with her daughter. What had happened?

Jack tapped his watch. His black expression told her everything she didn't want to know.

"What's the matter?" She jumped from the truck and ran to the car. "What's happened?"

Kelly and Jack exited the car with less panic, but Jack still slammed his door, even harder than Kelly had. "Where the hell have you been?"

"My truck broke down last night so I stayed at a friend's house."

Jack pointed at Kelly. "Get the keys from your mother and take your stuff inside."

Kelly scowled at both of them. She extended her hand to Annie, who passed the keys. "What's going on? Kelly? Jack? Is someone going to explain this to me?"

"Kelly, go inside. Your mother and I have some things to discuss."

Kelly stomped to the house, where four bags were already waiting outside the front door. After watching Kelly kick and throw the bags inside in true tantrum form, Annie turned to Jack.

"Tell me what's going on. Now."

"I should have known you'd be out drinking last night. You were so drunk you had to stay somewhere, didn't you?" Jack shook his head as he jerked his hand through his hair. " I don't know what to do, Annalisa. I don't have an option, but I don't want to leave Kelly here either. I mean look at you. Is that jam in your hair? Did you pass out in your breakfast?"

Annie raised her hand to where Jack's stare burned into the side of her head. Something sticky coated her hair. Jack was right. It *was* jam, raspberry jam to be exact.

"What kind of mother are you?"

She clenched her fist, too stunned to formulate words.

Jack shook his head again.

"That's enough." Annie slammed her fist against the hood of her truck. "Tell me about Kelly."

Jack stared at her, as if nothing in his life would ever be as clear-cut as it had been a few months ago. Things had changed on him, and he didn't get it. "I can't do it."

"You're kicking her out?"

Jack was breaking their daughter's heart, the way he had broken hers. Broken promises. That's all he delivered. She couldn't stand the sight of him right now.

Oh, look … A nice fresh patty of cow dung sat a few inches from Jack's polished Oxford.

At some point there had to be retribution.

Jack sighed. "I don't have any place else to take her. It isn't working with us."

He'd used nearly the same phrase when he'd left her.

Annie's skin crawled. She'd never seen Jack like this before—as the creep he'd become. "You're kicking her out," she said again, no question even implied. She squinted up at the window to what would now be Kelly's room. What must Kelly be thinking? Feeling? Annie knew firsthand about Jack's rejections, but this was different and so much worse. Jack was Kelly's father. "Why?"

"They went skiing at Christmas, remember?" Jack stared at her and waited for her nod. "Well, no one's parents went."

"You didn't ..." How could he have not phoned the other parents, followed up on the vacation plans?

"They were partying and carrying on with boys, alcohol ... Then they got tossed out of the hotel on Christmas Day. I had to drive all the way out there." Jack drew his hand over his face.

"That was almost a week ago. You should have called me immediately."

Jack ignored her. "Then, last night ..."

She clamped her tongue between her teeth and waited for the rest of his story.

"The police found her. She had been drinking vodka, waiting for the fireworks. I had to leave Abigail. It was before midnight, and Abigail had to find her own way home. Can you imagine? Everyone from work was there."

Her mouth dropped. Her mind reeled in a million directions. "You're telling me all of this now?" She thrust her finger into Jack's chest and he let her. "What have you been thinking?"

"Don't blame this on me. You were already in a state about Christmas. You're out of sync with everything, being out here in the middle of the bald-headed prairie."

"She's our daughter." Annie waved to Kelly's window. "And you are the one who moved to a different city to begin with."

"Seeing how you spent your night, I think I made a mistake. This isn't the place for Kelly, is it?"

"This isn't about me, Jack. You messed up. Admit it for once in your life."

"I should have taken her to my mother's."

Annie took a deep breath and tried to count to ten in her head, but her countdown was interrupted by a string of curses she didn't realize she knew. "What about school? Did you think about that? The new term doesn't start until February. You're uprooting her again, all on your whim. It's always about you, Jack, isn't it?"

"Not everyone moves when they're supposed to, Annalisa. It can be figured out." Jack leaned over her. "Are you going to drink in front of her?"

"For Pete's sake, Jack, I had one glass of champagne at midnight." She clenched her hands into fists and squared her shoulders. "Do you want a blood sample? A breathalyzer? A list of witnesses?"

Jack studied her. "Truth?"

"If you're dating Abigail Wilson, I'd be more concerned about your reputation for dating the office slut than anything Kelly or I could do. You're a little young for a midlife crisis, but here is yet another new car and everything." Annie swept her hand toward the shiny sports car.

"I'm not here to discuss my life." Jack folded his arms across his chest.

"You aren't here to discuss mine either." She braced her fists on her hips.

They stared at one another for a full sixty seconds, then Jack nodded. "Point taken."

"What does Kelly say about all this?"

"Not two words."

Annie rubbed her arms. She should be cold standing outside without a jacket, but heat throbbed through her veins like molten lava. She could explode any second. This fight was something they'd never had when they were married. They'd never had it when they separated either. It was a long time coming.

"What the—?" Jack had moved, stepping right into the cow dung. His pretty little leather shoe sank to its matching laces in fresh cow plop.

Some of the heat eased from her blood. Such a petty, insignificant little thing shouldn't matter, but it gave her hope there was justice in the universe after all.

Jack pulled his foot from the pile with a curse. He'd started to rub the brown crap from his shoe onto her truck's tire, when another car turned into the drive. Jenna and Ryan had finally arrived. This rusted, dented sports car was much closer to what Annie had imagined Ryan might drive.

As soon as the car stopped, Jenna jumped out. "What's happened?"

Jack didn't respond, being too absorbed in the task of trying to clean his shoe.

"Kelly is moving in," Annie said.

"What have you done?" Jenna charged at Jack.

"Jenna, don't. It's okay. We're going to sort this out." Annie tried to place a hand on Jenna's arm, but she shook it off.

Jack acknowledged Jenna only when she stood right in front of him. He continued to rub his foot on the ground. "Jenna. How nice of you to join us. Whose backseat did you roll out of this morning?"

Jenna slapped him. "Stay away from us Bingleys, Jack. You stay away."

Annie waved at Ryan apologetically as he left.

Jack sneered. "Gladly." He glared at Jenna as he returned to his car. He didn't notice another cow pile until he was up to his laces again. Jack cursed.

Annie glanced up at Kelly, who had finally made an appearance in the window.

"I'm sending the rest of Kelly's belongings on the bus. What won't fit, she can collect the next time she visits." He opened his car door and sat in the driver's seat. He unlaced his shoes and set them on the driveway beside his car. An instant later, all that remained in the drive were Jack's shoes.

CHAPTER 27

It'd been hours since Kelly had locked herself in her room. She'd let Jenna in for a little while, but she'd told Annie to go away.

"It's okay, Jenna," Annie said, and almost meant it. "It is more important Kelly feels she has someone to talk to, even if it isn't me."

Jenna's eyes brimmed with guilt. "I tried to get her to talk to you."

What was there to say? Annie remembered all too well how it felt to be hurt by Jack. It was raw and bone deep. She stirred the chopped celery into the minced onion.

"She'll come around. Give her time."

"Don't you think I know that?" Did Jenna forget Annie had been Kelly's mom for the last seventeen years?

Jenna opened her mouth as if to say something, but bit her lip instead.

"What?"

"She doesn't want to hear that you told her so."

"I'd never say that to her. Where would she get that idea?"

"It is in your every expression."

"I appear smug?" What could be more horrible than that?

"No, not smug exactly. Jack is an ass, we all know that, but no one wants their dad to be an ass … least of all to be an ass to them, do they?"

Annie stirred the celery and onion as they sautéed, but Kelly's stomping down the stairs erupted over the sizzling on the stove.

She smiled at Kelly. There was so much they needed to talk about, but for now, Annie just wanted Kelly to know she was safe.

"Hi, sweetie," she greeted.

Kelly grunted.

"We're having pork chops in sauce with potatoes."

"I'm not hungry." Kelly opened the fridge door and peered inside. She shut the door, then opened the freezer door.

"Okay."

Again, Kelly shut the door without taking anything out. The bell ornament on the door handle jingled.

"Jesus, Mom, what the hell is up with all the Christmas crap?" Kelly took the ornament off the handle and tossed it on top of the fridge.

It was her turn to bite her lip now. She turned to the stove.

Jenna stepped forward. "Kelly, your mom's worked hard to make the place nice for Christmas."

Kelly scowled at Jenna.

"I want it gone." Kelly turned to her mom. "I want that tree out of my room. Gone." Her voice cracked as it grew louder.

"Kelly." Jenna's tone held a warning. She was trying to intervene, trying to keep things calm, but Annie felt the air shift. Something dark was about to sweep across them all.

"Gone. All of this shit. Jesus. How can you wonder why Dad left you?" Kelly's voice had crescendoed to a scream.

The phone rang. Annie was frozen, and apparently so was Kelly. Neither of them moved. Someone needed to get the phone—it could be Jack calling to apologize. She pursed her lips. When would that ever happen?

Jenna answered the phone.

Kelly stared at her.

Annie turned off the stove. "There are lots of reasons why your father and I—"

"We both know, Mom. Quit pretending. What kind of person wants to live in a house like this? It's like a horrible old lady lives here. He left you because you act like you're eighty. He's turned his back on us all because of you."

Annie swallowed and tried to find her voice. The wooden spoon shook in her hand. She set it on the countertop and walked toward her daughter. "Kelly, honey, I know you are hurting right now, and I wish there was something I could—"

"It's all your fault. All of it." Kelly was still screaming, but now tears cascaded down her flushed cheeks. "He doesn't want us because of you." Then Kelly turned and ran from the kitchen.

Annie watched her leave. Cold sweat pierced through her skin. She let out the jagged breath she hadn't known she was holding. Kelly was right—this probably was her fault.

Jenna stepped into the room then. Annie turned away from her to face the wall, and blinked away her tears. "Who called?"

"Quinn."

"Oh."

"He said you could call him later."

"Sure, later." Annie nodded. Without a doubt, he would have heard everything.

CHAPTER 28

Valentine's Day

Annie pressed the letter again, carefully, gently, folding the paper into thirds along the same lines as it had originally been folded. They were uneven and slightly skewed, but she resisted the urge to refold the paper properly.

She'd read and re-read the letter and still couldn't believe her luck. Sure, Claire had told her that her article ended up in a monthly Christmas magazine more quickly than anyone had anticipated—apparently there had been a problem with one of the articles that had been slated to go to print, and Claire's article had been the same length so it was used instead—but Annie hadn't considered what that meant. The reality of it hit now. Her house … her decorations … her *creations* had been shown to hundreds, possibly thousands of people. And those people were now interested in what she did.

After inserting the letter into the envelope again, she set it on her worktable. She hadn't done any crafts since Kelly had moved in—particularly after the Christmas outburst—but her life now resembled a grilled cheese sandwich without the cheese. Something was missing in her days and nights. She craved it.

She'd resisted temptation for over a month. She didn't want Kelly to think she was an out-of-date 80-year-old. She didn't want Jack to call her Mrs. Claus in a derogatory way. She didn't want to be that person.

So why did she miss it?

She eyed the letter again, then reached for it. She started to extract it from the envelope again, but she didn't need to. She knew what it said—someone wanted to buy what she made. More than one person, even.

They'd tried to find her products online, but couldn't. They'd contacted the magazine, who must have received her address from Claire. That was a lot of trouble for someone to go through just to see if she sold her products.

Now that was something to consider.

She'd been surviving financially off a bit of savings and the money she received monthly from renting the city house. It would be good to supplement. After all, the other alternative of returning to accounting sent shivers down her spine.

No. Morning Lake symbolized new beginnings. Even new beginnings for Kelly, if she'd let herself have them. It was worrying about Kelly that'd kept Annie awake every night. How could she make things better for her? A little extra money in the house would help. They could go on a holiday or something.

She glanced at the clock. There were still a few hours before the school bus would come.

Pushing the letter to the side, she stared at her empty worktable. What if she did start her own business?

She'd have to incorporate.

She could write off her supplies.

A bubble of excitement filled her chest. She could have a business. Annie Bingley could be an independent business owner. Annie, the entrepreneur.

She pulled a notebook and markers from the shelf beside her. What would her logo be?

Oh—and her business name? Anything related to Mrs. Claus was out, for obvious reasons. She needed to sound younger than 80. What would sound sophisticated? Morning Lake Design Inc. Nah, that didn't seem right. What about something based on her address? The rural route number? 238 Studios? She bit her lip. That seemed a bit *too* sophisticated. Umm ... Bingley Creations? Second Chances? Glitter Inc.? White World? Elves Inc.? Stockings R Us?

She sucked at this.

Good grief, what had she drawn? A Santa hat? She put a big black "X" across the hat, then turned the page.

Fresh start. Okay. What about Red and Green? The Art of Giving? Hmm ...What about alliteration? Perfectly Pleasant? Beautiful Boughs? Noel Novelties?

Ugh.

Gah, she'd drawn another Santa hat.

Hmm, it didn't look too bad. What about AKA Mrs. Claus Inc.? Maybe it wasn't a horrible idea to reference the jolly elf's wife. Hmm …

A drone broke into her thoughts. It was too early for the bus.

Leaving the markers on the table, she got up to investigate. She couldn't see anything from the window in the craft room, so she went to the living room.

The windows were too frosted to offer more than a blurry silhouette.

She started to scrape the window, but stopped when a car door slammed.

Surely it was too cold outside for door-to-door religious types or salesmen. She went to the front door and opened it.

"Good. You're home," said the bundled figure walking up the walkway, carrying two boxes. No skin, no eyes, no identifiable characteristics were visible, but she knew only one person who had a car like the one parked in her driveway.

"Uncle Milt."

"Who else would it be?"

She stepped out of the way, while Milt entered the house and set his two boxes on the floor. When he shut the door, Annie noticed the boxes were moving.

"Are those ...?" She'd forgotten the cat and dog's names. They were something awful, but she couldn't remember.

"Well, the temperature is too cold for them, and the heater in the car is on the fritz." Milt tugged his scarf from his head, and shrugged off his coat.

"Umm ... where is Aunty Merry?"

Milt had bent to take off his boots, but at the mention of Merry's name, he seemed to shake.

"What's happened?" Annie clutched her fingers tight. "Where is she?"

Milt shook his head. His eyes were soft with unshed tears.

Oh no ...

"She's gone and kicked me out," Milt confided at last.

Not the answer she'd expected. "I don't understand."

"Bette Anderson died last week," Milt declared, as if that explained everything. He adjusted his boots so they were square with the wall.

"I don't understand," she said when she figured out Milt didn't plan to expand on his explanation.

"Ernie's single." Milt shrugged. "She wants to try her chances, I guess. Ernie's allergic to animals, so the three of us got booted."

Milt opened the top box. The cat sprang out with an irritated meow. It twitched its tail and started to sniff the perimeter of the room. Then Milt opened the bottom box. The dog leapt free, its body and tail wiggling so much it couldn't stand.

Then she remembered its name. "Dumbbell."

The dog whined.

"Yep, that Merry didn't want the lot of us, did she?" Milt looked at the cage and the dog whined again.

Annie put her hand on her forehead where it throbbed. "She was so frail at Christmas. How could you leave her?"

Milt recoiled. "I'd never leave her if I figured she'd be in trouble."

"This isn't making sense to me."

"The doctors fixed her medication, got it all at the right doses. Now she figures she's got a second wind." Milt shook his head again.

"But why are you here?"

Milt's shoulders drooped. "You told our Merry you'd take care of me if something happened to her. Don't you remember?" Milt held up his hand. "No, no, that's okay. I understand. We'll stay tonight, if that's all right. Then we'll be on our way. I just thought, well, it ain't no matter what I thought."

She grabbed the wall. "I didn't mean to say you weren't welcome. Of course, you are welcome, all of you. I'm sorry I hurt you. This is just such a surprise. I think I need to talk with Merry. She doesn't seem to be acting like herself."

His hunched body shuffled into the kitchen. Dumbbell and she followed him.

"Whatcha gotta drink in here?" Milt started opening cupboards.

"Milk, orange juice ..."

He waved away her suggestions. "No. I mean the good stuff."

"You haven't drunk hard alcohol since you retired."

He crossed his arms and stared at her.

"Okay, okay. Here." She opened the cupboard above the sink where she kept the liquor. "What do you want?"

Milt pulled out an unopened bottle of rye. "This'll do."

After pouring himself four fingers of booze and a splash of water, he took the bottle and his drink into the living room. "I don't mean to cause any bother. I'll sleep here for a bit until I figure out what to do."

By the time Milt sat on the couch, he'd swished down the last of his drink. An instant later, the glass was full again, with straight rye this time.

It made her ill to watch him. "I'm going to be in the other room."

"You betcha, my girl. I'll be here. You don't need to worry about me."

She hurried to the kitchen and picked up the telephone. She'd only dialed four digits of Merry's number when she heard another vehicle.

The bus.

She put down the phone. She tried to peer out the kitchen window, but it was too frosty, too. She needed to change the windows in this house. She could call Quinn—

Nope, she didn't need to think about him right now on top of everything else. She harbored too many mixed emotions on that front.

She should be fair to Quinn. He'd told her he was trying to give her a bit of space to help Kelly adjust to life at Morning Lake. And it wasn't like she hadn't seen him. He came over every snowfall and cleared her driveway, after which he'd stay for supper. She'd started to hope for snow in the forecast.

But he never stayed overnight. He never kissed her goodbye. Then again, under Kelly's pouting presence, it was awkward for all of them. At least Kelly seemed to like Quinn. That was a good start.

They also met in town for lunch every Friday, but that was awkward, too. Too many neighbors stopped by their table to find out what was going on.

With so many eavesdroppers around them all the time, it was hard to be entirely at ease. And there were no PDAs, as Jenna would say. Not that Annie *just* wanted to be naked with him, but it seemed they were edging a little too close to platonic. Was their relationship in hibernation like the groundhog? Or was it fading away? Annie knew that their attraction and their passion hadn't been a dream. Her sudden affinity for raspberry jam was evidence of that.

She scraped the frost with her thumbnail, clearing a little square of window through which to peer.

The taillights of the bus were disappearing around the caragana hedge, and Kelly trudged up the walk. She didn't even spare a glimpse at Milt's car. She didn't look at the window either, though Annie forced herself to stay there, smiling ... just in case.

A moment later, a gust of cold air raced across the floor and whirled around her feet as the front door was opened, then slammed shut.

Annie resisted the urge to go to meet her. She knew how much it annoyed Kelly to have her waiting inside the door, so she paced the kitchen. Then there were two thumps as Kelly's boots hit the floor, followed by another thump as her book bag joined them.

"Heya, Uncle Milt," Kelly said, when she entered the kitchen. She walked around Annie and began rifling through cupboards. "Where are the cookies?" she asked.

"I didn't know we were out." Guilt stabbed at Annie, just under her sternum. She'd always baked fresh cookies for Kelly, the way her mother had done for her. It was one of her favorite memories. Today, though, she had been playing with business ideas.

"Whatever." Kelly turned to the fridge and opened it. She moved things around until she found a jar of dill pickles.

"How was school?"

"Some stupid hoedown is going on." Kelly opened the jar, and stretched her fingers inside the mouth to reach her prize.

"A school dance sounds like fun."

"Why would I want to go hang out with a bunch of hillbillies?" Kelly plucked out a pickle and started eating it.

Annie pressed her lips together, and grabbed a napkin and fork for Kelly. She passed them to her daughter, who accepted them without comment.

"Don't you want to go?" she asked carefully after Kelly finished her first pickle and started fishing for a second one, again with her fingers.

"I never said that."

"Do you want to go shopping for something to wear to it?"

Kelly shrugged. "It is tonight."

"Tonight?" Annie glanced at the clock on the stove. "What time?"

"Seven."

"Are you going?"

"Melody's mom is going to give me a ride."

"Who is Melody? Why didn't you say anything? We should have talked about this before now."

"It's just a stupid hoedown," Kelly muttered. "Mel said you knew her parents ... I don't know ... Cathy something."

"Cathy and Chris are her parents?" Annie calmed. A little.

Kelly pulled out another pickle then put the lid on the jar. As she crunched on the pickle, she placed the jar in the fridge.

Annie studied her daughter. Was it possible Kelly hadn't asked because she assumed she was still grounded from what had happened at Christmas? Her antics had been pretty bad, but it was more important her daughter start making new friends at school.

"Okay, you can go tonight, but next time let's talk about it a little earlier than the night of."

Kelly shrugged.

"Is this a Valentine's dance?"

A bright red blush shot over Kelly's neck and cheeks. If Annie was reading this right, it looked like her daughter had a crush on someone.

"I'm going to get ready," Kelly announced as she turned and left the kitchen. Her fork and napkin were left, unused, on the kitchen table.

Annie smiled. Kelly was settling in at Morning Lake. When she clapped her hands, Dumbbell barked at her feet. She'd nearly forgotten about the dog. Right, she still needed to talk to her aunt.

She picked up the phone again to call Merry, but before she could dial, it rang.

"Aunty Merry?"

"Nope, it's me," Jenna answered. "What's up with Merry?"

She peered over her shoulder to check she was alone. "I've got some news. You'll never guess what happened." Finally, here was someone she could talk with about her letter.

"Did something happen to Merry?"

"Well, yes, but that's not it. Well, I suppose you should know ... Milt says Merry's kicked him out."

"Have you talked to Merry?" Jenna asked, but her tone suggested she didn't care. That was odd. Then, before she answered, Jenna asked, "Did something happen to Kelly?"

"Kelly is going to a dance tonight, and I think she might have a crush on someone."

"Well, that's good," Jenna said.

"Yes, and—"

"I'm late."

"Ah … right … We can talk another time." From the other room, she could hear Milt removing the cap from the bottle, followed by the clink of the bottle against his glass as he poured himself another drink. She needed to intervene. "How about tomorrow night?"

"No. I'm *late* late."

Annie's mouth dropped open but no words came out. She glanced around the room. The shower was still on upstairs and Milt hadn't left the couch, so she was essentially alone, but she still walked to the far corner of the kitchen and turned toward the wall. "You mean you're pregnant?" she whispered.

"Maybe. I don't know ..."

"Well, get a test and find out," she said. "Who is—? Oh!" It had to have been Ryan on New Year's Eve.

"Who is the father? I'm going to pretend you didn't try to ask me that. How many people do you think I sleep with? Next you'll be asking me how this happened, and I'm pretty sure you know."

"Okay. It's a surprise, that's all." They weren't supposed to have had sex that night, but then again who was she to give lectures on that topic.

"Well, it's a hell of a surprise for me, too."

"Okay, calm down. Go and get a test right now. Then call me when you get back from the store, okay? I'll be here. Waiting."

Jenna swallowed on the other end of the line.

"It'll be okay. You aren't alone, Jenna. I'm here for you."

"Right ... Okay, I'll call you soon."

Annie set the phone on the counter and stared at the frosted window. Good grief. A baby? At least Jenna had a good job as a teacher in a private school, which meant she had a good paycheck, benefits … and she loved kids. She'd be okay.

What to do while she waited for Jenna?

She should call Merry, but she couldn't be on the line when Jenna called again. Merry would have to wait until tomorrow.

Annie stared at the phone for a few minutes. It didn't ring. Jenna probably hadn't even left to go to the store yet. After all, she knew her sister well enough to know she'd have to fix her hair and makeup, and change her clothes first.

She put the phone on the charger. She might need to have a lot of battery power tonight. Then she pulled out the ground beef she'd taken from the freezer earlier and started preparing supper.

Two hours later, Milt was passed out on the sofa, Kelly had left for the dance, the dog had puked on the living room floor, the cat had broken a vase and she had listened to Jenna while she peed on twelve pregnancy tests and then cursed them all. The plastic sticks all confirmed she was pregnant.

Through it all, Annie's mind kept returning to one thought: She could never have peed while someone listened to her, even if it was filtered through the phone.

"Wash your hands now."

"I know, I know," Jenna muttered. "What if I try another brand?"

"Jenna, you're pregnant. It's okay. It seems a little scary right now, but it's going to be okay."

"What am I going to do?"

"Have a baby?"

"That is *so* not helpful," Jenna cried.

"Does the father know?"

"How could he? I just found out."

"You need to talk to him. Tell him."

Jenna sighed on the other end of the line. "I know."

"Listen, I know it'll be awkward—" Wait, was that a vehicle outside?

"Is something going on?"

"Kelly shouldn't be back yet, but it sounds like someone is here."

"Okay, I'll let you go. I suppose I need to talk to Ryan anyway. Thanks, sis, for being there for me."

"I'll always be here for you, you know that," Annie replied.

As soon as she hung up the phone, a crisp knock resonated through the house. She stepped over the dog, which apparently didn't care about strangers coming into the house because he didn't even raise his head or open his eyes.

She opened the door. Quinn. A rush of desire swept through her—just the sight of him aroused her.

"You have company." He looked over her shoulder.

"Yes ... Well, no, I guess not really. Uncle Milt is here. He's moving in."

"Oh, so you're busy then," he said, and he rubbed his hands as if he were cold.

"Where is my head? Come in."

"I don't want to be in the way if you've got company."

Annie reached out and grabbed his forearm. She tugged him into the house and shut the door behind him. A lopsided grin broke out over his face.

An instant later, Annie was all over him. His cold parka pressed against her warm body and she tasted that goofy grin of his. When had she last seen him alone? New Year's? That was a long, long, long, long time ago.

She yanked down the zipper on his jacket and had half a mind to tackle his pants zipper, too, when he caught her hands in his.

"Umm ... Annie? Shouldn't we …?"

Her cheeks were hot in a flash. Hot enough to melt the snow from the whole yard. "Oh, gosh ..." She pressed her fingers to her cheeks. She stumbled back.

Then it hit her—she could have gotten pregnant the same night Jenna had. It could have been Quinn and her having a baby. Sure, she was sitting on the outskirts of that possibility, but all those Hollywood types were having kids into their late thirties and early forties. Her heart started to pound in her chest.

"Is something wrong?" His concern touched her.

"I'm sorry ... I ..." Then she started crying. "I ..."

He drew her into a hug and brushed his hand over her hair. "You don't have to be embarrassed. I have to admit I've never been greeted quite like that when an uncle was in the house, but ..."

She smiled, then she started to cry again. "Uncle Milt ..."

"Okay, babe, you need to tell me what's going on."

She gave him a tight squeeze before stepping out of his embrace. "Come in. I promise not to attack you."

"I didn't mind, you know." He grinned as he shrugged off his jacket and kicked off his cowboy boots. His were the only ones at the door that weren't winter boots.

For some reason, that made Annie smile again. They looked so good sitting there next to her insulated faux fur things.

He followed her into the kitchen. He didn't stop or ask about Milt lying on the couch snoring.

"Cathy told me you've been pretty busy."

Annie narrowed her eyes. "Cathy told you to come tonight, didn't she?"

"I think she mentioned something about date night."

Her heart slid. Quinn wasn't here because he wanted to be. "Oh ..."

"Ah, I said that wrong, didn't I? I did want to see you. I didn't think you'd be entertaining ..." He glanced over his shoulder to the living room.

Her heart slid a little further. Was this about sex? Had he come for a nookie run? Did people even say that anymore? Did it matter what it was called? Or, more importantly, did it matter if Quinn wanted to jump her bones?

That would be nice.

After all, she'd hardly let him into the house before she'd tried to strip him.

Heat stung her cheeks again as she filled the kettle with water. "Milt showed up today." She put the kettle on the stove. "He says my aunt kicked him and the animals out."

She swallowed. Quinn was focused on her, listening to her. Really listening.

"I haven't had a chance to talk to Merry yet, but Milt says she's decided to chase after some other guy." It was nice to talk to someone about this.

"He brought the animals here?"

"Dumbbell and Tiger." She grabbed a dishcloth off a hook by the sink and started weaving it between her fingers.

"Is there anything else bothering you?"

"I think Kelly is attracted to someone at school, but she won't talk to me about it."

"That's normal, isn't it? For teenagers, I mean."

"I suppose ..." The kettle started to whistle. She took it off the burner before she pulled out the hot chocolate and two mugs. "I didn't even know about the dance until tonight after school."

"I see."

She counted out the teaspoons of hot chocolate mix into the mugs and poured the water in. After she stirred them, she placed three marshmallows in each mug.

When she set the cups on the table, Quinn raised his eyebrows but took one of the mugs.

They sat and drank their chocolate while Annie told him about Merry and Milt, Jenna and a bit more about Kelly. What else had happened? Something tickled the back of her mind, but she couldn't remember.

He made the suitable "I see" and "oh" comments at the appropriate times. But it wasn't that he was being dismissive. In fact it seemed quite the opposite. It was all rather mundane and comforting at the same time. Jack would never have sat and listened to her. He would have been solving things ... or rushing her ... or waving things off as unimportant.

Quinn didn't.

By the time they reached the bottom of their cups, she expected him to run for the door, but he didn't.

"Family's important," he said as he washed out his mug in the sink. Then he reached for her cup and washed it, too.

Jack had never done the dishes, never even moved a dirty glass from the living room to the kitchen. Tears rose again. Good grief, she'd devolved into a blubbering mess of a woman. More importantly, how could she have ever believed she loved Jack? She blinked quickly to get rid of the tears before Quinn noticed.

It didn't mean she loved Quinn.

He was considerate. That was appealing.

He was also elusive. After all, how long had it been since they'd been alone? He grabbed the tea towel from her hand, and she was too surprised to grab it back. Mouth gaping, she watched him dry the mugs. He even put them away in the cupboard.

Jack had been predictable—a Valentine's card, the "I love you" on anniversaries, the night out on her birthday, and, really, how sincere was the "I love you" on their last anniversary—two weeks before he announced he'd rented an apartment and would be moving out.

Annie wasn't even sure if Quinn liked her, but when she saw him close the cupboard door on the mugs he'd washed and put away—holy smokes. Now that was one heck of an aphrodisiac.

She laughed.

A big laugh-until-you-cry kind of laugh. She couldn't keep it in.

"Annie?" Then a smile broke across his face. "Now, how am I supposed to be serious when you're rolling on the floor?"

She laughed harder. When had her life turned into a sitcom? Milt, Merry, Jenna, Kelly ... and Mrs. Claus. How could she have forgotten about the business thing? She blinked, and started to float back to earth.

"Why do you want to be serious?" she asked after a minute or two had gone by. She was still grinning.

He kept his smile in place. "Well, I had planned to say I'd understand if you wanted to concentrate on family for a bit. You know ..." He nodded toward the living room.

She waved one hand through the air. "What? Isn't this normal?" She laughed again.

"You're getting quite a houseful. I'd understand if you want to concentrate on that for a bit." He turned surprisingly serious. "Family's important."

"I know it's important. It's the whole reason I moved here, but ... I need a bit of Annie to live here, too."

He cocked his head to the side. "What do you want?"

"You." That one word was simple, honest, and the most embarrassing thing she'd ever said. Part of her brain told her to take the word back. Avert her gaze. Run away. She ignored that part and listened instead to the part that wanted him to stick around. She didn't even reach up to touch how hot her cheeks were.

Quinn smiled. "Me?"

She nodded.

"Well, what do you want from me? To change these windows."

"Of course."

"Anything else?"

What the heck? When had she last taken a chance? When she moved here probably, and it had turned out pretty well, overall. She smiled then and leaned into him. "I bought some raspberry jam. A full jar, never been used—I mean opened."

He laughed as he walked over and pressed his body against hers.

"Well, we should do something about that ..." His words ended on a kiss as long and strong as his body.

A moment later, Annie tiptoed by her snoring uncle. She felt like a teenager again, except she'd never done anything bad in high school. She'd never skipped a class, never snuck out in the middle of the night, never did much but what had been expected of her.

Quinn walked normally, annoyingly so, as he followed her to the bedroom. Did he watch her walk up the stairs? Men in romance novels always watched women walk. She resisted the urge to put a bit more "oomph" into her hip sway. It probably had enough sway already ... and jiggle and wiggle ... and—oh dear, did she have a panty line?

She sprinted up the last few steps and down the hall to her room. Her hand lingered on the doorknob a second. He stood right behind her. He stopped and watched her. If she was going to turn back, now would be the time.

He'd helped her refinish the floors up here, so he'd seen the room before, but this was different, more intimate. After all, how many nights had she dreamt of him being there with her?

She threw open the door. It sprang from her hand and whacked the wall.

"Oh, dear ..." She hurried to examine the wall. It'd survived intact, without a doorknob-shaped hole in the wall. Thank goodness for doorstops.

He smiled at her. "You okay?"

"Yep, and so is the door." There was no sense trying to pretend she was a seasoned seducer. It wasn't in her genetic makeup.

"Are you sure?" He hovered at the threshold.

She scowled and dragged him inside. "Yes, I am absolutely, positively, certain." She flung the door closed. It vibrated in the doorjamb, but stayed closed.

He raised his eyebrows.

"Did I scare you?" she asked, lifting her hand from his arm. "You don't have to ... well, you know ... if you aren't sure."

"Absolutely, positively," he murmured as he pulled her close and stared into her eyes, "certain."

"I'm starting a business."

He nuzzled her neck.

"I forgot about it when we were talking earlier." She leaned back to give him easier access as she grasped his shoulders. They were muscular. Mmm.

"It's about time," he whispered in her ear.

"You don't think I'm crazy?"

"Of course you are crazy." When she stiffened, he chuckled in her ear before he nibbled on her earlobe. "I like it."

Just like that, her tension dissipated. She smiled and leaned into him. "Good. Me, too."

It seemed like such a novelty to be able to touch him, and have him touch her. Her heart pounded. She was ready to drool. Then he brushed his thumb over her collarbone, and started playing with the buttons on her shirt.

The blood in her veins jingled like Christmas bells. Wait.

"What's the matter?" He stopped his kisses.

"Do you think of Mrs. Claus when you think of me?"

He gaped at her like she'd lost her mind. "What?"

She backed out of his embrace. "Okay, that was a bizarre question, I know." Why had she opened her mouth? "Never mind."

She leaned forward to kiss him again. His kiss was soft, tentative.

She put her hand on his chest and broke the kiss. "It's just, well, I've been told I'm like Mrs. Claus." Was she really asking him if he found her sexy? Why did she do this to herself? "Anyway, she's not someone people want to take to bed ..."

He didn't laugh at her, bless him. He took her face between his hands. "I don't know about Mrs. Claus, but I want to take you to bed."

"Are you sure?"

He raised his eyebrows. He did that a lot around her. Then he sighed, which sounded rather resigned. "Annie, you are beautiful. You look nothing like what I'd imagine Mrs. Claus to look like. You are a vibrant woman." He tilted his head. "What is this all about? Do you think I don't want you?"

Heat flashed across her skin. She was an idiot. Of course he wanted her. His kisses showed her that much.

"It's been a long time since I've wanted to be with anyone. I want to be with you, Annie. You. Just the way you are. You don't have to try to be something you're not. You are not Mrs. Claus. You are Annie, and at some point tonight I'm hoping you'll be naked with me in that bed." He tilted his head. "Soon."

She grinned. "I think I can do that."

CHAPTER 29

Under Quinn's soft caresses and murmured endearments, the carefully constructed protection Annie had built around her scarred heart slipped to the floor with their clothing.

They stood in the middle of the room, and even with her bedside lamp casting their bodies in soft light, she didn't feel the embarrassment or anxiety she had the first time they'd been together.

She was bared to him, both body and soul.

Before her confidence could run and hide under the bed, she reached for Quinn's face and stared into his eyes. The room was quiet as they stood together.

Then it hit her.

She wasn't sure when she'd fallen for him, but she had.

And tonight, she wanted to show him how much he'd come to mean to her. But when she tried to form the words, they wouldn't cross her lips.

Her heart's last defense remained defiant.

"I've missed you," she said. It was close to what she'd wanted to say. "I know we see one another quite often, but I miss being alone with you."

That twinkle in his eye sprang to life as he grinned.

"Not just in the bedroom," she amended, as heat swept over her face.

"Have I mentioned that I love it when you blush?" he whispered as he traced circles on her arm.

She rose on her toes and kissed him. He tasted of the hot chocolate they'd shared earlier, and she smiled. Her lover tasted of chocolate—he really was perfect for her.

His arms circled her, drawing her closer. Her desire to have more escalated, when he spread his hands over her lower back and pulled her against him. She groaned into his mouth, which elicited a similar response from him.

His fingers dug into her flesh, and the space between their bodies was eliminated.

She broke the kiss and turned her head to whisper in his ear. "Bed" was the only word she managed before he lifted her and moved them to the bed.

He spread his body over hers. Sandwiched between him and the soft mattress, she felt safe and protected, which was strange since it was hardly as if she was at risk in her daily life. But when Quinn pressed against her, she was imbued with a sense of security and belonging she hadn't felt in a long time.

When he continued to hold himself still, she traced her fingers over his arms. "Quinn?"

"I wanted to go slow, to show you how beautiful you are to me." His tone was deep with emotion. "But I don't know that I can." She shuddered under the implication of his words—he was always in control with her.

"I—" *love you, too,* "—want you every way. Slow—" she drew her hands over his back in a tantalizingly leisurely pace, "—or fast," she shifted her legs to drape one over his, allowing his body to fit against hers, "—and every way in between." She brought his face down to hers.

His control evaporated when their lips met.

She stroked his body, trying to feel every part of him, memorize the feel of him beneath her hands, while he built within her a need that was unlike anything she'd experienced before. When they pulled apart long enough to fumble for a condom from her bedside table, she saw the same desire in Quinn's eyes.

When their bodies joined, their gazes locked. Her every emotion was bared to him. And when their releases crashed over them and he shouted her name, she believed he loved her, too.

CHAPTER 30

Ahh, her body was warm and satisfied. This was much better than hot chocolate. Annie snuggled closer to Quinn until her head rested on his shoulder. They wouldn't be able to stay like this for long. The man was like a stoked fireplace.

For now, though, it was good. Very, very good.

She let her hand drift over his chest and twirled the coarse hairs around her finger. With his free arm, he reached up and held her hand to still it. Ah, he must be ticklish. She smiled. She took a deep breath and was about to blow it across his chest.

Crap—was there another car coming into the yard? At this time?

Oh no—Kelly! It had to be Kelly. Annie bolted to a sitting position too fast. Dizzy, she swung her legs over the side of the bed. No modesty this time. There was no *time* for modesty.

She grabbed the first piece of clothing she found. She shook it out and tried to stick her arm into the shirt when she realized she was holding Quinn's. Her exasperated cry was cut short when she heard a car door slam.

She swallowed and tossed the shirt at him while she scanned the floor for her clothes. They couldn't have gone that far.

Behind her Quinn laughed. *Now?* How could he? She glanced at him. How could he be dressed already? Well, nearly anyway. His shirt hung open to reveal the curly little hairs she'd been playing with a moment earlier.

Even through her panic, she felt a jolt in her blood—no, there was no time for that.

"Help me," she whispered. "I can't find ..."

He was still grinning when he stood. What was he doing? He pulled something from the lamp. Her shirt. And was that—t? Yep, her pants were balled up in the corner behind the chair.

She seized the clothes, meeting Quinn's smile with a scowl. She was about to hold out for underwear but then the front door's telltale squeak announced she'd run out of time. Kelly was in the house, and Annie was buck-naked with Quinn in her bedroom. She couldn't even contemplate the rumpled bed.

She threw on the pants and the shirt.

"Mom, where are you?"

"Just a minute, honey." What kind of parent was she? Why wouldn't her fingers work properly?

She sent a pleading look at Quinn. He stepped forward—by the expression on his face, Annie knew he was still not taking this as seriously as he should—and buttoned her shirt over her bra-less boobs. She could only pray that Kelly and Milt wouldn't realize she'd been sans bra in a room with a man. In that light, it seemed seedy somehow going around without a bra. She wouldn't have thought about it under normal circumstances, but her nipples were overly sensitive at the moment and sticking out like marbles under her shirt.

She swept her fingers through her hair, and wished it didn't feel like a million degrees in the room right now. Wasn't it winter? Weren't they supposed to be cold?

"Are you upstairs?" Then there were footsteps on the stairs.

Annie dashed to the door. After opening the door a crack, she slipped through and closed the door firmly behind her. She turned to Kelly with a big smile.

"Hi, honey, how was the dance? Did you have a good time? Did Cathy want to come in for a coffee? Were all the people in your class there?"

Kelly raised her eyebrows. "Sheesh, Mom, are you on some kind of uppers or caffeine overdose or something?"

"What do you know about uppers?"

"Nothing. But seriously ..."

She pasted on a smile again. "I'm happy you had a good night. You did have a good night, right?"

Kelly tilted her head. "I suppose."

The expression on Kelly's face told Annie she was acting peculiarly. She did feel a little nuts for the second time in one night … or was this the third?

What did Quinn think about being stuck in her bedroom? Hopefully he'd stay in the bedroom ... until when? A love slave trapped in her room ... no, no, no. No thoughts like that in front of her daughter.

"Yeah, well, I'm going to stay at Mel's, okay? She and her mom are waiting outside."

"I ... okay ... I suppose that's okay. Are you sure Cathy is okay with this?"

Kelly rolled her eyes. "She's waiting in the car, isn't she?"

She followed Kelly into her room. Kelly kicked around some clothes on the floor until she unearthed a backpack.

"You had a good time?"

Kelly shrugged as she tossed a few things into her bag. "Kind of lame, but okay, I guess."

Annie smiled. That had to be the best thing Kelly had ever said about her new school. "That's good."

"Where is Mr. Quinn?" Kelly asked, as she rolled a magazine and tucked it into the bag.

"Mr. Quinn?" Annie's voice squeaked.

"His truck is outside." Kelly stopped shoving things into her bag long enough to study Annie.

"We were examining the windows. We need to replace them and Mr. Quinn is good—" no, she wasn't going to say he was good with his hands, even if he was, "—he's good at doing repairs." Her cheeks ached from this stupid smile.

Then Kelly turned and muttered something. It sounded a lot like damn.

"What's that, dear?" Annie's voice was at least two octaves higher than it should be. There was no way she sounded natural.

Kelly shook her head. "Now I owe Aunty Jenna. Man." Kelly grabbed two bottles of fingernail polish, threw them on top of the bag, and then zipped it up.

"What do you owe Aunty Jenna?" Annie remembered again about Jenna—poor Jenna. She'd probably gone to the all-night drug store to buy even more of their pregnancy tests.

Kelly tsked. "I thought you'd wait 'til summer, but Aunty Jenna, she knew what you'd do. Heck, even Aunty Merry and Uncle Milt were wrong—they, or at least Aunty Merry, thought you'd do it in secret."

Annie's chest seemed to be tightening around her lungs. A shot of anger pierced through her, followed quickly by humiliation. "What?"

Kelly hoisted her backpack over one shoulder. "You and Mr. Quinn, of course."

Annie didn't trust herself to speak.

Kelly let out a long sigh. Then she stepped in front of Annie and put her hands on her hips. "Aunty Merry thought you'd be sneaking off with Mr. Quinn all secret-like after I moved in, but as far as I can tell you haven't done that. I figured you'd hold off until I turned eighteen. You know, that *is* only another five months from now. Aunty Jenna believed you'd try to hold off but then would end up jumping his bones all of a sudden, unexpectedly. I know I lost the bet and all, but, seriously, it is about time. You and Dad have been apart for ages."

Annie's jaw was firmly embedded in the ground by the time Kelly stopped talking. Heat scorched her cheeks—no, it was more than heat. It was like she'd been hurled into the sun. She couldn't possibly be having this conversation with her daughter. She snapped her jaw closed. It seemed safer.

Behind her, floorboards were creaking in her bedroom. Quinn. Her heart thundered in her ears. She needed to get control of this. "I don't know what you think has happened here tonight, but rest assured I will be talking to both of your aunts first thing in the morning. Of all the ridiculous—" she waved her hand through the air, "—farfetched—"

"I knew I'd get that one." Kelly smiled.

Annie clenched her teeth.

"I knew you'd deny it." Kelly stepped up to her. "Anyway, Mom, no worries. Mel's mom says Mr. Quinn is nice and I think so, too." She grinned and Annie wanted to hide. "I have to run. Mel is still outside with her mom."

Annie's stomach fell to her feet. The whole community would know. "You don't say anything to anyone about your silly ideas until we talk about this tomorrow and I have a chance to talk to your aunts."

Kelly shrugged and kissed Annie on the cheek as she rushed out of the room.

"See you tomorrow." Then, in the hallway, Kelly said more loudly, "Bye, Mr. Quinn."

"Bye, Kelly," his voice came from behind the closed bedroom door—*her* closed bedroom door.

Kelly's footsteps faded down the stairs, and a moment later she was gone.

Annie's feet were rooted to the floor. How could she face any one of them? Even Quinn. What had he heard? He must think she was a terrible parent. After all, her teenager had talked about her affair as if it were common practice. If only she could fade into the wall and come out in say—what? Ten years? By then she may not be quite so embarrassed about being caught by her teenager. How could she have lost track of everything?

No, she knew exactly how that'd happened. Her blood churned again at the thought of his kisses, of what they had done ...

She took a deep breath as she exited Kelly's room. She turned off the light and shut the door. She took yet another deep breath and studied her bedroom door. All this deep breathing did nothing to settle her nerves.

Then the floor creaked, a second before the door opened. He was fully dressed. His appearance, though, didn't even hint that he'd just had a tumble. That was rather disappointing, considering her daughter had figured her out in a glance.

He leaned against the doorjamb and hooked his thumb in his pocket. Yum ...

Stop that.

She swallowed.

He grinned.

"Did you—?" The best approach was a direct approach. "My whole family has been betting on me ... on ..." *Us* was such a couple sort of word. "Well, on if you and I ... if ..." Her tongue wouldn't work. Her whole face had to be fire-engine red by now, right to the roots of her hair. When people had a terrible fright, they sometimes got white streaks in their hair. Considering how embarrassing this night had been, she would probably have hair the same crimson as Santa's hat by morning.

"I heard." Quinn hadn't moved. His cheeks weren't flushed. He seemed perfectly at ease, just waiting for her to return. He was waiting for her to decide what she wanted to do. Well, she didn't want to make this decision. Why couldn't someone else?

No, she didn't want anyone else to figure this out. Jack had always done the deciding.

She could do this. She lifted her chin. "Are you staying? Or are you leaving?" Okay, that wasn't making the decision, but at least she got out a bunch of words without tripping over her tongue.

"Do you want me to?" He tilted his head and watched her.

God, he'd put it back to her again. "No."

He pushed himself from the doorjamb and started to walk down the hallway.

"You're leaving?"

He stopped at the top of the stairs and paused before he started to descend. "You said—"

"I said no, as in I don't want you to leave."

He studied her for a minute. Then he nodded, but he didn't move off the top step.

"I'd like you to stay," Annie declared. What did it matter now, after all? The damage had been done. Kelly hadn't believed the whole window thing, which shouldn't have been a surprise. Annie had always been a terrible liar. Her heart pounded—again. Her life was turning into an effective cardio workout. "I want you to stay the night with me."

"I don't know if you're sure about this."

This conversation was almost as frustrating as the conversation with Kelly. "Yes."

"Okay."

Her heart bounced in her chest, partly from excitement and partly from fear. After all, it seemed suspiciously like she'd just begged him to stay the night, and earlier she'd nearly ripped off his clothes as soon as he'd walked in the door. Did he even want to be here? "Well, I mean, if you want ..."

His mouth kicked up in one corner. "I don't do much I don't want."

The way he said it, the way his gaze drifted over her body when he said it, the way his voice was all quiet and deep, made her body respond as if they were naked in bed again.

"Oh ... okay, then ..." Annie said. "I'll go shut off the lights downstairs and stuff then." Yep, she was an eloquent flirt.

His eyes crinkled in the corners. He was laughing at her … again. At least he didn't laugh aloud. He stepped out of her way as she moved past him to climb down the stairs. His hand brushed against the small of her back as she passed him.

"I'll be waiting."

She swallowed, but didn't look back. She'd probably fall down the stairs if she didn't concentrate on putting one foot in front of the other.

She raced through the rooms, turning off one light after the other to the sounds of Milt's rumbling snore. She checked the lock on the front door, threw a blanket over Milt, ignored the cat, who was using the couch as a scratching post, and walked past the dog, who was gnawing on one of her slippers. Sometimes you had to have priorities.

By the time she got to the top step again, she was panting as if she'd just run down that stupid road again the way she'd tried to do at New Year's. She needed to get in shape.

Who was she kidding? This wasn't about being in shape. The house was dark all around her, but there, at the door, was a sliver of glowing light. Quinn was waiting for her—in her bedroom.

When had that last happened?

Okay—it happened at New Year's, but tonight they were in her house, her bed. No man had ever slept in this particular bed. She'd bought it new, along with the sheets, the pillows and the bed frame. Tonight everything would change.

She swallowed and stepped to the door. It was ajar. She nudged the door, and it swung quietly.

Quinn straightened and turned from the window. He'd managed to pry it open, even though she hadn't been able to budge it since late October when the nights had started to cool. The cold air circled around her, but she didn't notice it. The heat from her earlier embarrassments still churned in her blood.

And there was also something heat-inducing about seeing her lover standing in her room, waiting for her.

CHAPTER 31

Annie listened to the quiet of the morning and marveled at how wonderful it was to wake to the crisp fresh air from the open window and the cozy warmth of Quinn's embrace. She smiled and resisted the urge to snuggle in closer. She'd need to get up soon, but she didn't want to wake him yet. If only she could enjoy the intimacy a minute or two longer.

Her back was pressed against his chest. His body moved with each breath he took. His legs were fitted against hers. Jack and she had never slept this way—he'd always been protective of his side of the bed, his portion of the blankets, his pillow ... Jack didn't know what he was missing.

She curled in closer to Quinn, unable to stop herself.

He moved in response. She held herself still and waited to see if he would drift back to sleep. He shifted again, pressing them even closer. Then he traced his fingers over her arm, leaving behind a whole new level of being awake.

When his mouth found the side of her neck, she shivered and tilted her head to give him more access. He groaned into her skin and her body tingled. As he continued to explore her body, she became aware of an unfamiliar noise.

A dog was barking.

Quinn lifted his head, and stopped his ministrations as if listening to what was going on downstairs.

Immediately she missed his mouth. She turned to face him. His cheeks were darkened with the shadow of stubble, his hair was flattened on one side of his head and puffy on the other but his eyes were alert. Had he been waiting for her to wake, too?

"It is just Dumbbell," Annie explained. "Uncle Milt will take care of him."

He bent his head to her, and claimed her mouth with his. All she could hear was the beating of her heart.

A scant moment later, a screech filled the room. Annie bolted straight up, banging her head against Quinn's. She shook her head and tried to focus on the figure in the door. "Jenna?"

"Oh, my God. I'm sorry." Jenna's voice was at least two octaves higher than normal. She laughed awkwardly, her face flushed. Meanwhile, Dumbbell ran in circles at her feet.

"What are you doing here?" Annie tugged the comforter higher over her body. Although her sister had seen her naked more times than she could count, the situation begged for modesty. Quinn groaned beside her and pulled away. She yanked the comforter higher yet.

It was 6:30, for pity's sake. It was way too early for Jenna, particularly when Jenna would have been driving for two hours already to get here. Out of the corner of her eye, Annie saw Quinn lean against the headboard, arms crossed over his bared chest. Oh dear, his body was covered with hickeys. Oops.

"I—oh, Annie—I've been fired." Jenna stepped closer to the bed. Tears welled in her already red eyes.

"What are you talking about? I just talked to you last night."

"I bumped into one of the parents at the drugstore, and then ..." Tears drizzled down Jenna's cheeks, and she wiped them away. "Then the superintendent called. He asked if I was in the family way. He surprised me, so I didn't think. I told him the truth ..." Jenna wrung her hands.

"They can't fire you," Annie exclaimed.

"It's a private school ... and, well, before we broke for spring break, there were rumors going around about upcoming cuts ... and, well ... I guess I'm being cut. They don't want an unwed mother with their children."

"They can't do that." Annie clenched her fist. "That's wrong and we can report—"

"Oh, fine." Jenna threw her hands up in the air, and started pacing. "I quit, okay? I quit because I knew that's what they wanted. They are horrible biddies. I couldn't stay there and watch them whisper behind my back. Besides, they would have fired me. My dismissal was just a matter of time, and I prefer to do this on my schedule."

"Oh, Jenna." She was about to say, come here, and offer her sister a hug when Quinn cleared his throat beside her. "Jenna, you go downstairs and I'll be there in a flash. We'll get this all sorted out."

Jenna hugged her arms over her chest as she glanced at Annie's bed partner. "I'm going to guess you're the Quinn everyone's been talking about? Sorry about this."

He nodded, but he stayed leaning against the headboard until the door closed and they were alone again.

Annie threw off her covers. Her body still tingled and ached with wanting him. "I'm so sorry. I wish ..." But of course he knew what she wished so she let the thought end on a shrug.

"Darlin', you need to set some boundaries."

"She couldn't have known you were here," she said. "Still, it would have been nice if ..." The memory of what they had been about to do sent delicious shivers through her body.

Quinn reached for her and held her gently. He stared into her eyes for a moment and then he brought his mouth to hers. The kiss lacked the heated passion of a few minutes earlier, but it brought an instant and immediate longing to the surface. She circled her arms around his neck and pressed her body against him. He responded with a groan. Then he eased out of the kiss. He held her gaze with his for a moment, their breath mingled between them. Heat radiated and she was sure they could explode from that moment alone.

He frowned slightly. "Boundaries."

He was probably right, but this was family. This was Jenna. Jenna had seen her through the worst of her divorce. She'd seen her through her fears and anxieties.

"I'm sorry about this morning, but I am happy you stayed last night," Annie said at last.

Something changed in his eyes. They softened, and it was almost as if she could see his memory of the night they'd spent together play out in his mind. Was she blushing again? "Me, too."

Then he brushed the side of her cheek with his fingertips. His every fleeting touch mesmerized her. "We should get dressed and go downstairs."

Her sister needed her, but somehow giving up the morning with Quinn still left her with a hollow feeling of disappointment. Like the Christmas Kelly had told her Jack had purchased something for her from the jewelry store. She had been so excited. Diamonds? Sapphires? A tennis bracelet? A locket? Something romantic and beautiful? When she opened the box Christmas morning, she found a watch. A watch? She supposed it was nice in its way, but it was still a watch—a dreary, practical, presumably costly, time-keeping reminder their romance was dead.

Five minutes later, Annie entered the kitchen to find Milt filling a cup with Irish Cream followed by a quick splash of coffee. "Good morning, Uncle Milt, how did you sleep?"

"Good, good." He smiled, but his bloodshot eyes and ashen face revealed his lie. She needed to talk to Merry today. She crossed through the kitchen to get cups for the rest of them. Behind her, she could feel Quinn. He'd followed her downstairs.

"Who might you be, young man?" Milt asked. She spun around in time to see Milt giving Quinn a quick study.

"I forgot you haven't met yet." She quickly made the introductions. The men shook hands and Quinn sat. Oh boy, this would be a long day.

A moment later, she poured a coffee for Quinn and an orange juice for herself. "Where is Jenna?"

"Said she's getting something from the car." Her uncle shrugged. "Tell me, Mr. Quinn, what are your intentions?"

"Uncle Milt, stop that," Annie said shrilly. "We should see what's keeping Jenna. She might need some help."

Quinn's eyes twinkled at her, but he didn't say anything.

Annie rolled her eyes and stood from the table. She crossed the room and pushed the drapes aside to peer out the window. Jenna was trudging to the house with two big suitcases in her hands.

Muttering to herself, Annie went to the front door and swung it open. Sitting on the front step were three more suitcases. The snow crunched beneath Jenna's boots as she climbed the stairs, making a path through newly fallen snow. Annie slipped on her own boots and stepped outside to retrieve some of her sister's belongings. "Jenna, what is all this?"

"What are you doing outside? You need a jacket."

Annie brought one suitcase inside and went for a second. Jenna squeezed past her with her load.

"Are you moving in?" Annie joked as she bent to pick up another suitcase. When she turned around to see Jenna's serious face, she realized it wasn't a joke. The smile faded from her face. "You're moving in?"

"You said you'd help. Oh, Annie, I can't stay in the city. I don't have a job. How could I afford my apartment without a paycheck?"

Annie tried to smile as she set a suitcase in the living room. Jenna went to get the last suitcase from the front step. "Is there anything else to come in?"

"Nothing that can't wait." Jenna shut the door. She stomped on the floor to loosen the snow from her boots, before she shrugged off her coat and hung it over the door handle.

"Listen, I know this is unexpected," Jenna said, "but I didn't have anywhere else to go."

"Oh, sis, of course you can stay here, as long as you like, but it can't be all bad. You have your savings. Things will seem a lot better tomorrow when you've had time to adjust."

Avoiding her gaze, Jenna slipped past her and went into the living room.

"Jenna?"

"I'll need to get the rest of my things before the end of the month."

"Don't make any hasty decisions."

Jenna stared at her.

Oh, no ... "You've already given your notice, haven't you?"

"What savings? Do you know how much it costs to live?" Jenna shrugged. "I put my notice under the landlord's door before I left this morning."

Annie swallowed. Maybe Milt had a good thing going with the Irish

Cream. "Of course, Jenna, of course you can stay here until you get your feet under you. It won't take long, you wait and see."

Jenna rushed to Annie and hugged her tight.

CHAPTER 32

St. Patrick's Day

"Green icing is supposed to taste like mint," Jenna complained as she swept her finger into the bowl and drew out a big gob of leaf green icing.

"I don't like mint," Annie said, "and the cookies are shaped like shamrocks, not mint leaves so it doesn't matter about the flavor."

Jenna frowned and muttered, "It doesn't seem right, somehow."

Annie agreed. A lot of things weren't quite right. The last month had been full of adjustments. Milt had settled in, Jenna had settled in, and Kelly was settled in at school. The only one who had been unsettled was Annie. Jenna couldn't sleep in the basement without throwing up every hour because of some mysterious odor that no one but she could smell. So Annie had relinquished her room.

The sofa bed in the basement was horrible. She hadn't had a proper night's sleep since she'd moved down there. Each morning promised a headache and deeper bags under her eyes.

Things changed again when she couldn't handle seeing Milt's dirty socks and balled-up underwear in her living room any longer. That was when Annie moved him into her craft room—well, into what *used* to be her craft room. She had originally thought he might move to Kelly's room temporarily, but he'd refused. He said the stairs were too much for him, which was a specious argument since the bathroom was upstairs, but then he emphasized that he didn't want to put anyone out. She had nearly cried when her supplies were packed and stowed in the basement.

At least they surrounded her. Every night she stared at the stacks of boxes clustered around her pullout bed, but there was nowhere to work on anything.

AKA Mrs. Claus Inc. was defunct before it even got started.

Family was more important than that. Everyone was here with her. They were welcome to stay as long as they wanted or needed. Even the cat and dog were slipping into a routine.

Tiger caught a mouse every Saturday night. He'd eat half of it right beside her bed. There was nothing quite like the smell of half-eaten mouse to get you going in the morning.

Ugh.

At least the one routine she'd kept was her lunches with Quinn in town, and he still came to dinner once a week, too. But Annie couldn't help but feel their relationship was on slippery ground. They hadn't been alone since Valentine's Day, and Quinn was always painfully polite when they were with other people. Then again, he was probably taking his cues from her. And after being caught in bed by her teenage daughter *and* her sister in one weekend, she'd been trying to keep things a little more neutral in public. The problem was that they were *always* in public.

"Jenna, you're acting like a little kid. Don't eat so much icing. You'll make yourself sick."

"Nope, the icing seems to be what I need right now. I think this little guy is going to have a sweet tooth." She patted her stomach.

"You could help me. Kelly will be down any minute. She already told me she doesn't want a fuss, but cookies should be safe, shouldn't they?"

"She'll like the cookies. Is my tongue green?" Jenna stuck out her tongue, while Annie spread the icing on the remaining sugar cookies.

"Yes. Now, can you at least help me with the dishes?"

"You know I can't put my hands in yucky, murky dish water. I'll dry."

Annie arranged the last cookies on the plate. "Why isn't Uncle Milt back yet?"

Jenna shrugged. "He said he was going to town for dog food."

It had been a month since she'd been alone with Quinn. Whenever she washed dishes, she remembered that night. Quinn had swept her off her feet with little things like washing his cup and buying her a table. He was the only person in her life who seemed the least bit interested in her thoughts and ideas. She bit her lip and passed a clean, dripping bowl to Jenna. Oh, what she wouldn't give to have a quiet conversation with him again, to talk about something other than morning sickness, homework or Merry's infidelity, which were the usual topics in her life now.

"I hope people come to Kelly's party tonight."

Then Kelly came around the corner. Her hair was still damp from the shower. She was scowling. "Mom, what are you doing? You promised."

"Honey, they are just cookies. I didn't stick out leprechauns or green streamers."

Her daughter had her hands on her hips. "Fine."

Annie held up her hands. "I made cookies, nothing more."

Kelly came into the kitchen and grabbed one from the plate.

"You're ready?" Annie asked.

"What are you doing tonight, Mom?" Kelly licked the icing off the cookie and waited for Annie's answer.

"I know, I know." She sighed and handed the last dish to Jenna. "I'll stay out of sight."

She watched Kelly's reflection in the window above the sink. Kelly took the plate of cookies into the living room and out of view.

"She's a teenager," Jenna said. "She doesn't mean to be rude."

Annie pursed her lips again.

Jenna didn't say anything for a minute. She dried the dishes and set them on the counter for Annie to put away. Annie took a deep breath. Their mother-daughter relationship had improved a lot since Christmas, but there was still a lot of hurt and distance.

"You know, Uncle Milt has been gone a long time," Jenna said.

"He'll be fine." She peeped into the yard again. With the warmer weather, she was able to see out the windows again, which was such a novelty, but there wasn't anything to look at tonight. Not yet, at any rate. The driveway was empty. "I hope people come to her party," Annie said again.

She had been a little concerned when Kelly had mentioned her friend Melody's boyfriend Jay was a few years older than Melody, already finished high school, and had moved here from the city, all of which Annie found unsettling. Since Kelly and she had just moved from the city, her apprehension was hypocritical, but it was what it was. Perhaps she needed to get to know the kids before she restricted who could come. The photographer, Claire, had mentioned something about the boy when she'd come to the house after the Christmas sale. If Annie remembered correctly, it seemed that Jay lived with Claire and her husband. They seemed nice, so maybe she didn't need to worry about him.

The movie party tonight was a first step in Kelly reaching out to the other kids. And Annie would meet Kelly's friends, and see how Kelly was fitting in at the same time. She rubbed her hands on her pants for the tenth time. She was more nervous about this than Kelly. She just wanted everything to go perfectly.

Half an hour later, the lights were out in the living room.

She and Jenna stared at one another. They couldn't talk over the heavy bass of the horror movie music, which was vibrating the floor.

Then her sister began turning a few shades paler than the icing she'd eaten earlier. Annie poured Jenna a glass of ginger ale and set a box of crackers beside the drink. In the last few weeks, there had been less and less of a need to put the crackers in the cupboard. The box just sat on the counter.

There wasn't much opportunity to talk with the movie blaring so loudly, but Jenna didn't seem to have much to say anyway. Were they all living together but lonely at the same time? How did they bridge that? Or could they?

No one was here because they wanted to be. They were here because they didn't feel they *could* be where they wanted to be. Well, everyone except her.

And didn't that just break her heart?

Jenna opened the box and pulled out one cracker. She sat it on the table in front on her and stared at it. Oh, dear, she was going to cry. Again? This was getting to be a daily occurrence.

There was a screech from the living room. It didn't seem connected to the movie noises.

"*Mom.*"

Jenna was still focused on the wafer, but Annie hoped she'd be okay for a few minutes.

When Annie entered the living room, she avoided looking at the TV screen. She hadn't been able to stomach horror movies since junior high school. Even though that was a long time ago, her aversion to the blood and guts hadn't changed.

Kelly was standing close to the front door. The other kids were just heads in the darkness.

"Mom, Dumbbell—"

Two of the eight teenage heads turned to them. "That's your dog's name?"

Kelly put her hands on her hips. "Not my dog. And, yes, that's his name." Then she turned to Annie. "He peed on Marc's shoe."

One of the boys turned around and shrugged. "It's all right. Probably smelled my dog on my stuff."

"No, Marc, it isn't okay. Mom ..."

"Of course we can't send you home with—never mind, I'll throw your shoes in the washing machine and dryer. They'll be dry before you know it."

"Thanks," Kelly said. The thanks didn't sound like thanks—it was more like *deal with it.*

Annie bit her tongue. She needed to have a chat with Kelly about her attitude.

She went to the front door and turned on the light. Groans reverberated from the living room, groans only a roomful of teenagers could generate. Sure enough, two shoes were sitting in a pale yellow puddle. The ends of the shoelaces extended beyond the puddle, so she grabbed those. Urine dripped onto the floor. Lifting the shoes, Annie held them away from her. It was a toss-up what was worse, the dog urine or the teenage boy foot smell.

Jenna bolted from the kitchen and up the stairs just as Annie hurried to the basement with her gag-inducing package. As she threw the shoes into the washing machine with some soap, she realized she probably wouldn't see her sister for the rest of the night.

Hmm … now what? She could work on a craft. She hadn't done that in a long time. The idea made her giddy. If she set up the ironing board and sat on the edge of her bed downstairs, she could do a small project like ... a Christmas ball.

She studied the boxes to find the Christmas balls. Where were they? She'd shifted and dug through three boxes when a beep announced the washing machine cycle had ended.

Right. Marc's shoes.

Still thinking about how to move the boxes in the tight space to get to the box in the middle, which had to be the one with the balls, Annie changed Marc's shoes to the dryer. Annie jumped with each thump, thump, thump noise as the shoes tumbled in the dryer. She wouldn't get anything done in this racket. If she smuggled something to the kitchen table …

No, Kelly would kill her if she took up her Mrs. Claus persona tonight. Huh. She trudged up the steps and closed the basement door. The thump, thump, thump was still audible, but the racket was muffled and tolerable. She walked to the kitchen and fell into a chair at the table. Jenna still hadn't made another appearance. What could she do?

A wet dog nose pressed into her arm, then Dumbbell nudged her hand. He let out a small whimper.

Where was Milt? He should have returned with the dog food by now. If he'd forgotten about his errand, what would they do? There was a bit of steak left from supper, but the last time they had given Dumbbell human food, it hadn't turned out well. Not well at all.

Shoot. She hadn't cleaned the puddle from the front door yet.

"He'll be back soon," she informed the dog, and tried not to question the sanity of talking to a furry four-legged creature. She grabbed a fistful of paper towels and some bleach and headed to the entrance. With another round of groans when the light was turned on again, Annie wiped the puddle while trying not to gag. The last thing they needed in this house was a competition for the toilet, particularly since Jenna still hadn't emerged from the bathroom.

Kneeling on the floor, serenaded by horror movie screams, wiping up dog pee—every woman would love a night like tonight. Something wet was seeping through the paper towels on to her hands. Ewww.

Please let it be the bleach and not the pee.

The phone rang. Annie tried to stand without touching the walls as she listened to the ringing continue. No one else was going to answer the phone. She scurried to the kitchen and plucked up the phone with her empty hand.

She couldn't make out the words—there was too much background noise.

"Milt? Is that you?" Annie raised her voice.

"It's Quinn. Milt is here."

"Quinn?" Her heart fluttered. She smiled and went to touch her chest with her hand. Gah, she still held the pee and bleach-soaked paper towels. She turned up her nose and held her hand away from her body, then yanked on the phone cord and tried to reach the garbage. But even stretching, she couldn't quite get there. Where was the cordless?

"Hey, baby, who are you talking to? It's your turn to break."

Wait a minute—that was a woman's voice. Annie froze, one arm stretched to the garbage, one hand pressing the phone even tighter to her ear.

Baby? What? Her heart plummeted. She'd been wrong. There was another reason to explain why he was so distant when he came around.

"Annie, are you still there?"

Words failed her. She nodded, then remembered he couldn't see her. A chorus of screams rose from the living room.

"What was that? Is everything okay?"

She blinked away a few tears and tried to steady her pounding heart. "Yes. You called about Uncle Milt."

"We're at the Shining Whistle. He's had a few. Do you want me to drive him home?"

She glanced around the room and considered all the things going on in the house: Jenna was still cuddling the toilet, and a troop of teenagers was itching to touch one another. She couldn't leave them unsupervised.

The hairs on her arm quivered, as if all the germs from the paper towels were marching up and up. "I can't collect him right now. Maybe in another hour or two."

"Come on, baby," the woman said again. Her voice was crisp, clear and excessively sultry. What, was she nuzzling his neck? Kissing his mouth? Annie's legs wobbled.

"I can bring him home," Quinn said.

She tried to figure out from his tone of voice if he was upset about that prospect. She swallowed. "You don't—"

"I'm coming."

Then the line was dead. She stared at the phone for a minute. Quinn was out at the bar with a woman, and Annie was wiping up dog pee. As soon as she hung up the phone, she crossed the kitchen and threw out the paper towels. She was numb. What had happened? Quinn was breaking her heart. Just the way Jack had. Why hadn't she remembered this pain earlier? How could she have left herself vulnerable again?

She couldn't break down. Not now. Not with Kelly's friends here.

Annie forced herself to blink. Remember what she'd been doing.

She could do this. She could pretend she was okay. She'd been practicing for years, long before Jack had moved out.

She scrubbed her hands, three times, as far up as she could reach without getting the sleeve of her T-shirt wet. She ignored her reflection in the window above the sink. If Quinn wanted to go out with other women, there wasn't anything she could do to make herself more appealing. No one found Mrs. Claus sexy. It was that simple.

She checked on the teenagers. Some of the heads had disappeared behind the back of the couch. She stepped in closer. Wait a minute.

She turned on the lights in the living room. Eight heads turned to look at her. Kelly was scowling.

"No blankets," Annie said.

"We're cold," Kelly complained.

"No blankets. Bring them to me now." She stood still and beckoned with her hands. The last thing she needed was some teenage grope-fest in the living room.

Kelly's face was bright red. "We're cold."

"Then turn up the thermostat."

A moment later, Annie had a big bundle of blankets in her arms. Had Kelly stripped every bed in the house? Kelly scowled at her as she placed the last blanket on Annie's pile, and then she turned out the light. Annie spun around and went to the basement door. As she left the living room, one of the boys, maybe that older boy named Jay, said, "Your mom took that well. Mr. Trent would've lost it."

Somehow, Annie didn't think Kelly would view it in quite the same way. Maybe that kid was okay after all. She got to the closed basement door. Right, she'd shut it the last time she'd come up. The thump, thump, thump of the shoes in the dryer still resounded from behind the door. She dropped the blankets to the floor and opened the door, but she didn't feel like walking downstairs again. She shoved the blankets down the steps with her foot. A moment later, she shut the door and returned to the kitchen.

She peered out the window, though she wasn't sure why—Milt and Quinn wouldn't be here yet anyway. It would take at least fifteen minutes to drive and they'd have to pay their bills and maybe have one last game of pool.

She ran her hand through her hair and started to pace.

CHAPTER 33

When Quinn's vehicle rumbled into the yard, Annie slipped on her boots and ran out to meet them. Her heart did another little tumble at the prospect of seeing him again. Then she scowled.

She put her hands on her hips and waited for Quinn to maneuver his truck into the driveway between the teenager's vehicles, which were parked at every angle. The younger generation wasn't terribly efficient at arranging the cars and trucks.

When the truck stopped, Quinn got out. No one else did. Where was Milt? She walked to the truck. Milt's head was pressed against the window, his mouth gaped open, and his eyes were closed.

"Did he pass out?"

"He fell asleep as soon as I poured him into the seat."

She sighed. "We can't take him in through the front door past the kids. We need to use the back door."

"It's good to see you, babe."

It was good to see him, too. The sight of him in the imperfect light cast from the front porch made her drool. "Thanks. You, too." Then belatedly, she remembered he was letting her go.

She turned to Milt. She grabbed the door handle as Quinn reached her side.

"Here, I'll help you," he said.

When she opened the door, Milt sagged. Quinn unbuckled his seat belt. A moment later, he hauled Milt from the truck. This wasn't going to be easy.

"Do we need a wheelbarrow?"

When Milt's feet hit the ground, though, he came to life.

"Annie, my beautiful niece." Milt sounded like a drunken leprechaun. "Luck o' the Irish, that's what I have."

Then Milt started to sing. It was hard to tell what he was saying between the slurring and the fake accent, but listening closely, she could hear some homage to green beer, Merry, a pot 'o gold and more green beer.

Oh, boy.

Quinn pulled Milt's arm over his shoulder.

"What about the dog food?" She peered hopefully into the cab of the truck.

"I didn't know anything about dog food."

She pursed her lips and shut the door.

He steered Milt to the back door. It seemed to take an eternity to get Milt over the path, up the steps, through the door and into the room that had recently become his bedroom.

At their destination, Quinn deposited Milt on the single bed, then turned in a circle. His low whistle bespoke his surprise. "What happened in here?"

She peered around her former craft room as she loosened one of Milt's shoes. Along the far wall was a jumble of Jenna's furniture and all the stuff they didn't have space for in the rest of the house. Jenna, Milt and Kelly all had boxes, most of which were stacked on the table Quinn had purchased for her. Luckily, Milt hadn't had any furniture. Well, that wasn't technically true, but after all these years of being with Merry, he had let her keep it all. Too painful maybe.

Most of the shelves Quinn and she had assembled for the craft room had been dismantled. Only one remained, and Milt seemed to have fashioned it into a makeshift dresser, with cardboard boxes as drawers. One of the boxes was pulled out, and inside, its contents were folded with neat precision. Even Milt's bed was made without a wrinkle. It probably had hospital corners and all the rest, too. She wondered for a moment if Milt had ever been in the army. Or was this the way he was after so many years with her aunt?

She shrugged as her gaze met Quinn's. "He needed some place to sleep."

She dropped one of Milt's shoes to the floor and then moved to take the shoe off his other foot. A moment later, Quinn and Annie left the room. She turned back for a moment and watched Milt. He seemed to be sleeping fine. Good. Then she glanced at the room again. This wasn't a home—it was a warehouse. Milt was living on the surface, which probably wasn't much different from what Jenna was doing in the upstairs bedroom or Annie was doing in the basement. This wasn't a home.

She'd failed.

Her heart caught in her chest as she turned out the light and closed the door. Quinn was watching her, she knew it, even though she couldn't meet his gaze. She started to step around him, but he reached for her arm.

"Thank you for bringing Milt home," she said. "I don't know why he was pretending to be Irish, because he isn't. He's Polish. His birth name isn't even Milt, it is Milosz or something—" She caught sight of Quinn shaking his head and stopped her babbling.

"Can I help?"

Great, he thought she needed charity. "Nope." She put a bright, albeit false, smile on her face. "We're great. It's all working out great."

He opened his mouth as if he was about to say something more, but there was a "Mom" shouted from the living room again.

She shrugged and he let her go.

By the time she returned to the living room, some of the teenagers had already left. It was almost midnight. Where had the night gone?

"Marc needs his shoes." Kelly had adopted her hands-on-hips pose again. "Mr. Quinn, when did you get here?"

"Hi, Mr. Quinn," Marc said.

Annie smiled at Marc. "I'll go get them."

She went to the basement door and was about to charge downstairs but the blankets were still all balled up on the steps. She should have taken them downstairs and folded them properly the first time. She kicked the blankets. They rolled another couple of steps. She kicked them again and again, until they were in a soft heap at the bottom. With one last punt, the blankets were out of her way. The thump, thump, thump of the shoes in the dryer still bounced over the bare concrete walls. Hopefully the shoes were wearable. She opened the dryer door and reached in as the smell of warm rubber wafted out.

She grabbed the shoes and thrust her fingers inside. They were warm and dry. She turned around and stopped dead.

Quinn was sitting on the steps. He peered around the room, and then his gaze landed on her. She swallowed.

"Are those boxes your crafts?"

She glanced at the stacks in the room. Two narrow paths, one from the steps to the bed and the other from the steps to the washer and dryer, cut through the ruin of cardboard mounds.

"Yes, those are the crafts."

"Annie ..." Quinn's sympathy was not what she needed right now.

"Isn't it silly to have so much useless stuff?"

"What about your business?"

She shrugged again. "I'll get going on it in a couple of years."

He watched her for a minute. She fiddled with the laces in Marc's shoe, weaving them in and out of her fingers. Quinn motioned to the bed and asked, "What about that?"

"The bed?"

"You're sleeping there." It wasn't a question, but a statement that seemed to hold a great deal of disapproval.

"It is better than you might think. It is dark and quiet down here." She pasted that fake smile on her face again, but who was she kidding? He seemed to see everything she was feeling and thinking anyway, and really, sleeping in the small, unfinished basement was not the dream she had been trying to build when she moved here.

He was quiet for a moment, then he whispered her name.

She put up her hand before he could say anything more. "Don't say it."

"Boundaries, sweetheart, you need boundaries."

She blinked, and continued to hold up her hand.

"Mom," Kelly yelled from the top of the steps.

"I'm coming, dear." She walked to stairs and climbed up, stepping around Quinn, who still stayed seated on the tread.

Kelly took the shoes from her hand and gave them to Marc, who was the last kid to leave. Kelly was smiling a lot as she watched Marc put on his shoes and tuck the laces into the side.

Marc was smiling, too.

So this was the boy who made Kelly happy. No wonder Kelly had been a little Napoleon tonight. Still, the night seemed to have worked out just fine for her. Maybe things were turning around.

At least for one of them.

Had Quinn left? He hadn't followed her to the living room. He must have gone out the back again.

Wow, it really was over between them. Her heart banged its panic against her chest, but she couldn't acknowledge it. Not yet.

Annie went to the kitchen to let the teenagers have a minute alone.

She rolled her shoulders before she started to tidy, not that there was much to do. Jenna must have come down when they were dealing with Milt. The crackers and ginger ale were on the table again. Poor Jenna. At least the morning sickness should pass by the time Easter rolled around.

She cleaned for the next ten minutes. Not that she wanted to watch the clock, but how long did it take Kelly to say goodbye to Marc? When Annie rinsed the washcloth and hung it over the faucet, she turned and found she was being watched.

"Quinn, you're still here?"

He was sitting at the table with his arms crossed over his chest. She had no idea how long he'd been there. "What's going on?"

She mirrored his posture, well aware Jack would not approve of this tactic—all of his body language for better business psychobabble scuttled around in her head—but this wasn't a tactic. It was more akin to self-preservation. "What?"

He narrowed his eyes. "Beyond the fact you're living in your own house like a squatter?"

She ignored his question and turned to the sink to grab the washcloth again. "So, you found Uncle Milt at the Shining Whistle?"

She wiped the countertops again, keeping her back to him. She couldn't look at him right now.

He didn't answer. He simply walked to her and put his hands on her shoulders.

She froze.

Then he touched the back of her head.

"No," she exclaimed.

He let go and she spun around. He put a hand on either side of her, essentially pinning her between him and the counter. He didn't touch his body to hers. He didn't have to. His proximity was distracting enough.

"What is this all about?" he said.

"I don't know what you mean." Annie lifted her chin.

"Yes, you do."

She stared into his eyes. They still seemed so ... trustworthy. How could she have fallen for a handsome face?

Handsome? That was a bit mild, but still ...

How was she going to survive being tossed away again?

She crossed her arms in front of her chest.

"Talk to me." His voice was quiet.

She shook her head. "It's not my place."

His face twitched, like he was holding something back. "Try me."

She couldn't be the nagging wife. Not with Quinn. "You can do whatever you want."

He tilted his head. "I know."

She shrugged. "That's settled then, isn't it?"

He raised his eyebrows, but waited for her to continue.

"Why are you making me say this?" She tilted her head back and stared at the ceiling. "Fine. Who were you playing pool with? You should go be with her."

She continued to stare at the ceiling, even though every intangible bit of her soul begged her to stare him down. Make him feel her wrath. Hell hath no fury and all that.

"Hmm."

"That's all you have to say?" She scowled at him then.

One corner of his mouth kicked up. "You're jealous."

She clenched her teeth, biting down her anger. Between her tight lips, she managed to squeeze out the word, "Ass."

Instantly she was horrified. Her mouth dropped open and she covered it with her hand.

"Oh, my," she said, the words coming out more like a moan beneath her fingers.

His lopsided grin turned into a full-out smile then.

"I'm sorry," she muttered through the fingers covering her mouth. "I didn't ..."

"Annie, it is okay. It is okay to feel things." He dragged his finger along the side of her neck. He knew precisely how to send wicked ripples through her body.

"Don't touch me."

"You heard a woman when I was on the phone with you, didn't you?"

She stared at him, unwilling to expose herself any more than she already had.

"It was my cousin."

She frowned. "She called you 'baby.' "

"I'm the baby of the family." He continued to drag his fingertip over her skin, down to her collarbone. His gentle touch was doing wonderful, awful things to her.

"No."

"Trust me. I'm not dating my cousin Edie behind your back."

"But—"

He smiled. "I'm seeing you, Annie. That's it." The expression in his eyes was sensual beyond description, like dipping into a vat of melted chocolate or falling on a bed of marshmallows. "You're the one, the only one."

"Oh." She could have melted into a puddle at his feet.

"Exactly."

As he leaned down to kiss her, the front door banged shut. Shoot. Kelly was finished saying goodbye to Marc. Annie ducked under Quinn's arms. What if Kelly saw them from the living room?

Sure, Kelly knew they'd been together, but every time Annie had tried to talk to her about it, Kelly changed the subject. It didn't leave Annie with much confidence that her daughter was okay with this, in spite of their odd conversation when Kelly'd come home after the dance.

A scant moment later, Kelly passed by. She didn't even peek into the kitchen. She was already typing something into her cell phone. "Good night, Mom. Good night, Mr. Quinn."

"Good night, honey."

"You can't keep running from things," he whispered as they listened to Kelly's heavy steps going up the stairs.

"Oh?"

"In the meantime, I'll take that kiss you were offering a minute ago."

"I didn't offer—"

Then he lowered his head to hers, and she forgot what she had been saying. The man had a way of doing that to her.

His lips were soft, slow and warm, and when he put his hands on her waist, they were strong, careful and attentive as they moved along the sides of her body. She pressed her body against his and he groaned.

Her self-control was slipping away like trying to hold sugar in your fist. She was about to suggest they take it upstairs, but she didn't sleep upstairs anymore. She slept in the basement on a bed that wouldn't hold the weight of two people, particularly if they were … moving. Her face grew hot.

He drew back and pressed a short kiss on her forehead.

"You need to think about things," he said.

She knew he wasn't talking about them. He was talking about her life. Her priorities. Her *boundaries*.

When he pulled away, she wanted to cling to him. Instead, she watched him leave.

CHAPTER 34

She stood in the kitchen, while hollowness seeped into her heart. The emptiness was at odds with the tingling that still rippled through her body from Quinn's kisses. Annie swallowed and washed her face with her hands.

The house was quiet.

She forced herself to move forward. She climbed the steps to the upstairs rooms. Kelly's room was dark, as was Jenna's. No sounds came from either. She doubted Kelly was sleeping yet, but the lights-out message was clear. Kelly didn't want to talk to her. She rested her hand on the door. She hoped Kelly had had a good night.

Then she faced Jenna's room, turned the doorknob and peered in. A soft snore emanated from the bed. She smiled. Jenna would hate to know she snored.

Not much else to do here. She closed the door quietly and went to the main floor again. Then she did the same thing at Milt's room. He was still passed out in the same position as she and Quinn had left him. Tiger and Dumbbell were curled beside him on the bed. Everyone else in the house was settled for the night, but Annie felt as if her true self was scratching on the inside of her body, begging for freedom.

After she'd turned off the lights and checked the doors, she hadn't much left to do but go to the basement. The stairs creaked with each step she took. One, two, three ... lower and lower she went into the bowels of her own house. She *was* living like a squatter amid her boxes and bare concrete.

Why did Quinn have to come and make her feel bad about things? She had been fine before. Truly. She rolled her eyes.

Was there any sense in lying?

Quinn. Man, oh, man, he had the most spectacular way of kissing, but this one was a little different. Goodbye? She had had a goodbye kiss before, which, if memory served, hadn't been quite the same. Or had it?

She couldn't very well kick out her family, so where did that leave things with Quinn? Annie slumped. No, he wasn't asking her to choose between him and her family. He was just trying to ... What? Make her lose her sanity? Boundaries, boundaries, boundaries. He could harp as much as he wanted, but there wasn't much to be done, was there?

Was this the end of things between them? Her breath caught in her lungs. Her heart tripped. *The end?*

Her heart had experimented with that scenario earlier, and it had been awful.

A few minutes later, Annie crawled into bed. This wasn't some place she could expect Quinn to stay. Could she expect *anyone* to stay here? Well, besides herself, that is.

She stared at the unfinished ceiling above her bed. The wood beams and joists were stained with water, leaks she hoped had been fixed over the years. There was no light fixture, just a bare bulb hanging from a wire. Cardboard boxes crowded in from every direction. To top if off, a wayward metal coil had broken free from the rest of the mattress and was trying to skewer her in the middle of her left shoulder blade.

What had happened to make this all turn out this way? What happened to the magazine living? To the joy? To the simple pleasures? To having a *home*?

She shouldn't have moved out of the city. Sure, that house on its suburban cul-de-sac was littered with memories, but there would have been room for all of them. All of them and her crafts, too.

She sighed and started hunting for phantom faces in the grain of the wood in the beams. It seemed easier than trying to count sheep. Yep—there they were—distorted, aghast and looking as dismayed as she felt.

Returning to the city was an option. She still owned the house. She could let the property managers know. They'd need something like 30 days to kick out the tenants. Or was it 60 days? Hmmm, she should have read the paperwork in more detail, but she had been convinced that was the end. She didn't think she'd ever want to move back.

She sighed. She still didn't. Besides how could she be so far from Quinn?

She'd kept the other place for a bit of future income, but it wasn't generating much of anything yet and it wouldn't, not until the mortgage was paid out two years from now. Should she sell it? No, that wouldn't solve anything. They still wouldn't fit here, not with all the furniture and boxes and ... and with the baby coming. Wow, that'd make five of them.

She turned out the teddy bear light she'd placed on one of the cardboard boxes. Yes, this was all pretty high-end. Cardboard boxes for night tables. Who did that? College students? Even they probably had more sense of style than that.

The bed creaked as she shifted, trying to move off the metal jabbing into her. Then her bum sank in the mattress's hole, while the middle of her back arched over a big lump.

At least the dismal wood faces weren't peering down on her anymore. The darkness accentuated the wet musty smell, like too many loads of laundry were left to mold in the washing machine, and the smell had seeped into the basement and would never be released.

Was that the smell Jenna found disturbing? Who knew? Maybe Jenna didn't like the dark.

The furnace kicked in then, a rumbling purr from the corner. Annie closed her eyes. If only the hum could lull her to sleep.

Sleep. Exactly.

Was Kelly having sweet dreams about Marc?

Annie sighed. She couldn't disrupt Kelly's schooling again. They couldn't move now. She'd already changed schools once this year. She needed stability in her senior year.

And Milt? He couldn't stay in his room like that any more. How had she not realized how dreadful it was?

No, she knew how. She had been blinded by how sad she'd been to tear down her craft room. Hmm … just thinking about her craft room made her fingers itch.

She needed to work harder at building a home for everyone. She'd let things slide that she shouldn't have. And then there was Quinn and his *boundaries*. Maybe he meant she should give herself a few things, too.

Hmm … maybe she should.

That's what she needed to settle down tonight—a little project. She turned on the light again, then rolled over and read the labels on the ends of the boxes.

Fifteen minutes later, Annie had rearranged the boxes and found the one with her glass balls. She sat the ironing table by the bed, and spread the craft paints out at her side. She smoothed her fingers over the soft hairs at the end of her favorite paintbrush.

A little sense of homecoming settled over her heart. This was perfect. A little something to occupy her hands while she waited for the sandman.

CHAPTER 35

Easter

The Internet was a fabulous but frightening thing. Not only did it reveal to Annie she had no way of financing an expansion on the house without selling a million Christmas balls—okay, perhaps not a million, but close enough—it also intimidated her. Did she register to sell things online correctly? What if she didn't? What if someone else got her money? What if she typed the address in wrong? It was silly, she knew, to be anxious about these things. After all, how many people used the web to sell things everyday? She couldn't be stupider than those millions of people, could she? Then there was the fact everything she'd seen suggested she needed a website. How would she create such a thing? She thought she'd figured out how to register something called a domain name and hoped that meant what she thought it did.

Because who would she ask?

No one knew she had been staying awake all night working on her crafts in the basement. There was joy there, even if there didn't seem to be a lot of joy elsewhere. She refused to think about the fact she holed up in her basement in the city and did the same thing, because it wasn't the same thing. She was starting a business here.

Anyway, she couldn't tell them. They would all think she was crazy. Jack would start being snide again on the telephone when he talked to Kelly—not that those conversations were well received yet, but she had to give him credit for at least trying. Annie could almost say or think his name without wishing him to the devil. It was a step up. However, that could change if he started mocking her again.

At least Kelly and she were on semi-normal ground … but that might not last if she discovered her mom was doing crafts again. Annie still had a pang in her chest when she remembered Kelly's outrage at New Year's.

No, she couldn't tell Kelly yet.

She needed to prove to them glitter and glue could do something. Be something.

Over the last few weeks, her days and nights had been packed full.

She'd tackled Milt's room, Jenna's room and Kelly's room. Everyone complained about the paint fumes, but no one complained about the results. What probably helped more than anything else was that she'd managed to rent a small storage room for all the extra furniture that she hadn't wanted to store in the leaky barn.

Then, every night in the wee hours of an otherwise sleeping household, she worked on her crafts.

Her plan was coming together.

When it did, she'd buy a new bed for the basement and get a bit of rest. But she didn't have time for that. Not right now. Besides, no one commented on the circles under her eyes—of course it seemed that Quinn had started studying her closer, but he hadn't actually uttered words of concern—so she probably wasn't as tired as she felt. It was all in her head.

All she needed was to turn her full attention on her business, then it was sure to blossom. If she could sell some of her items sooner rather than later, it would be great. It'd be the jingle in her bell, so to speak.

After two weeks of listing things at a few online auction sites, she'd only sold one measly ball. No wreaths. No stockings. No Santas.

Sure, it was Easter and most people weren't in the Christmas spirit right now, but shouldn't a little goodwill toward men carry through the year?

Why hadn't she made something to sell for Easter? She'd known spring was coming. The evidence was everywhere—they hadn't had a snowstorm in five days, the flower bulbs she'd planted last fall were starting to poke through the ground, and the only moldy, dirty snow left loitering around the yard was on the north side of the house.

To make it even more miraculous, Annie had purchased little pots of tulips and hyacinths for the windows, and even Kelly didn't complain. It was spring and the world was shaking off the dreary winter and embracing all things pastel.

She'd even planned her Easter menu. There would be baked *babka* bread for Milt, lots of eggs to boil for Jenna, who was finally starting to get over her morning sickness, and a big juicy ham for Kelly. Jack wouldn't be attending this holiday. Not that he had attended the other holidays, but for this one, he was specifically not invited. She wasn't even sure he'd noticed.

Of course, Merry had to come. Sure, it would terribly awkward with Milt living here, but Merry was family. Somehow they had to stick together. Milt and Merry would just have to figure it out. Annie, on the other hand, would have to figure out new sleeping arrangements. Perhaps Kelly could sleep on the sofa.

If only another bid would magically appear on her set of matching

Christmas stockings. She tapped the edge of the desk absently, before she stretched and sat back from the computer.

She rolled her shoulders and glanced out the window. Over the last couple of days, the snow had melted from the field outside her window. When the last of the snow was gone, then spring would arrive in full, followed by summer … and then she'd be broke.

Gritting her teeth, Annie turned her attention back to the computer. How could she entice someone to buy? Maybe she needed to put Easter things on. But Easter was almost finished. Then what? Victoria Day? Were there even any decorations associated with Victoria Day? She'd never heard of any, and if there was some traditional but obscure decoration, who would buy it?

The sunlight glinted through the living room window and into her eyes. She sighed. It was time to get the day going. If the sun was coming up, everyone would be getting up soon and begging for coffee.

She stretched. The sky was red. When was the last time she'd seen such a beautiful sunrise? She listened for movement from the others, but no one else was awake to enjoy the dawn with her.

As she shut down the computer, she reviewed her checklist again before folding her notebook closed. Why did it have to be so difficult to set up a business? Jack would know what to do, but she wasn't about to ask him for help. She bit the inside of her lip as she slid the notebook into the bottom drawer of the desk.

It was quiet. Even the dog and cat were contented, since she'd fed them as soon as she rose. She smiled and stood.

Dizzy.

She braced herself on the desk. She'd been light-headed the day before, too. What was wrong with her? She closed her eyes for a minute until the spinning ended.

If only she liked coffee … it brought the rest of the family to life in the morning. Maybe she needed to give it another try. Bile surged up her throat at the thought. Okay, not coffee, but she needed something.

She glanced out the window again. The dawn was a real explosion in the eastern horizon. Golden sunrays pierced through the red-tinged clouds. Stunning. The clouds crept through the heavens. It was almost hypnotic.

Her vision blurred. She wobbled on her feet.

Get a grip. She didn't have time to sit with her feet up.

In the recesses of the house, a door opened and closed. It must be Milt getting up to watch his golf or soccer or whatever kind of sport was on this early on a weekend.

She shuffled into the kitchen. The day was starting, and everyone would want coffee. She measured out the grounds and then topped up the sugar bowl.

The coffee had brewed and still Milt hadn't come in yet. She poured a cup for him and carried it into the living room.

"Milt, what are you doing?"

Milt winked at her. "I needed to change the furniture a bit for the boys."

"The boys?" She frowned. "What boys?"

"The boys. They're coming to watch the Masters."

She raised her eyebrows. "Who are the masters?"

Milt shook his head and pushed the couch until it sat directly in front of the television. "The Masters, you know, golf."

"You invited people to watch golf?"

Milt shrugged and moved to one of the chairs. He nudged it beside the couch and angled it toward the television. "Is there a problem?"

"No, no, you live here and can invite people over. I'm just surprised you didn't say anything."

"It came up last night. Jimmy Curie was supposed to do it, but his kid knocked their TV over the other night and it's getting fixed. Though I don't expect there is much to be fixed. Expect they'll have to buy a new one."

"How many are coming?"

Milt shrugged. "We were talking at the Whistle, and I'm not sure who was gonna come in the end."

"The patrons of the Shining Whistle? All of them?" She glanced around the house again.

"Don't you worry about a thing. I've got it all under control." Milt waved at the dining room.

She peered into the room. Milt had been busy. All kinds of liquor bottles were laid out as well as chips, dips, and all sorts of things. When had he gone and bought all that? More importantly, why was this the first she'd heard of it? She needed to get ready for Easter dinner. She needed to polish silverware, bake buns, fold napkins, chop vegetables, and a million other things.

In the midst of it, Milt had invited the bar crowd to her house for a party on a Saturday morning. Just seeing the alcohol displayed at this time of day made her queasy.

She turned around and returned to the kitchen. She set Milt's coffee on the countertop and blinked. How was she supposed to respond to this? This seemed to fit under the boundaries category Quinn was so fond of talking about, but Milt needed to feel this was his home, too, didn't he? He was entitled to have friends and interests.

She braced her shoulders. Milt and his buddies would be in the living room. The kitchen was her domain. It'd be okay.

By the time Kelly stumbled into the kitchen, a dozen men were in the living room. Annie tried not to listen, but Milt's loud voice, greeting each man and offering him a tequila sunrise, was hard to miss.

Kelly didn't ask about the crowd in the living room as she grabbed the coffee pot and dumped the coffee.

"That was a full pot."

Kelly's eyes were still puffy with sleep, but clear enough to form a scowl. "It was burnt. Gross. I can't drink burnt coffee."

Annie pounded the bread dough. When the doorbell rang again, Milt bellowed out another greeting. She pummeled the dough with more force. Flour shot up from the kitchen table in a fine cloud.

She concentrated on the dough and tried to ignore everything else. When someone cleared his throat at her side, she nearly jumped out of her dough-crusted skin.

A good-looking man was eying her sheepishly. He held his baseball cap with both hands. What did he want? What had happened now? When he smiled, she realized it was Ryan, father to Jenna's unborn child. *Clueless* father, Annie amended, since Jenna was still trying to get to know the man and had decided she had another month or two before things became too obvious and she had no choice but to tell him.

"Sorry," he said, "didn't mean to surprise you."

"Er … hi … may I help you?"

"Is Jenna around?"

Annie shrugged and glanced at the clock on the stove. "She probably won't be up for another hour."

"I was hoping you'd say that." Ryan grinned. "Where's her room?"

Her brain formed ten refusals in less than a second, but in the end, Annie sighed. Ryan had already seen Jenna in the morning, hadn't he? Wasn't it a little too late to put up roadblocks now? "Up the stairs, on the left."

As Ryan shot out of the kitchen, Annie turned to Kelly. Kelly's mouth was hanging open. Annie pointed at her. "Don't you think you can have boys up to your room, young lady."

Kelly closed her mouth, then she held out the coffee can to Annie. "Can you make another pot?"

Annie wiped her hands on a dishcloth before taking the container. "I just follow the directions on the package," she said as she measured coffee grounds into the machine.

"I know, but it tastes better when you make it." Kelly flopped into one of the kitchen chairs.

Annie added the water to the reservoir and turned on the machine. A moment later, there was a scream from upstairs followed by a hearty round of laughter from the living room. Ryan had found the right room. She shouldn't have let Ryan go upstairs. *Too late now.* She washed her hands and dried them before returning to her bread.

"Who was that?" Kelly whispered.

"Jenna's boyfriend."

"Boyfriend?" Kelly leaned forward. "Is he the father?"

Annie frowned. "Don't say a word about that today, okay?" She sprinkled flour over her hands and started kneading the dough again.

"Why are you cooking now?" Kelly said, with a voice that suggested she'd just realized her mom was making bread.

"Well, it has to get done sometime." What did everyone think? That the kitchen magically produced things? As far as she knew, house elves only lived in stories.

"Umm … Mom? I was talking to Marc last night … and well, can he come to Easter? His parents have to go out of town for some wedding."

"When did you talk to Marc?" Annie placed the dough in the bowl for its second rising.

"Last night."

"You need to get sleep. What do his parents think of the two of you staying up all night talking?" She laid a dishtowel over the dough.

Kelly shrugged. "So, about Easter?"

"Yes, Marc can come to Easter dinner," she said. "One other thing, Kelly, try to keep the phone calls limited to before ten only."

"You're kidding. Ten?"

"Okay, I'll give you until eleven, but no later. You need sleep if you are going to learn anything at school."

Kelly yawned and pulled her cell phone from her pajama pants' pocket. As she poured coffee into a mug with one hand, she tapped a staccato rhythm on the screen of her smart phone with the other.

For the next several hours, Annie tried to ignore the fact Ryan and Jenna still hadn't emerged from her bedroom. *Jenna's* bedroom. It was no longer hers. Still, Annie knew the second she got back into town she'd be buying new sheets and pillows … again …

Maybe they weren't doing naked things. *Please let them just talk.* She swallowed. No, those two didn't seem to talk much, or else they wouldn't have ended up with a baby in the first place.

Annie was even happy Kelly had settled in to watch the golf with the Whistle people. At least she wasn't upstairs, where she could potentially hear things she shouldn't. Why did Jenna have to be so irresponsible? Could she be a worse role model?

Gah. She was starting to sound like Jack.

How long was a game of golf? Shouldn't everyone be leaving? They'd been here for hours. She scanned the kitchen. She'd done everything she could do in here today, and now she had a few minutes.

Quiet as a mouse, she crept through the back of the living room to the basement door. The little creak of the door was muffled under the cumulative "ahh" from the golf-watching group. Something must have happened in the golf game.

She closed the door and went downstairs. She sat on the edge of her sofa bed. That morning she'd had an idea: She needed to make wreaths. After all, wreaths weren't only for Christmas, so they could be her first year-round merchandise item.

Now, which box contained her floral wires? She studied the stacks. She searched five cartons, then forgot why she was doing this.

What was she searching for? Floral wires? Right.

Why was she having such a hard time remembering things lately?

CHAPTER 36

"Mom." Kelly screamed from the top of the stairs. "Are you down there?"

Annie bolted upright. "Hmmm? What? Yes." Rubbing her forehead with the heel of her hand, she swung her legs over the side of the bed. A pair of scissors dropped to the floor as she pushed the ironing board back out of the way. How long had she been asleep?

"Aunty Merry is on the phone."

She trudged up the stairs and took the phone from Kelly's outstretched hand. "Aunty Merry?"

"I'll be at the bus depot at seven o'clock," Merry said. "I'll see you then."

"Wait, that wasn't what we'd talked about," Annie said quickly. "You're coming by bus? What time will you be here?"

"Seven, dear. You come by and pick me up at seven. I have to go now, though, or I'll miss my connection."

Annie nodded and was about to say something more when the line went dead. At least it didn't sound like Milt would have to worry about Merry having a date for Easter. Annie hung up the phone.

The living room was quiet, and the men had all gone home. Milt was asleep on the sofa with one leg hanging off the side and the remote clutched in his hand. He was snoring.

She swallowed and stepped farther into the living room, which was in worse shape than she'd feared. The floor was sticky with spilled drinks. Potato chips lay wet and wilted in puddles on the wooden coffee table, which would now have little puddle-shaped stains. Someone must have knocked over one of those tequila sunrise drinks, because there was a splatter of orange going up the wall. She didn't need to enter the dining room to know it'd be in much the same shape.

How could everyone have been so careless with her home? Probably because everyone who lived here didn't care about it. Hurt, and something that seemed suspiciously like anger, stabbed through her chest.

Her living room had morphed into a pub at closing time, and not a nice little Mom-and-Pop kind of pub. Ew, what was that? A pale brown blob glistened on the floor by the couch. Cat vomit? The dog was licking it. Annie's stomach rolled.

Fresh air. She needed fresh air. She hurried to the front door. Swinging it open, she stepped out in her bare feet. She knocked something with her toe and gasped. An ashtray skidded over her porch. She didn't own an ashtray, but one was sloshing all over her pretty little porch. Someone must have poured something into the ashtray, and now little cigarette butts bobbed in the murky, ashy liquid—hell's version of boats on the ocean.

Then she noticed the world beyond the porch. White, wet globs of snow slapped into the earth. All the little shrubs that had been leafing out were bowing with the heavy snow. And Merry was coming. That meant Annie would have to drive to town in this. She slumped against the doorjamb.

That's what living in the country meant. You had to take the bad with the good. It just seemed like there had been more challenges than not lately.

"Mom."

She put a big smile on her face. "Yes, honey?"

"My room is leaking. Aunty Jenna's is, too."

When she got upstairs, she determined their description was an understatement. Water was beading along the ceiling and bubbling beneath the paint in the walls. There was even water in the light fixtures. Did they condemn houses for things like this? Would the water short out the electricity? Would there be a fire?

And why now? What had happened? They'd survived the snow melting off the roof, so what was causing this?

They all stared at the ceiling in silence for a few minutes.

Her beautiful home was falling to pieces. Just like her life. Annie wanted to curl up in a ball and cry, but Jenna and Kelly were looking to her to fix this.

She couldn't fix a roof in this weather—no, amend that, she couldn't fix a roof in any weather—but she had to do something, or else the ceiling and the walls would have to be ripped out and replaced.

By the time she found a ladder tall enough to get her to the roof, the sleet had seeped through her winter coat and her fingers were numb.

This was what homeowners did when things happened. They fixed them. At least they fixed them enough to get by until people who knew about roofs could be hired. She extended the ladder. The roof was a long way up. She climbed the ladder, hauling a giant patchwork of tarps. This temporary fix was the best thing she could think of to get them through the weekend.

Jenna and Kelly watched from the bedroom window as she tried to heave the tarp up the ladder. It took the better part of two hours for her to get the tarp onto the roof, spread out and nailed in place.

As soon as Annie got into the house, Kelly was shoving her out the door again and telling her to collect Merry, with not so much as a cup of tea to warm her.

Her teeth chattered as she got into the truck. A bath would be great tonight. A nice hot bath.

She turned the heater on in the truck, but it only threw out cold air. She hit it, but the air got colder. The knobs must be stuck. Annie shivered and peeled off her wet mittens. They fell to the seat with a slap.

The windshield wipers squeaked and squealed against the glass, but she still couldn't see more than blurred outlines through the front window. With white knuckles, Annie drove into town.

Arriving at the gas station that doubled as a bus stop, Annie looked for Merry. The bus must be late. She went in to check the schedule. The attendant told her the bus had come and gone, and that no one was waiting. He did seem to think there was an older woman who got off the bus, but he thought she'd been picked up already. He wasn't sure by whom.

Annie went to pull out her cell phone to dial home, but it wasn't in her purse. Gah, she'd been in such a rush to pick up Merry she'd forgotten it. She had to beg the attendant to let her use his phone. The reception was awful, but it was clear enough for her to know Merry was indeed at the house.

Gees, couldn't she have called?

But at least she could go home again and maybe have that bath she'd been dreaming of all day. Annie shivered again and started the truck. The cold air flooded over her. Fiddling with the controls didn't work. Her drive was going to be colder than a sleigh ride through the North Pole, and much less jolly.

Steering the truck down the road she'd just taken, she squinted through the windshield. The sleet had turned to plain old snow. The wet roads would soon be icy.

She breathed on one of her hands and then the other. The windows were fogging up on the inside. She reached forward and wiped the window with her hand. The typical late day sunlight was obliterated by the blizzard, so it was darker than normal, almost like a moonless midnight. The white snowflakes seemed to be shooting forward at her through the blackness. She wiped the window again.

With both hands on wheel, she leaned forward.

Then the truck was moving in a new direction. She yanked her foot off the gas and clenched the steering wheel tighter. The truck continued to slide over the slick road.

A moment later, she and her truck were in an infernal ditch. Again.

CHAPTER 37

Annie blinked through the window. The front headlights were masked by snow. The whole ditch seemed remarkably quiet. Peaceful. Cold, true, but pleasant.

A strange barking, snorting sound filled the cab. It took her a minute to realize she was laughing. She was probably in shock, but couldn't bring herself to care.

She flexed, then wiggled her fingers and toes. No aches or pains. Much like when she slid into the ditch that first day she'd met Quinn. He'd been so sexy standing on the road. Yummy. Lean hips. Strong arms. Eyes that could make you melt, reminding her of chocolate in her palm. Yummy, yummy, yummy.

Yep. She must be in shock.

She should probably try to get the truck out of the ditch. It was the right thing to do, even though she was kind of enjoying the moment.

Foot on brake. Change to Reverse. Foot on gas.

The truck didn't move.

Not a surprise. She'd known it wouldn't before she'd even tried.

She tapped her fingers on the steering wheel.

Oh, right. She should try to get out and go for help. She put the truck in Park and turned it off. Blissful quiet engulfed the cab.

After five minutes, Annie realized she still hadn't tried to open the door.

Right. The door.

She wrenched the handle. Nope. No budgy… She laughed. A budgie was a bird.

She should hang out a bit. Stay with the vehicle. That's what her dad had always said.

When she unbuckled her seatbelt, she swung her feet onto the bench seat. What a weird way to sit, but quite comfy, really. People should sit this way more often. It was strange that she'd found this so uncomfortable that first night when she'd moved to Morning Lake. She'd obviously been crazy at the time.

She wiggled her toes.

They were cold. Her whole body was cold.

She sat and stared at her boots. They were quite ugly. Jack would find them disgraceful, which made her want to bronze the boots. She'd done that with Kelly's baby shoes. Where were they? She should put them out somewhere—a strange little sculpture of toddler footwear. Everyone wanted one of them gathering dust on their end table.

Well ... Jack hadn't really ... and probably Kelly wouldn't ... and, oh, there would be another set coming soon.

Her chest tightened. Yep, soon there would be another body in the house. Another mouth. Another mess. Needing another room that wasn't there.

Baby. A baby was good. Jenna's baby would be wonderful.

Deep breath in and out. All good.

She leaned back on the door.

This was quite lovely. She should stay in here all the time. Move into the truck. She bounced. Yep. Better springs in here than her current basement bed.

She cocked her head to the side. Hmm. She should have seen the opportunities before now. She could string Christmas lights around the cab, one of those kinds that plug into the lighter. She nodded. Yes, this was certainly worth some consideration.

It was quiet. No one around. No cat puke. No doggie puddles. No uncles passed out. What else started with "p"? No sisters puking. No wait, she'd used puke already.

She rolled her head against the window. It felt strong. Not her head. The window. The truck as a whole.

It helped her to change her life. It carried her and her precious things to a new beginning. It was a beautiful creation.

"To the truck." She lifted her hand in an imaginary toast. Hmm ... the truck needed a name. It was not some fussy Bella, Betsy, or Susie. No, it needed a manly name, like Jupiter.

She laughed. Jupiter. A Roman god. Powerful.

Where had that come from?

It didn't matter. It was right. It was good. Yep. "To Jupiter." She lifted her hand again.

Hmm ... were the windows fogging up more? It was getting pretty dark outside. She should sleep for a little bit.

Smiling, she leaned into Jupiter, cradled between his steering wheel and seat.

"Annie."

She waved her hand through the air. "I'm going to sleep. Leave me alone." That felt good, so she shouted it. "Leave me alone."

"Annie. Oh, my God. Annie, talk to me."

A bright light sliced into the cab of the truck, showing her breath hanging in the air. Right there. She reached up to touch it.

"Talk to me. Oh, God, not again."

She curled into Jupiter. Why didn't they go away?

"If you can hear me, Annie, I'm going to break the window."

Break the window? Something hit the truck. "No, don't hurt Jupiter. Stop."

"Annie?"

She frowned. She couldn't find peace anywhere. Not even in the ditch in the middle of the night. She sighed and turned toward the window. With one finger, she cleared a spot on the window the size of a quarter. It sure was bright out there.

"Annie. Oh, thank God."

Something in her brain was starting to come to life. "Quinn, is that you?"

"Yes. Are you hurt?"

Glancing at her body, she wiggled her fingers and toes again. "Nope."

"Roll down the window. I can't open the door."

She did as she was told, and sure enough, there he was. "Hello, Quinn."

His warm fingers touched her face. They were pretty hot. He had a fever.

"Listen to me," he said. "I need you to climb out of the truck. Can you do that?"

"You want to peek down my shirt again." She laughed.

"You bet, babe. Show me what you've got." He wasn't laughing, though. He seemed pretty serious.

"Are you okay, Quinn? I think you might be sick." She scratched her head. "If you need to, you could stay at the house. You shouldn't be alone when you're sick. I could make you some chicken noodle soup. Yes. Chicken noodle soup. Oh, but the baby. You couldn't be near Jenna. She's having a baby, you know. So if you're sick, that won't work. Hmm ... We'll figure it out. I'll make you chicken noodle soup."

"I'll eat a whole pot of soup, if you just climb on the seat and let me help you out of the truck. You remember how we did this last time, I know you do."

She patted the dashboard. "This isn't Truck. This is Jupiter."

Warm fingers on her chin guided her face toward the horribly bright light. "Annie. Climb onto the seat."

She crawled onto the seat, grumbling the whole time. He was sure not himself tonight. He was being all Mr. Big Boss. No fun at all. She needed to introduce him to Jupiter. They had quite a lot in common when you thought about it.

"Now, are you sure you haven't hurt yourself?"

She rolled her eyes.

"Okay, I'm trusting you're telling me the truth. Now, lean out the window and grab my shoulders. I'll take care of the rest."

She did as he told her, and a moment later, she was in his arms.

He hugged her tight, until she squirmed. "Quinn?"

He pulled back to look at her. The light cast from his headlights silhouetted his head, but she could see his face. It was wet. She brushed her fingers over his cheek.

"I think you might be hurt," she whispered.

He laughed then, but it wasn't a normal laugh. It sounded a bit desperate.

"Do you need a doctor?" She was getting a little worried about him.

He swept her into his arms and carried her out of the ditch. "No, I'm good. After my heart settles back into my chest again, I'll be right as rain. No." He frowned. "Strike that. When I get you to the hospital, *then* I'll be okay."

She frowned as he opened his truck door and settled her into the passenger seat. He reached over and fastened her seatbelt. "I don't need a hospital."

He kissed her forehead, then stepped back and closed the door.

She watched him go around the truck and get into the driver's seat. "What about Jupiter?"

His face was tight with fear as he threw his truck into Drive.

"Quinn, don't drive so fast. The roads are slippery. First, there was sleet. It was all wet and then the snow came along and froze it all up."

He shook his head, but a smile crept on his face. "I'll get you there safe."

She craned around to see her truck. "What about Jupiter?"

"Annie, it's a truck."

"I know that, silly. His name is Jupiter. We can't leave him there. I'm thinking of moving into his cab. I have a few more details to sort out, but it'll be wonderful. Hmm … well, I haven't figured out about the business yet. It won't fit into the cab with me." She scratched her head. "I told you I'm in business, right? Need money and all. Do you know how much it costs to feed four adults? More than you'd think, I think. Hmm … I can't move into Jupiter when he's in the ditch somewhere. Then again, at least his roof doesn't leak. Oh, but the window. Jupiter will be all wet inside. Quinn?"

He didn't say anything. His lips were pursed as he turned the heat to high and blazed over the frozen road back to town.

CHAPTER 38

Several hours later, Annie was sitting beside Quinn in his truck again and they were returning to her house. The roads had gone from frozen solid to a slippery muddy mess with icy bits. She clutched the handle above the door.

"I didn't even phone home. They are probably worried by now." Doubtful, but possible.

"I phoned your house, and the police, too."

"Why on earth would you call the police?" She turned to him.

"In case they found your truck and wondered what'd happened to you," he said. "We'll haul it out tomorrow."

She sighed. "It'll be ruined. The window was left open."

"You need to take it easy. Don't worry about your truck. It'll be okay." He rested his hand on her leg, and the weight was warm and oddly reassuring.

She leaned against the door. "I'm just tired. That's what the doctor said."

"No, the doctor used the word 'exhausted.' "

She shrugged. "That's the same thing."

He stared ahead at the road.

"Okay, I know it isn't the same. It is temporary though."

"Temporary." He glanced her way. "Okay, so when will it end? When your sister has her baby?"

She pressed her forehead against the cool window. The shadowy landscape rushed past. The horizon seemed sketched in charcoal and silver with dots of light scattered across the shadows. "I'm sorry I'm such a bother."

"You are not the problem."

She reached down and rested her hand on top of his. "When you found me ..." She swallowed. "You said 'not again'. I know you keep having to get me unstuck and I'm sorry."

He removed his hand from her leg and wiped his face. He didn't put his hand back on her leg. He adjusted the heater again instead. "You warm enough?"

"Yes."

He drew his hand over his mouth. "I wasn't talking about you earlier. I could pull you out of a hundred ditches—not that I want to you go into the ditch that many times. So don't take that as a challenge." He swallowed. "You scared me tonight."

"Oh," she said, unsure what else to say.

When the truck slowed, she realized they were already at the house. He steered the truck into the drive and parked it behind Jenna's car. He turned off the ignition. She went to open the door, but he put his hand on her leg again and stilled her. "I'm sure you know some of this … but my wife and daughters were …" His words trailed off. He didn't look at her, but his hand was still on her leg.

She covered it with her own. "You don't have to …"

He squeezed her leg. "My wife and daughters were in a car accident six years ago." His voice was soft. "I was out, and her dad called. He'd been drinking and needed a ride home." He cleared his throat, and she held his hand and waited. "It was late. I should have been home, but … I wasn't. She bundled the girls up and they all went out. The roads were bad, same as tonight. No one should have been out on them."

He shook his head.

"I found them. The accident must have happened shortly before I got there. They … They were all d—" His words stopped, as if his mouth couldn't form the word *dead.* "Gone. They were gone already when I got there."

"Oh, Quinn, I'm so sorry." Her heart broke for him.

"When I came across your truck there tonight, I …" He swallowed, then he turned to study her. "I wasn't honest with you before."

She stilled.

"When you asked why I didn't come to Thanksgiving." He squeezed her hand. "I mean, I guess it's true I didn't want to meet your ex—he sounds like an ass—but the other part of it was that I'd already started to like you and wanted to spend more time with you. It felt wrong, somehow. Like a betrayal … to Beth and the girls." His voice was getting steadily quieter and his gaze slid to where he held her hand in his. "It took me a while, I guess, to accept that it was okay to want to spend time with you."

She swallowed. "I'm glad you did. I want to spend more time with you, too."

He looked at her. "You understand?"

"Yes."

They sat in silence for a few minutes, holding hands. Then he withdrew his hand and patted her leg. "I'd love to take you home with me, but you need your rest." He was trying to lighten the mood, but his voice was still shaky with emotion. "You should get inside."

She stared at the house. The wind was tugging at the tarp she'd thrown over the roof earlier, shredding it along the spots she'd nailed. A new roof was going to sink them. An ache curled over her.

"I'll come in with you."

"Thank you," she said.

A moment later, she reached the front door. The ashtray was still there. Bent and broken filters remained bloated and swollen in the liquid. She took a deep breath, trying to dispel the growing ache inside her chest.

Stepping into the house, Annie was struck by the noise. The TV was blaring. The dog was barking. The cat was screeching. There was loud conversation. She slipped out of her boots and took another deep breath. The smell of freshly baked bread was gone. It had been replaced with burnt microwave popcorn and wet dog. At least someone must have let the dog out for a potty break.

She stepped into the living room. The orange splatter still climbed the wall. The floor was still sticky under her feet. The cat's hairball was half there. She shuddered to think what happened to the rest of it.

"Hi, Mom. Mr. Quinn." Kelly greeted them from the couch, which was still skewed from the golf watching this morning. Another three heads poked over the top of the couch, but she didn't hear anything from them.

She walked through the living room and stopped at the kitchen door. The room had been spotless when she'd left, but now the counters were cluttered with pop bottles, half-eaten loaves of bread, and dirty dishes where it appeared someone had tried to make spaghetti. In the middle of the table, there was a pile of burnt popcorn stacked into a little pyramid.

Her sternum. Right there. Ached. She rubbed her chest with her fingers. She needed to get out of these clothes and have a bath. Yes, a nice hot bath would be heavenly.

She went to the basement door and flicked on the light. She started descending to her room.

Something wasn't quite right. She blinked. Oh no, the floor was wet. No, more than wet. There was a shallow swimming pool in her basement. Sparkles glittered and floated on the surface of the water.

The sofa bed, an island oasis amid the soggy and drooping boxes, was only fit for a mermaid. Streaks of dampness were climbing the parts of the sofa that poked up like islands in this messy sea. There was no way it'd survive this new disaster.

Annie sank to the step. All her neat and tidy stacks of boxes containing her various goods, merchandise and dreams were doubled over, slumped and skewed. The bottom boxes, steeping in the murky liquid, appeared to be disintegrating, collapsing and sending the upper boxes cascading into the waiting pond.

A strange whimpering noise squeaked out of her throat, then all she could do was stare.

"Annie, what is—?" Quinn's voice came from behind her, but she couldn't respond. Then he simply said, "Oh."

Then Jenna and Kelly said something at the top of the stairs. Kelly laughed. "Holy shit."

Jenna snickered. "Come on, Annie. It's okay. There wasn't anything worth saving down there anyway. That sofa bed has been around since the dawn of time. We'll deal with it in the morning."

Quinn sighed behind her. At least she assumed it was Quinn. She hadn't sighed—she wasn't even sure she breathed—and she was sure the rest of them had gone back to watching TV. A hand squeezed her shoulder.

All her work was gone.

Stars shot across her vision. Then Quinn's hand was on her head. He was forcing her head between her knees. "Breathe. Take a deep breath."

She closed her eyes.

When she finally gulped in air, he stepped around her and into the basement. His feet sloshed through the water. His muttered words floated by her on the ripples at the foot of the stairs. Something clicked, then there was a humming noise. Somehow, she knew all this, but she didn't understand what it meant. And it didn't matter. Her dreams were destroyed.

The sloshing announced Quinn's return. He stopped at the foot of the stairs.

"Annie?"

She grunted.

He bent and kissed the side of her head. "It'll be okay," he whispered in her ear.

But he didn't understand. It was all gone. It wasn't going to be okay.

Then he walked up the stairs, stepping around her. She was alone, with that hum.

Behind her then, she heard something. His voice. It was far away, but this time she could understand the words.

"What are you doing?" he asked. "Get up. We need to get to work."

She'd never heard Quinn sound angry before.

"We'll get to it in the morning," Jenna said.

She could envision Jenna turning back to the TV.

Then it was oddly quiet upstairs, before a rush of "We were watching that."

"We need to get to work," he said again. "Now."

"Listen, young man," Merry reprimanded. "It isn't polite to …"

She didn't hear anymore. Blood was rushing through her ears. Pounding.

She found herself stomping up the stairs. She slammed the basement door. The painting of the house, which had inspired her move to the countryside all those months ago, vibrated against the wall, then crashed to the floor.

Her breath was coming fast again as she surveyed her family, who were all staring wide-eyed at her.

"What is the matter with you all?" Annie spoke softly. "There is a problem. I am not going to fix it this time. I am beyond fixing things. There is no rest to be had. Well, not for me at least." She bowed. "Yes, I am your servant. I am your maid. I am your slave. I am also your breadwinner, but there is no bread to be won. You've eaten it all.

"What are we going to do?" she continued. "There is no exotic fruit orchard in the barn. Where do you think the food on the table comes from? It doesn't magically arrive by elf courier. It has to be purchased. Made. Baked. It takes time and money." She was a bike at the top of a big, big hill. All these things whirled in her head, until they burst from her mouth.

Jenna and Milt were flushed and indignant. Merry inched toward the kitchen. Kelly shrugged.

"If you don't want us here ..." Jenna muttered.

"Arg. Don't be so self-absorbed. I love having you here. All of you. But, for Pete's sake, Jenna, when I was pregnant I worked until three days before I gave birth. Three days. I didn't take a nine-month sabbatical. Your baby is coming and if you think this is hard, wait and see. And you need to tell the father. He deserves to know what is going on.

She turned to Milt. "You aren't twenty anymore. You can't keep up with the crowd at the Whistle. You shouldn't try. Merry, you, too. What are you doing? You are too smart to be running all over hell's half acre after a rich widower, who, may I remind you, you didn't even like before his wife died.

"Kelly, you are not going to have sex with Marc as long as you live under this roof. You are going to quit texting into the night. You are going to study. And you are going to learn how to cook, so you can take care of yourself when you move to college. This is not a prison sentence. This is your home.

"Everyday there are things to do here. Guess who does them? Who walks the dog? Cleans out the kitty litter? Makes sure there is fresh milk in the fridge? Makes sure when you go to turn the light on in your room, it comes on and the electricity hasn't been cut off?"

"I've walked the dog," Kelly muttered.

"Once. You walked the dog once. These things need to be done everyday. They aren't all free. And now there is the roof." She waved toward the ceiling in a wide arc. "What do you think is going to happen to the roof? It needs to be fixed. We'll have erased my savings to nothing before I've even lived here for a year. Those savings should have lasted four years. So I went into business."

Four sets of eyebrows lifted.

"Did any of you even see the stupid magazine?" She pushed her hand through her hair, as her gaze darted over the living room. Then she charged over to the magazine rack, which had been pushed behind the TV. "Did you? I went to a sale and I made hundreds of dollars from my glitter and glue. Not a piddly bit of milk money. I made over five hundred dollars.

"Did you even know that this decrepit old house was featured in an article?" She seized the magazine from the rack and slapped it. "Right here. In these glossy pages. People read it and contacted the publisher. They wanted to buy what you all like to call my Christmas crap."

Jenna and Kelly glanced at one another. Merry was chewing her lips and shaking her head. Milt was about twenty seconds away from passing out again.

"Yes, and the stupid glitter and glue would help keep a roof over your head. Now it is ruined. Floating and destroyed." She threw the magazine to the floor, then lifted her hands to the air. They shook. "Along with all my hopes I had of keeping things going. I don't know. How much is that worth?" She punctuated the sentence with a string of curse words. Jenna would never again be able to tell Annie she wouldn't say shit if her mouth was full of it.

"Oh, sweet pea," Merry said. "You should have said something."

"Aunty Merry, please don't. I have to go." She held her hand up to stop Merry from coming any closer or saying any more. Her heart and head were pounding erratically. "The doctor told me to rest, and I'm pretty sure this isn't what he meant." Quinn had his hands in his pockets and was leaning against the wall close to the front door. "Can you give me a lift?"

"You bet," he said.

"I'll grab a few things and be right back." She spun around and ran up the stairs to the bathroom.

A moment later, with a plastic grocery bag full of toiletries, she fled the house.

In the truck, they sat for a moment in the quiet and stared at the house. "What have I done?"

"You know what, Annie?"

She rubbed the ache still flowering beneath her sternum. It was weird to think of stress as having a physical pain. Her nerves were pudding on a roller coaster. "What?"

"I think I might love you." Quinn grinned and started the truck.

Her mouth gaped open and then she laughed. By the time they reached the end of her drive, her laughter had morphed into tears, complete with hiccups and a runny nose.

When he parked in front of his home, the tears had ended and she was back to being numb again. She stared ahead, unmoving, as he exited the truck.

Quinn didn't say a word as he undid her seatbelt and carried her into the house, straight through to his bedroom. On some distant level, it struck her that he seemed to tote her about quite regularly, but she did nothing to resist him. With careful, tender movements, he removed her shirt, pants and shoes before laying her back on the bed. And she let him.

She knew she shouldn't. She should be capable of this.

A few minutes later, Quinn crawled into bed beside her. He pulled her close, so her back was flush against his chest. Then he started murmuring soothing words, which she let wash over her. Slowly, they cleared away all the anxiety she'd been carrying.

Cocooned within his embrace, she knew everything would be okay.

CHAPTER 39

The bed moved. There was a thumping noise immediately. The dog, right. Annie had almost forgotten. She rolled toward Quinn. He was sitting up.

"You stay sleeping, okay?" Quinn whispered as he reached and brushed his fingers across her cheek. Then he leaned over and kissed her where he'd just trailed his fingers. "Go back to sleep, babe."

She closed her eyes. When he tucked the warm flannel sheets around her, she smiled. He had such big strong hands. "Okay." It was wonderful here. She could sleep forever.

The next thing she felt was the kiss of sunlight on her face. She blinked. Good grief, the clock read eleven. The day was half over.

It was Easter. There were things to do. She had to clean the house, set the table, get the ham in the oven. The list kept growing in her head.

She threw off the blankets and scrambled out of bed. Why hadn't he woken her? She yanked on her jeans and shirt. She needed to get back to the house.

Oh, God, what had she done? She'd shouted such horrible things to her family. She was terrible. She didn't deserve to have Easter.

And Quinn thought he might love her.

After all the crazy and horrible things she'd done, he loved her. How could he? She'd yelled at her family. And he still said he loved her *after* that. She had to tell him she loved him too … because it was true.

A giggle erupted from her throat. When was the last time she'd felt rested? This was probably how Santa felt on Boxing Day. The air had been cleared and now she could set sail into the future.

Except there wasn't a future, because it was floating in her flooded basement.

Some of her spurt of happiness slipped.

Still, it could always be worse. It was worse the day Jack said he was leaving. It was worse the day Kelly said she was moving in with Jack. At least now there was always a silver lining. After all, now she couldn't care less if Jack took a long bungee trip off a short bridge. Okay, that was a bit extreme, but she had moved on, and Kelly had come back home.

She braced her shoulders. It was time to face the day. Throwing open the bedroom door, she marched into her new life.

The kitchen was empty and silent.

Where was he? She turned from the kitchen and followed the hallway, until she found Quinn and Digger. She had never been in his living room before.

Digger lifted his head when she entered the room. He tilted his head and his tail started thumping on the floor. Quinn had a pencil stuck behind his ear, and a book laid across his lap. He was sitting in a reclining chair with the footrest up. She had a clear vision of how he would age over the next forty years and she wanted to be there to see him.

"I'm hungry." He set the book aside.

On cue, her stomach rumbled. "I guess I am, too, but I should return to the house."

"Let's eat first. You can have your Easter meal late this year." He lowered the footrest and rose from his chair.

"You haven't eaten, have you? Because of me."

He ignored her question and went to the kitchen. She trailed behind. "What were you reading?"

He peered into the fridge and pulled out a couple of plastic packages filled with deli meat. "I found a book on marketing on the book shelf. I'd forgotten it was there."

"Marketing?"

He didn't reply, and she watched as he made a plate of sandwiches. When he was done, he set the plate on the table.

"Here. It isn't much, but I imagine you'll have lots of food later."

"These are great." When was the last time someone had made a meal for her? Probably when he'd made breakfast on New Year's morning.

She stared at the meal. Her eyes filled with tears.

"It'll be okay." Then he was in front of her, drawing her into a gentle embrace.

"You're always taking care of me, aren't you?"

She expected him to make a quip about how much she needed someone to take care of her, particularly given all that had happened. After all, this bizarre overreaction to sandwiches was hardly normal.

Instead he held her tighter. "I like taking care of you."

She wiped her tears away. "The doctor said I wouldn't be fixed after only one night's sleep. I think I may have run myself a little thin."

"It's okay." He patted her back and loosened his embrace.

"Let's eat."

When they sat, he looked at her. "I don't know if you are interested, but Beth took some small business courses by correspondence a few years before ..." He bit into his sandwich. He chewed and swallowed before continuing. "Anyway, I found the books this morning. You might find them helpful. I was reading the one on marketing, when you got up. It's a lot of common sense, but—" he shrugged, "—you can have them if you want."

"Thank you." She rushed out of her chair and jumped on Quinn. She kissed him lightly on the lips, then snuggled into his embrace.

He rubbed her back. "If they help, they're yours."

They sat quietly for a moment, Quinn cradling her in his arms. She never wanted to leave.

"Quinn," she said, sitting up so she could see his face. She could stare at him forever. "You're amazing, did you know that?"

He rolled his eyes. "I think you're getting delirious now. Do I have to take you back to the doctor?"

"No, I'm serious." Annie touched his cheek. His stubble was rough under her fingers. "I think I love you, too."

Quinn's lopsided grin broke over his face. "You can't take that back, you know. You can't blame that on your exhaustion."

"Quit teasing me. I'm being serious."

His eyes softened. "So am I. I love you, Annie, and I am the luckiest man in the world to have you love me back."

New tears cascaded over her cheeks now, but these were happy ones. Quinn gently wiped each one away.

"I don't know what I ever did to deserve your love, but I don't know what I'd do without it."

When his lips met hers, joy thrummed through her. She understood what it was to be cherished and to cherish. His mouth was soft, and she melted into him. Then he shifted and kissed her face, eliminating any lingering tears with his tender attention.

"You are beautiful," he said. "And I can't believe you don't know why I fell in love with you. I remember that first day we met. You were tearless, facing me down and blushing all at the same time. Your sweet blushes, though, those are what kept me coming back. They revealed your innermost wants, whether you realized it or not."

"My what?" She shifted, suddenly awkward.

"They whispered to me long ago that you liked me, then they hinted that you'd come to care for me, and now … they're telling me I was right."

"You love me because I blush?"

"No, I love you because of your determination to give yourself to the happiness of others and your belief that with enough effort everything will work out."

"I'm pretty sure I don't do that …"

"Yes, you do." His statement brooked no further discussion on the matter. Then he cleared his throat. "Don't worry, I won't ask what you love about me. After all, what's not to love?" He winked.

She laughed. "You don't know how true that is."

They sat holding one another in that kitchen chair for a long while before her thoughts turned once again to her family and everything that had happened the day before.

"I will need your help, to get that silly truck out of the ditch again."

"It's already out."

"When?"

He shrugged. "Earlier. It's back at your house."

"My house ..." She took a deep breath. A nervous panic rippled through her belly. "Can you take me over?" She lifted her hand to her face. It was trembling. "I'm not sure what to say to everyone, how to apologize."

"You might be surprised. I talked to Milt this morning, when we organized getting your truck out." He rubbed her hand. "Eat up, then we'll head over."

He would go with her. It'd be okay if he was there. She needed to apologize to her family, and anything that eased her nerves was good.

CHAPTER 40

Annie stepped into the house and her mouth dropped open. Every surface was covered with Christmas. Santa's workshop had nothing on this. Early afternoon sunlight pierced through the window and set the living room alive. It glittered and shimmered. It was beautiful in its chaos.

"Hi, sweet pea," Merry said from behind a pile of boxes.

The sofas had been pushed to the perimeter of the room, and in the middle were heaps of Christmas goods.

"Wow." Annie moved farther into the room. Then Jenna appeared in the door to the basement. She was carrying a soggy box.

"Got another one here," Jenna announced. "Oh, hi, hon. You've got quite the collection."

"Where are Kelly and Milt?"

"In here, Mom," Kelly called from the direction of the kitchen.

She made it as far as the threshold between the kitchen and the living room, and then she stopped again. Milt, Kelly and Marc had paper all over the kitchen table. Taped to the kitchen wall was a large piece of poster board with "AKA Mrs. Claus Inc." written on it in big block letters.

"We're working on your website and sales stuff. We've got lots of things to talk about with you."

Kelly came over and hugged Annie. "We're sorry, Mom, for everything."

She raised her eyebrows. Quinn had shed his coat and boots and was putting the business books on a small square of empty floor space. Then he sat with Merry and Jenna, who were extracting Christmas decorations from the box Jenna had just hauled up.

"Let's see ..." Kelly put her hands on her hips and looked around. "Aunty Jenna and Aunty Merry are sorting through the boxes that were in the water. You've got a lot, Mom."

She tensed. Kelly seemed to notice.

"It's okay. I didn't mean what I said at Christmas. I was mad at Dad."

Annie pursed her lips.

"They're sorting things and seeing what survived the flood. We're spreading the damp, salvageable items to dry. It's helped to have that—what did you call it, Uncle Milt?—a sump pump?"

Milt nodded.

"That's helped a lot." Then Kelly turned to the kitchen. "Then we found your domain name and business stuff on the computer. The company name is pretty cute, Mom. Lots of possibilities."

When had Kelly ever thought something Annie had done was good? Not since she was four, she was sure.

"I'm sorry I've been such a brat," Kelly said, again as if she read Annie's mind. "Did you know Uncle Milt was a salesman and I've taken classes in school about websites? Anyway, when most of the boxes were out of the basement, he and I started working on your business plan." Kelly glanced at Milt, as if to confirm she got the words right.

Milt nodded.

Annie put her hand on her chest. In a matter of a few heartbeats, the panic that had nestled there for the last two months eased. "Oh, you guys, I don't know what to say. I ... I'm sorry for all the terrible things I said yesterday. I love you all so much."

Merry shook her head. "Nonsense. You should have said something ages ago, sweet pea. We talked about that after you left yesterday. You see, now that we know what is going on, we can help." Merry looked straight into Annie's eyes. "We want to help … if you'll let us. "

They all grinned at her.

"Thank you," Annie said.

"Now, take your coat off and get in here," Jenna said.

CHAPTER 41

Canada Day

The fireworks at the Morning Lake Canada Day celebrations yesterday were nothing compared to the shocks of excitement shooting through Annie's nerves. Jupiter was loaded to the brim, and everything was secured under a bright orange tarp.

She was attending her very first gift show. The jury had accepted her and she had a booth. Milt's connections in the sales industry had come through for her, though Milt insisted she had been given a booth because of the quality of her products and the professional quality of her website.

"Do you think we should bring more stockings?" she asked. Quinn tilted his head back as if he were bargaining with heaven.

"Annie, you've got more than enough," Jenna said from her perch on the deck chair. She rubbed her baby belly. Kelly, who was dressed in her new work uniform, was sitting beside her. "Remember what Uncle Milt said—you're just getting orders. It is different from a craft sale."

"I know," she said. "Are you going to be okay?"

"Yes, we've already talked about this. I still have two months to go before the baby comes. That's a long time. Besides, I've got a break this week before summer school starts and I start tutoring again." Jenna grinned then. "Ryan will be here every day—we've got a lot to talk about before the wedding, and Kelly is here every night."

Jenna patted Kelly on the knee, but she was looking at Quinn. "You'll have to pick her up and throw her into the truck if you are ever going to get out of here. Uncle Milt and Aunty Merry will be wondering what happened to you. You are supposed to meet them at the venue at three."

Quinn grinned. "Come on, babe, we'll be late."

She walked around the bed of the truck again and checked the tie downs for the tarp.

"Annie, it's fine. Let's go."

"Hurry up, Mom. I want to see you off, but I'm going to be late for work if you don't get going."

She opened her mouth, but Kelly shushed her. "Yes, I know what you're going to say. I'll check the website and the e-mails twice a day for orders, like I always do. You have nothing to worry about."

"Okay, okay." She laughed as she turned to Quinn. "I guess we should go."

She walked to the driver's side of the truck and opened the door.

"Oh, no, you don't." He took her elbow and steered her toward the passenger side. "I'm driving. We don't have time to get stuck or drive into the ditch today."

"Sheesh," she said, but she was way too giddy to feel anything but happiness.

She climbed into the cab of the truck and waved at Jenna and Kelly. They waved back. Everything was picture perfect, good enough for a magazine or a painting.

Then, as Annie pulled on her Santa's hat and sat back in her seat, she decided sometimes real life was even better.

EPILOGUE

Christmas

"Twas the night before Christmas, when all through the house
Not a creature was stirring, not even a mouse."

Annie paused from reading Moore's poem and looked around the living room. Everyone was listening, even baby Joey, who was cradled in Kelly's arms.

In the few months since Kelly had been away at university, she'd taken on a quiet, simple sophistication that surprised Annie. Still, Jenna had been right. Kelly had come home right after her exams were finished—she hadn't wanted to miss another family Christmas.

Ryan and Jenna were on the sofa. His arm was around her shoulders and he caressed her neck. With each movement, his wedding ring glinted in the soft light shed by the Christmas tree lights. Jenna looked flushed and happy. Annie imagined Jenna would have been skeptical that happiness could be achieved without makeup or designer clothes just twelve months ago. When Annie moved into Quinn's place and set up her burgeoning business in his beautiful basement, Ryan and Jenna had rented the Geller place at a steal of a deal. They had made it a home of which they could be proud. She couldn't have wanted anything more for them.

Beside them, Merry was nibbling on a shortbread cookie. Her eyes were full of love and looking at Milt, who was sitting on an ottoman across the room. He hadn't had a drink since Easter. Merry and Milt and their furry companions were staying with Ryan and Jenna for the holiday, since Digger didn't like sharing his house, and Merry and Milt couldn't bear leaving Dumbbell and Tiger at home.

On the other side of the room, Quinn was stretched on his recliner. He winked at her.

It was absolutely perfect.

TITLES BY LORRAINE PATON

Morning Lake Series:
Chloe's Matchmaking Terrier
Devin's Second Chance
Annie's Christmas Plan

ABOUT THE AUTHOR

When Lorraine Paton finished her master's degree, she was tempted to sign on to do a doctorate, but then she realized she wanted to write fiction more. So, by day, she works in a hectic office, and by night, she lets loose her passion for writing romance novels. She lives with two cats who hate one another and a wonderfully patient man with a sexy Scottish accent in Alberta, Canada, which is where her contemporary stories take place. A diehard romance reader and writer, her goal is to bring happily-ever-afters to as many people—*or characters*—as she can.

Connect with Lorraine on:

- her newsletter (http://eepurl.com/tYuqP)
- her blog (www.lorrainepaton.com),
- Twitter (twitter.com/patonlorraine), and
- Facebook (facebook.com/LorrainePaton.Author).

www.ingramcontent.com/pod-product-compliance
Lightning Source LLC
LaVergne TN
LVHW090945080826
845145LV00003B/897

* 9 7 8 0 9 9 1 9 9 4 0 5 2 *